# WISH UPON A CRIME

# WISH UPON A CRIME

## CRIME FICTION INSPIRED BY
## FAIRY TALES

EDITED BY

## MICHAEL BRACKEN & STACY WOODSON

*For Temple*
*My Love, My Muse, My Everything*
*—Michael*


*To DWW*
*The person who believed I could be a storyteller before I did.*
*I wish you could be here to share this journey with me.*
*—Stacy*

# Contents

# Praise for Wish Upon a Crime

"Gritty and tense, this collection takes the classic stories we all know and love and spins them into a different dark and delightful gold.  The crime authors here blend a modern, stark reality with the magic lore of old, and as a result bring a new meaning to the word 'grim.'"—**Tara Laskowski**, Agatha Award-winning author of *The Weekend Retreat*

# Hansel and Gretel

By Joseph S. Walker

The simple, two-story homes on Woodlawn Street were built, decades ago, for factory workers and their families. The houses themselves might have been turned out by a factory, matching in everything but the colors painted on the porch railings. Now the factories were long gone, and the houses on Woodlawn were no longer identical. Some were burned-out shells. Some were abandoned, the walls stripped of copper and coated in years of gang tags. Some had been broken up into apartments that charged by the week and didn't require references. Some, Mallard knew, were shooting galleries or stash houses.

At two in the morning, splashed with alternating washes of blue and red light from three police cruisers and an ambulance, they all looked empty. Once upon a time, neighbors would have stood on their lawns waiting to learn the shape of the tragedy, many willing to offer help or comfort. The ones watching now sat in the darkness of untidy rooms, well back from the glass, some holding guns.

Mallard recognized the uniform on the broken sidewalk in front of 1622 Woodlawn but couldn't remember her name. She nodded him past without meeting his eye. "Upstairs," she said.

He found Viv Stallings on the second-floor landing outside apartments three and four. Four was open. The muted sounds from inside were as familiar to Mallard as his own breathing. Cops and techs, at work in the presence of death.

Stallings wasn't the best detective Mallard had run across, but she was far from the worst. She was like most of them, piling up paperwork and waiting for the pension to kick in. At least she didn't pretend it was good to see him or ask what he was up to these days. He appreciated the honesty of her disinterest.

"Rudy Knutson," she said quietly, taking his arm to turn them both away from the open door. "With a *K*. Remember him?"

Mallard kept his face blank. "Name's in my head somewhere."

"You arrested him last year. Possession, side order of resisting."

"I arrested a lot of people."

"He was released about twelve hours ago. His wife's in there on the bed, strangled. Knutson says he doesn't want a lawyer. He'll talk, but only to you."

"You tell him I'm not on the job anymore?"

"He doesn't care. He's willing to have me listen, even to be recorded, but you have to be there."

Mallard looked over his shoulder at the open door. "Who called it in?"

"Knutson. Called nine-one-one himself."

"You caught it, Viv. What do you want me to do?"

"It's two in the goddamned morning, Mallard. Don't ask questions you know the answer to."

* * *

Knutson sat on an ancient, lopsided couch, his hands cuffed behind him, wearing a pair of workout shorts and nothing else. His chest was sunken, his skin pale and mottled. Mallard remembered stringy hair, but Knutson's head was shaved smooth. People did that in jail sometimes to keep off lice. It gave him the look of a buzzard, his small head thrust out at the end of his long neck.

Two uniforms leaned against the wall across from Knutson. The only other furniture in the room was an aluminum lawn chair and a low, scarred coffee table. Mallard sat on the table, his knees a few inches from the cuffed man's. "Mr. Knutson," he said. "You wanted to talk to me."

Cops get used to angry looks, but Mallard had rarely encountered the depth of hatred he saw when Knutson met his eyes. "You." He had a high voice, thin, like he had trouble getting a real breath. "They said you're not a cop anymore."

"That's right. Have they told you your rights?"

"Yeah," Knutson said. "They read the little card to me."

"You know this is being recorded?"

"I don't give a fuck."

"Okay," Mallard said. "You got me here. What is it you wanted to say?"

"Wanted you to know this is your fault." Knutson licked his lips.

"What's my fault?"

"I killed her." Knutson's eyes went to Stallings. "Bitch is gone, right?"

"Yes, Mr. Knutson," she said. "Your wife is dead."

"Good." He looked back at Mallard. "Kill you, too, if I could."

"Why's that, sir?" Mallard asked.

"*Sir*," Knutson mocked. "Damned well no *sir* when you had me out in the street with your knee in my back."

"You want to kill me because I arrested you?"

Knutson's jaw tightened. "I wasn't here. I wasn't here because of *you*, and she couldn't do it. Couldn't handle them without me here."

"Handle who?"

Knutson started rocking back and forth. His arms strained at the cuffs. "The kids," he said. "My kids."

That quick, the image was in Mallard's head. Cuffing Knutson on the postage stamp lawn out front, then looking at the house to see the two faces watching. Wide eyes, blond hair.

"Mr. Knutson. Where are your children?"

"She threw them out," Knutson said. "Two weeks ago. Put them on the street. *My kids*. You know what happens to kids out there?"

"Jesus," one of the uniforms said. Mallard looked at Stallings, but she was already heading back to the landing, cell at her ear.

"Whatever happened to them, it's on you," Knutson said. "I wanted you to fucking know it." He leaned forward and spit, hitting Mallard's cheek, then burst into tears, sobbing as Mallard had never seen an adult man do in his life.

* * *

When Mallard left the room, after cleaning his face with a sanitary wipe one of the uniforms gave him, Stallings was on the landing, listening to someone on the phone. "Twins," she said, ending the call. "Eleven years old. Girl named Gretel, boy named Hansel."

"You didn't know?"

"He didn't say a fucking word about it until you got here. We'll check the local shelters. Talk to any neighbors willing to talk."

"Two weeks gone," Mallard said. "Eleven years old."

"Think you need to tell me?" Stallings nodded at the stairs. "Appreciate you coming down, Mallard. Now go home. That's what you want to do, right?"

* * *

Four hours later, Mallard was on his back porch, waiting for the sun, when the sliding door opened, and Tasha came out of the house with two mugs of coffee. She put one on the small table between the two chairs and sat. "I thought we were done with phone calls and you running off in the middle of the night."

Mallard was a cop for thirteen years, the last four as a detective in Major Crimes, mostly working embezzlement and fraud. The day he arrested Rudy Knutson was a rare shift on the street, covering for a friend who wanted to watch his kid play ball. Two months afterward, not many blocks from Knutson's apartment, a Black teenager who had shoplifted an energy drink was shot fourteen times by three cops. The day the DA declined to indict them, and the department restored them to full duty, Mallard handed in his resignation.

"Old case," he said. "Just a consult."

They drank coffee and watched the world getting lighter. Eventually, Tasha stood. "Off to the grind," she said. "Gonna put in some miles today?"

Tasha's marketing job paid enough for Mallard to drag his feet on finding a permanent new profession. He drove an Uber a few hours a day to feel like he was doing something while he waited for inspiration to strike. "In a little while."

She stepped inside but turned before closing the door. "Just a consult?"

"I hope so," he said.

* * *

The murder on Woodlawn was a one-paragraph item in the back pages of the next day's paper, Mallard being one of the few people on his block who still had a real copy delivered. It didn't make the TV news at all. There was no mention of the twins. Mallard waited two more days before he called Stallings.

"No trace," she said. "They're not at any of the shelters, anyway. Haven't been in school."

"Any other leads?" He felt idiotic as soon as he said it.

"*Leads?* Sure, Mallard. Exotic cigarette ash, tire treads with traces of a distinctive red clay." Her tone softened. "You know the job, man. I've pulled three other cases since I saw you, and there's no family to whip up the media. Patrol has their pictures. They'll turn up, or they won't."

"But probably they won't," Mallard said.

Stallings killed the call before he got it out.

* * *

In the middle of the afternoon, Mallard figured any virtuous residents of 1622 Woodlawn would be out in the world, and the others would be dead to it. The lock on apartment four was embarrassingly cheap, barely more than a push-button knob. A credit card had Mallard through in thirty seconds, into the weighted quiet of a home nobody is ever returning to.

He followed a narrow hallway out of the front room, past a bathroom and the bedroom where the woman was killed. The last room in the apartment, not much bigger than a closet in Mallard's home, had almost all its space taken up by a sagging bunk bed. Clothes were scattered on the floor, some folded and piled, most just strewn.

The walls, from floor to ceiling, were covered in drawings, all done in thick purple marker. A lot of them were just doodles, geometric shapes and squiggles, imitations of tags from around the neighborhood. In places there were people, little more than stick figures, but with detail on the faces indicating at least some degree of care in their composition. In several places there was a cat's head, drawn with quick, ritualized strokes to indicate pointed ears and whiskers, the narrow eyes malevolent. BAD CAT was scrawled under each, the stylized lines of the letters jagged lightning bolts.

The other bedroom, where Angela Knutson had died, was large enough for a queen-sized bed, a nightstand, and a small dresser. The TV on the dresser was so ancient that it had a tube. A plastic frame on the nightstand held wallet-sized school pictures of two children. Mallard couldn't remember the last time someone had shown him a picture in a wallet. Probably more recently than the last time he'd watched TV on a tube. He took the small photos from the frame. The girl's hair was to her shoulders, the boy's barely touching his ears. Other than that, they might have been two pictures of the same person. He put them in his pocket.

The rest of the apartment didn't offer any leads. He wasn't expecting it to.

* * *

"Quiet kids," Angelo Flume said. "Kept to themselves. Sat in the back."

"Smart?"

"Who the hell can tell? If they're missing, I wouldn't start the search at Harvard."

Flume looked like the "before" picture in an ad for a drug treating advanced burnout. His clothes were worn, he hadn't shaved in a few days, and his breath suggested there was a bottle of something fairly potent in one of his desk drawers, but he was the first teacher Mallard had talked to at South Elm Elementary who remembered the Knutsons.

"Any close friends? Someone they might go to if they were in trouble?"

Flume turned up his hands. "Mostly, they only talked to each other. Actually, mostly the girl was the only one who talked at all, and then usually to yell at somebody. She has a real hair trigger. The brother followed her around like a puppy. She got suspended for fighting once, and he spent the whole week without her, practically in a fetal position. All he really ever wanted to do was draw." He nodded at the corner of the classroom farthest from the door. "Take a look at his desk."

Mallard walked back. The entire surface of the desk was covered with the same purple doodles and swirls as the walls on Woodlawn. BAD CAT was dead in the middle. "Any idea what *Bad Cat* means?"

"I think it's just what he called himself. These days, they all have rap names or Twitter handles. Legal names are very twentieth-century." Flume stood and joined Mallard. "Damn purple markers. Take one away and he'd come up with another, Christ knows how."

"Looks obsessive. Is he maybe on the spectrum? Or ADD?"

"You tell me. Budget we've got, I can have about half a dozen kids a year tested, and then only if the parents care, and they don't. Mostly the job is to get them to June alive. Then they're somebody else's problem."

"Inspiring."

"Fuck you." Flume returned to the front of the room. "I'm in here every damn day with forty of them. Where the hell are you?"

"Driving an Uber."

"There you go. You got a BA? In anything? Stop at the office. They'll have you in front of a room Monday." Flume sat down and ran a hand over his face. "Everybody's got a finite number of fucks to give in their life, Mr. Mallard, then they're done. I'm holding on to my last couple. Trying to make them count. Think you're any better?"

"No," Mallard said. "No, I don't."

* * *

Mallard drove around the poorest parts of the city, working outward in a rough spiral from Woodlawn. He kept the Uber app open, but people in these neighborhoods walked or took the bus. At least he could tell Tasha he was working without actually lying.

Finding the homeless (the *unhoused*, he reminded himself, flashing on public relation memos) wasn't a problem. It was mostly a matter of shifting your gaze downward a few notches. When he saw one who seemed sober and coherent, Mallard pulled over and showed the pictures. A lot of them walked away as soon as they saw him. To the street, he was still a cop. The ones who would talk didn't have anything to say. He handed out some fives, partly to generate goodwill and partly so he could tell himself he was better than Angelo Flume.

On the fourth day, he left his car on the street in front of a scrapyard and walked a quarter mile to a railroad trestle over a wide, weed-infested ravine. There had been a homeless camp here for years. Occasionally, usually just before an election, the city cleared it out, knowing the homeless would be back as soon as the cameras were gone. The ravine had its own rough social structure, those with tents or other shelters up higher on the sides, single men and women with needles or bottles sleeping rough near the low, muddy center. A lot of them were gone in the middle of the day, but Mallard knew better than to be here alone at night.

He started on the east side and worked his way across, showing the pictures to people who shook their heads and looked away, when he could get their attention at all. He reached the western bank and was about to give up when he glanced at the underside of the trestle and saw purple. He climbed up, scrambling with his hands at one point. In the sheltered overhang where the tracks jutted out from the bluff, big steel beams curved up to support them. A three-foot length of one beam was covered with purple swirls and complex, intersecting lines, all of it branching out from the central figure. BAD CAT.

Mallard took a picture, then looked around. Ten yards away, a man in an olive-green canvas coat was sitting cross-legged on the ground, watching him. Mallard raised a hand. The man didn't respond.

Mallard walked over and squatted in front of him. "Afternoon. I'm interested in that purple graffiti on the bridge there. You see who did it?"

The man scratched at the stubble on his cheek, looked at the purple lines, looked back at Mallard. "Think it was your mama."

Mallard smiled tightly. "I've got money."

"Damn, man, me too. Let's have dinner at the club. I'll bring the Rolls around."

"Have I done something to offend you, sir?"

Mallard heard Rudy Knutson in his head, sneering at the *sir*.

"Knew the minute I saw those kids that somebody would be looking for them," the man said. "Couple of cute little blond kids. Cute little blond kids always got people looking for them."

"So you did see them."

"Nobody looking for the rest of us. Damn sure nobody looking for my ugly hide. You think I should bleach my hair?"

"Are they still here?"

The man looked away from Mallard, across the ravine. He shook his head, and something in him deflated. "Lemme hold twenty."

Mallard slid two twenties out of his wallet. The man took them without looking and they vanished into some inner pocket. "They were here for a few days, off and on. Got the feeling they were sleeping different places, moving around a lot."

"Didn't they get hassled?"

"Girl had a knife. Made sure everybody knew it too."

"When did you last see them?"

"Week? Week and a half? All kind of blurs together when you're busy, you know?"

"Yeah," Mallard said. He got out a card, wrapped it in another twenty, and passed it over. "You see them again, let me know."

The man grunted. Mallard stood and turned away.

"Might have seen them with Sister Patience once," the man said.

Mallard turned back. "Sister Patience?"

"Nun who comes around sometimes handing out food, bottled water, fresh fruit, shit like that. Only, if you want anything, you gotta kneel down and pray with her, and once she gets going, she rattles on until you forget what you're there for. Then you have to take a Bible and promise to read it. She always has candy for the kids, tries to get them to come with her so she can get them home. Me, I turn around if I see her coming. Can't stand that holy roller shit."

"Where do I find her?"

"She doesn't go anyplace regular, far as I know. Only shows up every couple months. Shouldn't be hard to spot. She always wears the full nun outfit, you know, rosary hanging from her belt and all. Look for a penguin in an old green panel van with a cross painted on the hood."

"Okay," Mallard said. "Thanks."

"Yeah," the man said. "You get done rescuing little blond kids, come on back. My ass could use some saving too."

* * *

Mallard spent the next morning making phone calls. None of the churches in the area knew anything about a Sister Patience. He couldn't even be sure that was her real name, or title, or whatever nuns have, legal names being so twentieth-century.

He started calling food banks.

"Yeah," somebody at the third one said. "I've heard about her."

Mallard sat forward. "You have?"

"Couple times. Never seen her. Near as I can tell, there's no rhyme or reason to where she shows up."

"She with any particular church you know of?"

"Nope. Hell, it's possible she's not even a nun. It's not like you need a note from the pope to buy a habit." The man warmed to his topic. "We had a guy a few years back who liked to dress as Jesus and offer to wash people's feet. Turned out he had a toe fetish."

In the next two hours Mallard talked to another dozen people. Two had heard rumors about the nun in the panel van. Nobody had any idea where or how to find her.

He took a sandwich and a beer onto the back deck to think about his next move. He could call Stallings, but lately she was letting his calls go straight to voicemail. She probably deleted them without listening. He couldn't think of anybody on the force who would still be well-disposed enough toward him to risk their job by running down the van through the DMV.

Tasha came around the corner of the house, back from her daily jog. She climbed the three steps to the deck, fell into the other chair, and picked up Mallard's beer. "Important to stay hydrated," she said, and took a long drink.

"I've heard that," he said. "Hey, listen, that grade school you went to."

"Holy Trinity," she said.

"The teachers were priests and nuns, right?"

"Not all of them. About half." She started peeling the label off the bottle. "Father Brian put a hell of a spin on *The Scarlet Letter*. Gave me nightmares."

"You know where they lived?"

"Sure.  There was a little hill behind the school with two small square buildings, like dorms. One for the nuns and one for the priests. At recess, we used to dare each other to run up and peep through the windows."

"But this was all torn down years ago."

"Was it?" Tasha squinted in thought, looking across the yard. "The school moved. All the well-off Catholic families went out to the northern suburbs, so they built a new school there. But I don't know that they ever tore the old place down." She shrugged. "It's probably a car dealership now or something."

* * *

It wasn't a car dealership, though there was one across the street and half a block down.  The school building was still there, in a part of town that hadn't quite fallen to Woodlawn levels but was well on the way. Most of the nearby businesses seemed abandoned, and even the used car lot showed no sign of life. Tasha's old school grounds were bordered by an eight-foot chain-link fence. Every twenty or thirty yards, it had a CONDEMNED PROPERTY—STAY OUT sign. The bluff behind the school was covered in scrub brush and young, sickly trees, but Mallard could see the top floors of the two small dorms. It was strange to think of his wife, as a young girl, running around in there with her friends.

Mallard parked in the lot of a restaurant supply warehouse and looked at the school, trying to figure out what was bothering him. Something about it brooded. He couldn't think of any better word. He got out of his car, went across the street, and started walking the fence. Up close, the signs of neglect were obvious. The parking lot was broken by lines of weeds, some several feet tall. Most of the windows were broken, and the letters of the old HOLY TRINITY sign over the main entrance had fallen off, leaving ghostly outlines on the facade.

Broken windows.

Mallard jogged back across the street and backed up, facing the school, until he could see the dorm buildings again. The one on the left, like the school, had mostly broken windows. The windows on the other structure were whole, reflecting the gray sky in solid squares.

He was pretty sure he could climb the fence, but he didn't want to do it at the front. This wasn't a heavily traveled road, but a cruiser coming past at the wrong moment would be awkward. He returned to the fence and went around the corner, following as it went up a mild incline and then a steeper one, the bluff the dorms sat on. The rear corner of the fence was eighty or ninety yards from the road. The school grounds backed onto a swath of dusty trees with scant undergrowth. Mallard looked at a map on his phone. The patch of woods was about a quarter of a mile wide, separating the school grounds from the parking lot of a shopping mall, barely clinging to life.

He didn't have to climb. Halfway along the back fence, a ten-foot section had been cut away. Two deep, muddy ruts, a car's width apart, came through the woods and went through the gap and around the corner of the dorm with unbroken windows. Mallard stood for a long moment, listening. Aside from a few birds, there was nothing to hear. Feeling naked and exposed, he went through the fence and followed the ruts, forcing himself to walk upright.

A green panel van with a cross painted on the hood was parked on the far side of the dorm, the open rear doors near a cellar entrance. The cellar doors were pushed back, and cement stairs descended into darkness.

He considered calling Stallings, but what would he tell her? For all he knew, Sister Patience owned this land and had every right in the world to be here. He couldn't even give Stallings any kind of rationale for trying to get a warrant. Judges were generally not persuaded by *the place felt really creepy, Your Honor.*

He went down the stairs slowly, letting his eyes adjust to the gloom. The short corridor in front of him ended in stairs going up into the interior of the building. There were two doors on either side, the first door on the right open. The small room inside was lit by a single bulb hanging from a cord. The walls were lined with stacks of crates and boxes. Some held basic kitchen staples—flour, sugar, cooking oil—but most held candy bars. The top box of each stack was open.

There was a sudden sound of footsteps moving across the floor above him. Mallard froze, holding his breath. The steps went still after a moment and didn't resume.

Mallard took a deliberate step across the corridor. He turned the knob of the door across from the storeroom and eased it open. Pale light filtered into this room from a window near the ceiling. It was enough to show three heavy iron cots, each bolted to the floor. Two were empty. On the one farthest from the door, Hansel Knutson stretched out on his back, one arm over his eyes. He was wearing only a pair of boxer shorts, and Mallard could see his ribs clearly outlined through his skin. A chain was padlocked to his left ankle and ran out of sight under the cot.

At first, Mallard thought he was too late. He stepped instinctively forward and felt a flood of relief when the boy moved his arm away and lifted his head. The relief ended when the boy's eyes shifted over Mallard's shoulder and widened. Mallard started to turn, but the base of his skull exploded, and the cement floor rushed to meet him.

* * *

Mallard startled awake, face doused with water. Sputtering, he tried to rise but sank back, skull throbbing. He touched the back of his head. The skin was pulpy and warm, and he smelled blood, too, dimly surprised his smelled like everyone else's. He blinked, fighting to bring the world into focus. He was on a rough canvas blanket, stripped to his underwear, something heavy wound around his left ankle. He lifted his foot and felt the weight of the chain, like the one on the boy.

"I'm glad you did not die, Mr. Mallard. It means you can still be purified." A petite woman in a black and white habit stood beside the cot, expression serene, with a bottle of water in her hand.

"Sister Patience," he said, his voice a harsh croak.

She put the water on the floor. "Rejoice, sinner. For your earthly troubles are ended. Here shall you be freed of the encumbrance of your earthly flesh."

"You need to let me go. I'm not some homeless kid. People are going to miss me." He looked around, his vision still blurred. There were only two cots, and the window by the ceiling was in a different place. The boy was in another room.

"I'm going to let you go." Her voice was light, with a singsong intonation. "Go to your heavenly reward. My love compels me, for to free you would be to condemn you to eternal suffering. Here you will earn everlasting peace by being released from your sullied form."

"She means she's going to starve you to death." A girl stood in the doorway. She wore a Catholic girl's school uniform, down to the white socks and patent leather shoes. Her hands were clasped demurely in front of her, and her long hair was shining and clean.

"Gretel." Mallard forced himself into a sitting position.

"Her name is Sister Virtue." Patience went to the doorway and put a hand on Gretel's shoulder. "My disciple. My assistant in the great work."

"What great work is that?" Mallard managed.

Patience's eyes turned to him placidly. "Men are made demons by their flesh," she said. "The flesh of the woman gives life. The flesh of the man, only death. Through privation, you will be freed of your sin, free to become a spirit eternal."

"Jesus Christ," Mallard said.

"Blasphemer. With your own lips you condemn yourself." Patience raised her hands, seeming prepared to go on, but Gretel interrupted her.

"I remember you. You arrested our father. You took him away."

"That's right. But I'm not a policeman anymore. I'm here to help you."

"We were left with Mother," Gretel said. "Mother isn't nice."

"I know," Mallard said, having trouble keeping the woman and the girl in focus. He tried to decide if telling Gretel about her mother was a good idea, but the problem seemed too complex to fix. "She's dead, Gretel. I'm sorry. Your father got out and—and he was very angry that you weren't there."

Gretel stared. "Is that the truth?"

"It is."

The girl looked at Sister Patience. "We need to leave."

Patience shook her head. "The work is not done, child. You have much still to learn. Your brother will be purified soon."

"You said you'd let him go before he died. You said you were only teaching him the weakness of flesh."

"Sister," the woman said. "I said what was needed to start you on your path. You may not turn aside now."

Gretel stood absolutely still, stared for a moment, then turned and disappeared.

Patience sighed. "You will be given water to ease your way, Mr. Mallard. We will pray together thrice daily—"

Gretel was back in the hallway, behind the nun, holding a baseball bat stained with blood. Mallard had the sick feeling some of it was his. Gretel reared back, swung the bat, and connected with the woman's head.

Patience jerked, eyes wide, then collapsed to the floor.

Gretel looked at Mallard. "Will you help my brother?"

"Yes," he said, stomach roiling.

Gretel knelt and reached inside Patience's clothes. She brought out a ring of keys and tossed them to Mallard, who missed catching them. "Get him out of here," she said. "Hurry." She took hold of Patience's wrists and dragged her out of sight.

Mallard bent for the keys. The movement made his head swim, and he fell from the bed, landing heavily on his side. There were five keys on the ring. The third one opened his padlock. He shook loose of the chain, tried to stand, and decided to crawl.

The short corridor was empty. Mallard crawled as fast as he could to the boy's room. Hansel was breathing but didn't move when Mallard shook him. This time, he got lucky on the second key. He sucked in a ragged breath and forced himself to stand. Steeling himself, he picked up the boy and staggered to the door.

Sister Patience was lying on the floor of the storage room. Her hands moved weakly at her sides. Gretel stood over her, holding a gallon jug of cooking oil. She upended it and poured the oil over the woman, the sickening smell filling the air.

"What the hell are you doing?" Mallard said.

Gretel looked at him as she tossed the jug aside. "Get him out." She slammed the storage room door, and he heard a bolt slide closed. He had no energy to break it down. Going up the cellar stairs was all he could manage, and with the boy in his arms, he almost didn't make it. A few feet past the van, he collapsed into the weeds, head jackhammering in pain.

He sucked in another ragged breath, forced himself upright, and turned just in time to see the building go up in flames.

* * *

"We'll probably never know who she was," Stallings said. "Body was burned so badly that even DNA is gonna be hard to pull."

She was sitting on one side of Mallard's hospital bed. Tasha was on the other, giving Stallings looks that the cop was diplomatically ignoring.

"Gretel?" Mallard asked.

"No sign of her. She got out somehow. But there were at least five bodies in that fourth cellar room, maybe more. They'll be digging for a while."

"And the boy?"

"Malnutrition, but they expect him to recover. Physically, anyway. Lord knows he'll need therapy, but he'll get whatever he needs. He's a celebrity now. The killer nun's last victim." Stallings clicked her pen. "You're going to be hearing from a lot of reporters yourself. Can probably get your job back, if you leverage it right."

"Pass," Mallard said, Tasha squeezing his hand. "I'm fresh out of fucks to give."

* * *

Two days later, Mallard awoke in the middle of the night, not knowing what had roused him. The chair beside his bed was empty, Tasha having gone home for the first time. Mallard turned his head and Hansel was standing there, looking down at him, hand holding an IV stand connected to the inside of his arm.

They looked at each other for a long minute.

"Thank you for getting me out," the boy whispered.

Mallard resisted the urge to say something flip. "You're welcome."

The boy nodded and stepped away from the bed.

"Hansel. Where do you think she'll go?"

The boy's eyes were huge, his skin almost translucent. "Someplace where she can hurt people," he whispered. "She's very angry. All the time."

Mallard found himself whispering back. "She's the Bad Cat, isn't she?"

The boy nodded. "Bad Cat," he said. Then he was gone.

Mallard didn't sleep again that night.

# Goldilocks and the Three Bears

By John M. Floyd

Officer Goldie Johnson was depressed.

Part of it was her job. Working as a cop in a quiet suburb of a midsized city had its good points—she didn't get shot at often, for one thing—but six years of low pay and few promotions and no challenges were wearing her down. That, and personal stuff. Money trouble, back trouble, weight trouble, marriage trouble. Admittedly, Goldie's backaches were probably weight-related (fixing the one might fix the other), and some of her problems were more serious than others (overdrawn bank accounts were worse than strained buttons on her uniform)—but even the minor irritants were getting to her. Like the time her nitwit husband Bernie had left out the apostrophe when he'd painted the sign LOCKES AUTO REPAIR over the door of his shop, or the fact that—although she'd kept and always used her maiden name—Bernie insisted on introducing her to others as Goldie Locke, which inevitably produced either smiles or smirks, and afterward Bernie seemed to consider it her fault.

Not only was Goldie feeling depressed, she was also feeling guilty about feeling depressed. After all, she did have gainful employment, boring though it was. Most of her work time was spent issuing traffic tickets and defusing domestic disturbances, the kind of low-risk/low-stress duty that would've suited most folks just fine. It certainly suited her assigned partner, Joe Bob Finkter, who wore her ear off talking about his model trains. But the point was, Goldie longed for more than a cushy job. She longed for some real police work, which was something she and Joe Bob never saw or heard about.

Well, almost never. Precious Everett, one of the file clerks at the police station and a friend of Goldie's since childhood, had given her an unusual piece of information the other day.

"I think something funny's going on next door," Precious said. The two of them had run into each other in the hallway after Monday morning roll call. Precious had a file folder in one hand and a coffee cup in the other. It was raining outside the station-house windows at the time, which did nothing to help Goldie's gloomy mood.

"Next door to what?" Goldie asked.

"My house, that's what."

"Funny how?"

"Funny peculiar," Precious said. And for the next ten minutes, she unloaded all her fears and concerns about the home she said was owned by the Barrett family on the lot next to hers on Hamilton Street. She'd never met the occupants in the two months they'd lived there, she told Goldie, and in recent weeks she'd noticed odd comings and goings at all hours of the night, cars parked out front when no one was home, rough voices she didn't recognize, delivery boys in and out all the time carrying covered boxes and cases, and—always—averted eyes and sneaky looks anytime Precious happened to spot anyone and offer a greeting. A strange and secretive bunch.

"What do you mean, voices you didn't recognize?" Goldie asked. "You just said you've never met the residents."

"I haven't, but I know what they sound like. It's a crowded neighborhood—most of our houses are less than ten feet apart." Precious paused and added, "Some of the after-hours visitors had guns tucked in their waistbands."

Goldie frowned. "You sure about that?"

"I work at a police station. I know a gun when I see it."

Both of them fell silent for a moment. Several fellow cops passed them in the hallway.

"What's the name?" Goldie asked. "Barrett, you said?"

"Yeah. Father, mother, one son. The parents are employed someplace, apparently—both leave in the same car every morning around eight and are gone till six—and the kid always catches the school bus in front of the house before they leave."

"How old's the son?"

"I don't know, ten, eleven? His name's Theodore. They call him Teddy."

"Teddy Barrett?" Goldie said. "You're kiddin' me."

"It gets better. The parents' names are Grennen and Sugar."

"Griffin?"

"Grennen." Precious spelled it out.

"Grennen Barrett? *Sugar Barrett?* Precious, you are the worst liar I've ever—"

"I'm dead serious."

"Right," Goldie said. "And you know their first names because…"

"Because I know the real estate agent who sold 'em the house. When they moved in next door to me, I asked her for details."

Goldie paused, realizing her friend wasn't joking. Could this story get any crazier?

"So, you said the house is empty all day?"

"Empty of people," Precious said. "Heaven knows what else might be inside. They could be holding handcuffed Venezuelan refugees in there for all I know. They could be making fake hundred-dollar bills or cooking crystal meth. They could be building a bomb in the basement."

"This is South Alabama," Goldie said. "Know how many homes here have basements?"

"Figure of speech, okay? I'm just saying something sneaky's going on in that house."

"For which you have no real evidence."

Precious shrugged. "Call it an educated guess. But I would bet my law-enforcement-file-clerk's nonexistent badge that there's a shitload of criminal activity taking place in a location practically right outside my bedroom window."

Goldie let out a sigh. Secretly, she was interested—intrigued, even—but she hesitated to let her over-emotional friend know that. After some thought, she asked the question she was already asking herself. "What am I supposed to do about it?"

Precious gave her the stink eye. "You're a cop—you're supposed to check it out. You and that gooberhead partner of yours."

"Check it out, how? Knock on the front door and question them? Bring them into the station? Stake the place out? Bug their phones? Search the premises?" Goldie, who'd been ticking off each item, stopped when she ran out of fingers. "How would we get a search warrant without probable cause?"

"Beats me. I man the phones and file paperwork. This is *your* job."

Having said that, Precious Everett continued carrying whatever she was carrying to wherever she was carrying it, leaving Goldie Johnson standing in the hallway.

But Goldie already had an idea in mind. She smiled to herself. Maybe this was just what she needed.

Hadn't she read someplace that the best cure for depression is a *challenge*?

Even her backache felt better.

* * *

The pain in her ass, however, remained. His name, appropriately, was Joe Bob Finkter. It was the only word Goldie'd ever heard that rhymes with a certain muscle.

"I realize it's not normal procedure," Goldie said to him. They were in their squad car with her at the wheel, cruising a street near the station. A few raindrops dotted the windshield.

"What it is," Joe Bob said, "is a crime in itself. We can't just break into somebody's house because you *think* something's going on there."

"Not we," she said. "Me. All I need you to do is stay outside and keep watch. And it wouldn't be breaking in. Precious says the back window's always open an inch or two, rain or shine. I just want a quick look around."

"How does Precious know all this?"

"The houses are close together. The window's right outside her own."

Her partner shook his head. "Sure sounds like breaking in, to me," he whined. Joe Bob, she'd found, whined a lot, even when things were going his way. "I say tell the chief about it and let her decide what to do."

"Old Stoneface? What she'll do is nothing, Fink. You know that." Goldie had taken to calling him Fink because she thought "Joe Bob" sounded even hickier than he was. "This could prevent what might be serious criminal activity"—she was beginning to like that term—"right here on our beat."

Joe Bob was still shaking his head like a tennis spectator, so she casually added, "I heard yesterday about an estate sale by the family of a train guy."

"A what?"

"A dude who collected model trains. A dozen fancy layouts, I heard. All of it has to go."

After a brief silence, he said, "You got the address?"

"Someplace. I could probably find it."

They stopped at a red light. Goldie could feel Joe Bob staring at her from the passenger seat. *Was this playing dirty?* she wondered. Everybody knew her partner was obsessed with model trains—actually, trains of any kind. It was rumored he watched old *Casey Jones* episodes on DVD.

It was raining harder now. Goldie turned on the wipers.

"I'd just be a lookout," he said finally. "Right?"

* * *

The next day at exactly nine a.m., Goldie Johnson snuck through muddy backyards until she reached the narrow space between her friend Precious Everett's house and the one next door. The morning was overcast but dry for a change, and sure enough, the back window Precious had mentioned was cracked an inch or so. Goldie pushed it up with one elbow to make a gap of about twenty inches. It would go no higher. Determined, Goldie sucked in her stomach and squeezed through. Her point of entrance, she discovered, was a laundry room.

Breathing deeply, Goldie recalled her promise to Joe Bob Finkter: I just want a quick look around. He was currently parked at the curb under a shade tree two houses away and was—hopefully—keeping an eye out for anyone,

22

Barretts or not, who might be approaching. She hadn't forgotten her friend's warning that people sometimes came to the house when no one was home.

Her first stop was the kitchen, the window also visible from Precious's house—the room she'd told Goldie was often used for meetings. *What kinds? Family gatherings? Planning sessions? Mission reports?* Goldie stopped in the doorway and scanned the room.

The first thing she noticed was that the three Barretts were not the tidiest of families. The table was littered with used silverware, a cereal bowl, two greasy plates, a glass, and two empty coffee cups. The three chairs around the table, instead of being a matched set, were of different sizes: one large, one medium-sized, one small. Carefully, since Goldie's back was killing her after the contorted climb through the window, she sat in the biggest chair to rest a moment, which was so hard and uncomfortable that she moved to the next smaller one—no better—while she examined the tabletop more closely. Nothing notable there, just the leavings of breakfast. At last, she settled into the smallest of the chairs, which fit her size best—she was wide but barely five foot two. It was then she spotted several items of interest.

With a groan, she rose to her feet—the chair groaning and cracking from her weight too—and crossed the room to the counter beside the sink with a plastic milk jug and other containers holding various amounts of water. Or what looked like water. Goldie pulled on latex gloves, gingerly dipped a finger into a container, and—hoping it wasn't poison—touched her tongue.

*Sugar water?*

She frowned, wondering if the liquid had something to do with drug production.

She pulled a small empty bottle from her pocket, poured the liquid inside, capped it tightly, and dropped the bottle into a plastic "evidence" bag.

Also on the counter were a box of graham crackers, a loaf of bread, a stack of potholders, a full jar of honey, and matched salt and pepper shakers. She set the evidence bag aside, picked up the crackers and the jar, looked them over, and took pictures with her phone. Then she methodically checked cabinets and drawers. Nothing there. Leaving the room, she dug out her phone again and punched in a number.

Precious Everett answered immediately. "Are you in?"

"Yeah," Goldie said. "Where are you?"

"Behind the dumpsters outside the station house. No one can hear me. Anything so far?"

"Maybe. I'll call you when I'm done." Goldie stepped over several boxes and papers that cluttered the floor. "You got some messy neighbors."

"Is Sphincter with you?"

"Finkter. He's in the car, standing watch."

"Okay," Precious said. "Over and out."

Goldie rolled her eyes, put her phone away, and examined the living room. More disorder, but nothing glaring. Here, too, were three chairs of different sizes: big, mid-sized, and small. She sagged into the largest, which she figured would be the most comfy. It wasn't. The middle chair was worse. Hard and lumpy. Only the small chair felt good. Goldie let out a tired breath and tried to relax her stiff back as she looked around the room.

She didn't have to look far. She immediately spotted something underneath a couch. With an effort, she rose from the chair, hoping she hadn't damaged this one as well, and moved to the couch, pulling out items she'd seen. One was a heavy chisel-like tool, another had a long handle with a sinister hook on one end. Stored with them were various clamps and racks.

What the hell were these things? Weapons? Torture devices?

They didn't look like tools for repair or woodworking or metalworking.

Things were getting curiouser and curiouser.

Goldie checked her watch. She'd been inside almost ten minutes. Fink was probably hyperventilating. She wiped the sweat from her face, checked the rest of the room, and left.

Next was a bathroom which yielded nothing of note, except a pyramid of Charmin toilet-paper rolls. The room after that, she figured, was a bedroom—but the door was locked. Frowning and wishing and jiggling the doorknob had no effect, and since she had no key and no time to look for one, she reluctantly moved on.

On the other side of the hall was indeed a bedroom, a large space with not one or two beds but three, side-by-side, one big, one regular, one fairly small. Again, the size difference wasn't surprising—nothing about this place seemed normal. What did surprise her was that young Teddy apparently shared a room with his parents. He probably had to, she realized, since the other bedroom wasn't available. Again, she wondered what the locked room was used for. Storage, possibly? How she wished she could've seen what was inside.

Focusing on what she *could* see, she checked this bedroom's closets, dresser, and night tables—and found six firearms. Four revolvers, two automatics. That seemed like five guns too many, but not necessarily illegal. She discovered nothing else of interest. She couldn't resist trying out the beds, partly out of curiosity and partly because her back had grown steadily worse—a byproduct of squeezing an XL-size woman through an L-sized window. But, as before, resting provided little relief. The beds couldn't have been more uncomfortable if they were covered with Hindu nails instead of sheets and blankets. Wearily, Goldie climbed off the smallest one, and only then remembered to check between the mattresses and under the beds.

And found something. From underneath the biggest bed, she pulled a long, wide cardboard box bearing no identifying information. It was already open, so she parted the flaps and peeked inside. What she saw was some sort of suit made of thick white material, with buckles, straps, zippers, gloves, and a hood. It reminded her of laboratory outfits she'd seen mad villains wear in science-fiction movies. This, somehow, disturbed her more than the locked room and the guns and other weird items she'd found so far.

Goldie took photographs of everything.

She remained kneeling for a minute, thinking hard. All this had become seriously creepy. Were these people conducting experiments of some kind? Were they plotting something, some deadly operation? Could they be terrorists, hiding out here, waiting for their opportunity? Whatever was happening, it was time for a decision. Maybe Fink was right—she needed to tell Chief Stonecipher. Maybe it could be done without revealing her little field trip and what she'd found and photographed. Goldie could just say she and Precious had heard and seen things that were suspicious from afar, enough to justify immediate action. In war-on-terror terms, if you see something, say something, right?

But that would come later. Right now, it was time to get the hell out of Dodge.

Just as she was pushing the Dr. No suit and its box back underneath the bed, her phone buzzed. This time it wasn't Precious. It was Finkter.

"Somebody's coming," Joe Bob hissed. "Get out, quick!"

Goldie almost wet her pants. Frantically, she finished stowing the box, stuffed the phone into her pocket, and headed for her escape hatch. On her way into the hall, she heard a car door slam; when she reached the laundry room, she heard steps on the front porch; as she approached the open window, she heard the click of a key in the door.

Then she thought of something that made her stop in her tracks.

*The evidence bag.*

She'd left it in the kitchen.

Frozen, Goldie heard the front door squeak open, heard someone enter the house.

Her vision blurred; her heart was in her throat. She couldn't leave the bag behind.

*Think*, she told herself. Whoever it was, where would he—or she—go first? Living room? Bedroom? *Kitchen?* Goldie could hear footsteps now, coming down the hallway. What could she do? There was no place to hide.

At that moment, she heard another door open, and close again. Not the front; an inside door, nearby. Who closes a door behind them in an otherwise empty house?

Then she understood. *The bathroom.*

Relief flooded her frenzied mind; her muscles unlocked. Quietly, she left the room, crept past the closed door of the hall bathroom, entered the kitchen, snatched her plastic bag off the counter, and retraced her steps. Just as she reached the laundry room, she heard the toilet flush, heard the bathroom door open.

*No more time!*

Trembling, she squeezed headfirst through the window and landed in a heap on the soggy grass below. Within seconds, she was on her feet, back pain forgotten, sprinting like a scalded ape away and around the corner of the house. She didn't slow until she was three houses away. It took her five minutes to calm herself enough to circle back to the squad car and her waiting partner.

Goldie opened the passenger door and collapsed into the seat before turning to look at Joe Bob. He gaped back at her. His face seemed to have aged ten years.

"From now on," he said, "you can keep your estate sales."

She sighed and pointed to the windshield. "Drive."

* * *

That afternoon, once she'd made sure there'd been no complaints of a prowler on Hamilton Street that morning, Goldie made her case to her superiors about the mysterious Barretts. She said nothing about her unofficial tour of the house or the "evidence" she'd gathered. She also neglected to mention her partner's participation. After considerable embellishment, some of which was fictional and most of which involved Precious's sighting of gunmen coming and going, she urged Chief Stonecipher to order an immediate raid of the home, and the only reason her suggestion worked was the mention of a "possible terrorist threat." She said the magic words in front of several witnesses, and after that, everyone knew that if they didn't do anything and something *did* happen, the whole force might soon find itself on permanent security duty at the city amusement park, with the chief guarding the Ferris wheel.

Goldie was allowed to accompany the raid, and at around six p.m. that day, half a dozen cops descended on the suburban home of Grennen and Sugar Barrett while the shocked residents watched their house searched from stem to stern. The final result, however, was not what Goldie Johnson—or Precious Everett, for that matter—had expected or hoped. It turned out, the Barrett family was not hosting some kind of evil and illegal enterprise.

The three Barretts were beekeepers.

Grennen and Sugar raised and tended bees every day at an offsite location between here and Montgomery, and even Teddy helped out on weekends. The strange and wicked-looking tools scattered about the house, including those with hooks and chisel blades, were hive scrapers and honey extractors. The scary white space-suit—each of the Barretts had one at the hive site— was a protective bee suit with a hood. The one under the bed was a spare. The locked room contained no bombs or bazookas or AR-15s. Inside was a dozen cases of honey in labeled mason jars. The handguns in the bedroom's dresser drawer were licensed, legal, and part of Mr. Barrett's collection that he and Sugar occasionally used for target shooting. And most of the unfamiliar liquids in the kitchen were indeed sugar water, a one-to-one mixture of sugar and water that the cops learned was used to energize and stimulate bees to produce a better product. In the end, the two parents and their young son were declared innocent of any wrongdoing. Sincere apologies were issued and politely accepted, and the team of crimefighters filed one by one out of the Barretts' home with tails between their legs and honey on their faces, so to speak.

But not before the chief of police—here too, by now—gave Goldie a long and meaningful stare. "You can ride back with me, Officer Johnson," she said. "We have some things to discuss."

Goldie barely heard the request. She was standing behind one of the uncomfortable living room chairs, heart in her boots, holding a labeled jar of honey she'd taken from a case in the corner of the room, a case that hadn't been there this morning. She figured it had been delivered that afternoon by one of the shady-looking workers Precious had seen earlier. Maybe the same one Goldie had heard come in during her own visit. She stared at the jar and wondered idly if any policewoman in the history of law enforcement had managed to commit career suicide so quickly and effectively.

By now, almost all her colleagues had left, filing somberly toward the parked cruisers. Goldie bent to replace the jar of honey—

And froze.

Slowly, she straightened, still studying the jar. The bottom was opaque, the lower half covered with a colorful label that said BARRETT FARMS—PURE HONEY.

Frowning, she lifted the jar and lowered it again, several times, like a dumbbell. Then, she turned and marched into the kitchen. The full, unlabeled jar of honey she'd seen on the counter this morning was still there. She picked it up and held both jars, one in each hand, raising and lowering them together.

The one in her left hand weighed more than the one in her right.

Goldie was vaguely aware the adult Barretts and Chief Stonecipher had entered the kitchen, all three watching her. She didn't care. With no hesitation, Goldie took out a penknife, slit the label on the jar in her right hand, and peeled back the paper.

The bottom third of the jar, visible now, wasn't honey. It was packed with fine white powder.

Slowly, Goldie and her boss turned to the Barretts. Both parents sagged into their chairs at the table, shoulders slumped, faces slack.

But Chief Stonecipher's face wasn't slack. The always-solemn chief was smiling now.

* * *

Two weeks later, Goldie leaned back in a lawn chair behind Precious Everett's house and gazed up at the cloudless blue sky. The weather had finally cleared, and the sun felt good. Flowers were blooming, birds were singing, and her back exercises seemed to be helping. In a matching chair six feet away, Precious stretched and sipped from a glass of lemonade. "This," she said, "is what Saturdays are made for."

"Bernie would disagree," Goldie said. "He's gone hunting with his buddies."

Precious gave her a look. "How're things going on that front?"

Goldie shrugged. "The usual. He told me this morning to mind his shop while he's out playing Daniel Boone, and I told him he could stick his hunting license up his ass. I'm not sure he's doing *that*, but I'm sure he's not at the shop, so I guess he called his brother in to help out for the day." She knew Bernie Locke would never change. A week ago, she'd finally talked him into adding the apostrophe to his sign, and he put it in the wrong place. "I'm divorcing him," she added. "When it's done, wanta go on a vacation with me to Tahiti?"

Precious grinned. "Is that in Alabama?"

Both of them laughed.

The truth was, they might actually be able to do that, Goldie thought. Ever since the Barrett drug bust, things had improved for them both. Goldie received the promotion she'd been hoping for, along with the associated pay bump, and thanks to her mention of who'd supplied the original tip, Precious Everett also got a raise. And since the two old friends had helped make the chief look like a genius, daily life at the station house had improved as well.

How could they *not* be heroes? As everyone soon learned, the secret and immensely profitable Barrett Farms cocaine network had operated for years and served three states. Now it had been discovered and dismantled, not by the DEA but by a file clerk and a patrol officer in the local PD. Sometimes, Goldie thought, good things happen to good people.

"How about Sphincter?" Precious asked. "I haven't seen him lately."

"You won't. He went to work for the railroad."

"Seriously?"

"Yep." And Goldie didn't mind a bit. On their way back from their unauthorized probe of the Barretts' home that fateful morning, Joe Bob Finkter had informed her that he wanted no involvement with what had happened or anything that might happen as a result. So, she'd kept his name out of it when she'd asked the chief for the raid. But when that turned out brilliant instead of disastrous, she didn't mention Fink then either. No involvement meant no involvement. Joe Bob pitched a fit in the squad room in front of the wrong people and was invited to take his already-doubtful talents elsewhere. She made a mental note not to book a train trip anytime soon.

Noises from the house next door snapped Goldie out of her thoughts. "What was that?" she asked, turning to look.

"Forgot to tell you," Precious said. "I have new neighbors."

"In the Barrett house?"

"Yep. Family of eight."

"Whoa," Goldie said. "Did you ask the real estate lady for their names?"

"No, but I got a look at 'em yesterday. Single woman and seven kids."

"Seven?"

"Yep. Odd little boogers, too. One looks bashful, one looks sleepy, one's happy, one's grumpy—" Precious paused, frowning. "What's the matter?"

"Nothing," Goldie said, raising her lemonade glass. "Here's to Ms. White."

"What? You know her name?"

Goldie smiled. "Call it an educated guess."

# Rapunzel

By Adam Meyer

I was standing out in front of The Whiskey Jar the first time I saw the girl with the golden hair.

I wasn't expecting to find her, not then. I kept looking down the sidewalk for Gabby, who was running late, when I felt the first drops of rain on my head and heard a faint ping. The text message was short and direct. Gabby wasn't planning to join me for the show tonight. She wanted to "move on."

Not a huge surprise. We'd only been going out a few weeks, and after a white-hot start, things had cooled quickly. Despite her lack of taste in music—she thought Taylor Swift hung the moon, and rolled her eyes every time I played The Clash—we had gotten along well, or so I'd thought. But while we had a good time going out drinking and listening to music, the breakfasts the next morning had always felt strained.

Well, no more awkward chats over burnt coffee and frozen waffles. Gabby was gone.

I wasn't exactly brokenhearted, but I felt a pang of regret. Somehow, I was about to slide past thirty without a steady girlfriend, a stable career, or a sense of where I was headed except to the next dive bar to see one more group trying to rise from Charlottesville's indie music scene to superstardom. This being a feat no one had done since the Dave Matthews Band, back when I was in diapers.

Turning from the street, I started to move under The Whiskey Jar's front awning and out of the spitting rain when I heard some distant singing.

A high-pitched, melodic female voice, chanting what sounded like an old-timey song—one I didn't recognize. The words might not even be English, though it was hard to tell. Whoever was singing sounded like an angel.

I stood there, listening, and as I started to turn toward the sound, I nearly collided with someone. A figure in a dark blue hoodie. Her shadowed face showed a flash of anger so intense I stepped back.

"Sorry," I said, putting my hands up in apology.

She dropped her gaze, and I studied her face more closely inside the hood. No trace of the fury I'd seen before. Either I had imagined it, or it had passed as quickly as it had come.

"It's okay," she said.

Her voice was high and melodic, and I realized: she's the singer.

The girl in the hoodie.

I squinted through the drizzling rain to get a better look at her. A long wave of straw-like yellow hair came down on either side of her face, her skin smooth and white like porcelain, her eyes cornflower blue. I'd never been one to believe in fairy tales, but when she looked up at me, I felt an instant connection. Or maybe I was still stung from Gabby's rejection and was trying to make myself feel better.

"I heard you singing…you're amazing. You in a band?"

She laughed, without humor. "Me? No."

"You sounded great. What were you singing?"

She shrugged inside the baggy blue fabric. The hood had started to slip off her head. Wisps of blond hair stuck to her damp face.

"I was just about to go in for the show," I said, gesturing at The Whiskey Jar. "There's a band called The Witches playing. Supposed to be pretty good."

She said nothing, looking down at her feet. Her shoes were simple and black.

"I'm going to write about the show for my *Substack*. It's called *Prince of the City*, 'cause that's my name, Prince. Aaron Prince. You into local music? Maybe you've read it, I've actually got a few thousand followers."

More like a few hundred, but who was counting? I closed my mouth to keep from saying more. In my efforts to impress this girl—woman, really, since she looked to be at least twenty—I had started blathering.

"Hey, why don't you come on in?" I nodded at the wooden doorway, the faint sound of voices wafting out. "Music might be decent, and at least it'll be dry in there. Plus, I owe you a drink for nearly knocking you down."

"Sorry, I can't. But thank you for the offer."

She pulled her hood back down, covering her face, and started edging down the street.

"Hold on. Wait up."

She ignored me, taking long strides away. "Hey!" I called, blinking away water as I chased her. "I didn't catch your name."

She turned, fixing her blue eyes on mine. "Zel. My name is Zel."

"Zel, forget the show. You want to grab a cup of coffee or something?"

She opened her mouth, starting to say no, but I charged past her down the sidewalk, leading the way to a brightly-lit storefront, the name GRIMM'S COFFEE etched into the window. I pulled the door open and waited for Zel to either step through the doorway or walk past me. I truly didn't know which choice she'd make.

Neither did she, from the look of it.

Her feet had stopped moving, one chunky black shoe aimed at the far corner, the other angled toward the open door. I started into the coffee shop, not looking back. A moment later, I heard squeaking shoes behind me.

"I can't stay long," she said.

I left Zel at a table in the corner while I went to the counter and ordered coffee for me and bottled water for her. When I looked back, I saw that she'd taken down the hood, revealing a wave of long blond hair. It streamed past her shoulders, glinting like spun gold.

When I returned to the table, I pushed the bottle of water toward her and smiled.

"Zel. Where'd you get a name like that? It must be short for something. Zelda?"

"That's two questions." She turned away, but not like she meant to hide anything, or at least not everything. "Yes, it's short for something. But not Zelda."

"What, then?"

She whispered her name. It was long and unwieldly, but also beautiful in its own way.

"What is it? Russian or something?"

"German. My mother was German."

"Was that a German song you were singing before?"

"Yes, an old lullaby my mother liked."

She looked sad, and I had the feeling our talk was about to be over before it had even begun. Changing course, I asked Zel about her favorite kinds of music. To my surprise, she loved classic folk singers like Joni Mitchell and James Taylor and Cat Stevens. But when I asked what she thought of Beyoncé or Billie Eilish, she stared at me blankly.

"Don't you stream new music?" I asked. "Or watch videos on YouTube?"

She looked down at the scuffed tabletop. "The only music I listen to is on the old records my parents left me. We don't have the Internet or anything like that at home...just a TV."

"But you've got a cell phone, right?"

She shook her head. "I don't have anyone to call...except the neighbors, I suppose."

I looked at Zel in disbelief. What she'd said was shocking, and yet I wasn't surprised somehow. Something about her seemed slightly foreign, like she had come here from another place or even another time.

"The truth is, I've never really made friends. I didn't go to school. I learned at home. My *Gothel*...she says there's so much filth out there and she needs to protect me from it."

"Wait, your what?" I asked.

"My *Gothel*." Zel looked down at the table again, folding her hands. "My godmother...my mother's best friend. They grew up together in the town of Hanau and came here to America after college. That's where my parents met. But they died in a car accident when I was only two and a half years old, and the truth is, I barely remember them. They always said if anything happened to them, they wanted my *Gothel* to raise me, and that's what she did."

"Zel, I don't mean to be rude, but your godmother…she didn't let you go to school? Or make friends? Or use a computer? I mean, she sounds more like a warden than a parent."

Zel's face flushed. "No, she's just looking out for me."

"Well, I guess. And she might be right, the world can be pretty messed up. But there's some amazing things in it too. Art and books and…" Before I knew it, I had launched into a long monologue about some of my favorite things, especially music, and Zel listened patiently but without much clue what I was talking about.

Finally, I realized the problem. Telling Zel about the songs I loved was pointless. I pulled out my phone and a pair of wireless earbuds. She picked them up, turning them over in her hands as if they were magic. I put one into her right ear, and then she nodded, sliding in the other.

"Okay, now I'm going to play some Beyoncé for you."

At first, she looked uneasy, as if the sounds flooding her ears unsettled her, and then her features started to relax. Now she was nodding to the beat. I took out one of the earbuds she was using and slipped it into my own ear. Together we grooved to the beat of "Love on Top."

When the song was over, Zel looked at me, her eyes wide. "That's… Beyoncé?"

"Yes. You like it?"

"Very much. Does she sing any other songs?"

I explained that, yes, in fact, Beyoncé had made many albums. We listened to more of her songs, and then I played some other female singers, like Adele and Amy Winehouse. All the while, I looked at Zel, watching the way the music seemed to enchant her, and felt anger twist inside me. Who was this godmother of hers? And why had she locked Zel away like a prisoner?

We had just started listening to some Alicia Keys when Zel pulled out her earbud and asked me the time. I told her it was nearly midnight. She stood sharply.

"I've got to go," she said.

"Don't tell me. If you don't get home in the next five minutes, you'll turn into a pumpkin." I smiled to show I was teasing, but she didn't seem to get the joke.

"It's just, if my *Gothel* wakes up and sees I'm not in my room—" Zel shook her head, her long blond hair shimmering. "I need to be there when she wakes up."

"She doesn't know you're gone?"

"She takes her medicines at night. I give them to her. Sometimes, I give her an extra dose of one of her pills…it puts her into a deep sleep… But if she wakes up and sees I'm gone…" She wrapped her arms around herself, shivering. "Thanks again for tonight. I mean it. It was…magical."

I reached out and touched her hand. She didn't pull away.

"Where do you live?" I asked. "Let me at least give you a ride home."

She shook her head. "No, I can walk. It's not far."

"Then I'll walk with you."

She said nothing, opening her mouth as if to say *no* and then closing it again. Sliding out from behind the table, she edged to the door. I watched her, hesitating, but after another step she looked back as if waiting for me. This time, I went after her.

* * *

As Zel had said, she lived only a short walk from the coffee shop. We didn't talk much along the way, but I was aware of the scent of Zel's hair and the sound of our footsteps. The rain had stopped, but everything gleamed with a wet sheen. She led the way down East High Street, past old single-family homes, and then down Third Street to the Castle Tower Apartments. The huge building had a medieval design with a brick façade and claimed half of a city block. It had an open courtyard in the middle and two tall towers at each end.

"Good," she said, pointing at a row of dark windows on the top floor of the near tower. "She's still asleep."

I took her hands in mine. They felt like they were made of ice.

"So, when am I going to see you again?"

She looked back up at the dark tower. "Aaron, I thought you understood. I can't." She let her eyes drop to her shoes. "My *Gothel*...if she finds out about you..."

She let the thought trail off, a trace of fear in her voice.

"Okay, listen, I've got an idea. You said you gave her an extra dose of pills, right?"

"Yes. But—"

"Do it again tomorrow. The coffee shop where I met you tonight is open late. I'll be back there at ten o'clock tomorrow night, and I'll wait for you."

"But that's..." She frowned. "Why would you do that?"

I thought of what to say, but instead I leaned in and kissed her quickly. She stared at me, shocked, and then smiled.

"I'll see you soon," I said, watching as she disappeared into the darkness.

* * *

I thought about Zel all the next day, even as I tried to finish an album review for my blog and worked on a playlist for an upcoming party that I was DJing. I kept trying to put her out of my head, but it was no use. Finally, I gave up on my work and searched online, looking up obscure old German lullabies, trying to find the one I'd heard Zel singing on the street. But I couldn't track it down.

I arrived at the coffee shop just before ten p.m., watching a cluster of blond coeds at the next table hunched over their laptops for a late-night study session. They seemed older and more savvy than Zel, and yet somehow they were pale imitations, bootleg recordings that didn't quite capture the live experience.

Zel didn't get there until almost a quarter past ten, pulling the hood off her long blond hair.

"Sorry, I'm late...it took forever for my *Gothel* to fall asleep, and when she did, I was scared she'd wake up again, so I waited...and besides, I thought maybe you wouldn't even be here."

I stood up, took her face in my hands, and kissed her.

Not a quick peck like last night.

When I pulled away, I looked into her blue eyes. She seemed both surprised and pleased. There was also a new emotion beneath it, one I felt deep inside myself as well, as I fought the urge to reach for her again.

Hunger.

"Do you want to listen to some music?" I said, thinking of the playlist I'd run through in my head earlier. But all of it seemed wrong now, and slightly irrelevant. "Or we could go for a drive. My car's only a couple of blocks away."

"A drive sounds nice."

We walked around the corner to my old Ford Bronco, which had rolled off the assembly line the same year Jay-Z first came on the music scene. Zel and I drove around the city for a while, listening to some Norah Jones on the Bluetooth stereo I'd installed a couple of years ago, and then I parked at a quiet spot over near Pen Park. I reached for Zel's face, kissing her again, longer and deeper than last time.

We soon made music of our own.

Although Zel was tentative at first, she quickly showed another side of herself. Intense and passionate. At one point, I looked at her and saw a kind of ferocity in her eyes. The same emotion I'd noticed ever so briefly the night before. But it was gone in an instant, leaving only the same wide-eyed innocence that had enchanted me since we met.

A little after one a.m., I took Zel back to the Castle and watched as she made her way across the courtyard, seeming to float.

When she had disappeared inside, I let my eyes run along the narrow windows of the apartment complex. About a third were dark. In the ones that were still lit, I saw the blue glow of television screens and the warm colors of bookshelves and framed posters.

Finally, a light went on at the top floor of the nearby tower.

A moment later, I saw Zel's face. She held up a hand. I blew her a kiss, spun away, and headed off.

* * *

I met Zel at the coffee shop every night for the next month. Usually, we'd follow the same pattern. We'd have a drink—coffee for me, water for her—listen to a few songs, then head back to my Bronco and take a short drive. As the nights piled up, we parked at the same place and got to know each other better. Not just physically, of course, but also through talking.

Zel told me about how lonely her childhood had been, how whenever she had a friend, her *Gothel* would find some way to keep them apart. She explained how the record albums left by her parents had been a lifeline to a family she'd barely known, and how she spent hours listening to them again and again. She revealed how she sometimes watched soap operas with her *Gothel* in the afternoons, seeing those couples in love and thinking she'd never have lives like they did.

I bought her a disposable phone so that we could stay in touch during the days, but she wouldn't take it. She was too worried about her *Gothel* finding it. Hearing that, I felt a sharp stab of anger, but also something else. Longing.

That was when I began to see what I'd tried to ignore: I wasn't just infatuated with Zel.

This was something more.

That night, we followed our usual routine, but everything felt different because of the constant thought echoing in my skull: *you love her.*

When I drove her back to the Castle, I parked at the curb and turned off the Bronco's engine. I looked at Zel, her face striped with shadows. I was scared to tell her the truth. Still, after all the risks she'd taken, it seemed like I ought to take one myself.

"Zel, I need to tell you something…I think I love you."

She turned away, long blond hair whipping across her shoulders.

"Don't say that."

"Why not?"

"Because I'm unlovable."

"That's not true." I pushed the curtain of hair from her cheek, tucked it behind her ear and kept my gaze on her face until she looked at me. "You are the most beautiful person I've ever known."

She stared out the windshield, seeming uncertain.

"You are so…so purely yourself, and somehow I feel like when I'm with you, I'm a better version of me." Hearing myself, I felt my face grow hot. "Never mind, I'm a walking cliché. I sound like a million bad love songs."

"That's okay." Zel leaned in closer. "I like love songs."

"I want you to stay with me," I said, running my fingers through her long blond hair. It was as soft as silk, my nerve endings coming alive beneath it.

"I'm right here."

"I mean for good."

She pulled away slightly. "I can't. My *Gothel…*she doesn't have anyone but me."

A line she'd been hearing her whole life, so often she'd mistaken it for truth. Or maybe it was true. But so what?

"You don't owe her anything. You've got a right to live your own life."

She looked at me, hesitant. Her eyes wide. Waiting for me to say the rest of it, or back away.

"Let's go off together. Get married. Make our own family."

I didn't know what kind of argument she'd make against it, but I was ready to push back with reasons of my own. She didn't, however. She leaned in and kissed me, and when she pulled away, her blue eyes stared deep into mine. In the dark, they looked like shiny black stones, the kind found deep in a cave where few ever went.

"I better go." She touched my cheek. "It's late."

She ran from the Bronco, hurrying across the Tower's front lawn. I wondered if I had just ruined things between us. But there was a bounce in her step that I hadn't seen earlier, and I knew deep down she felt exactly the way I did.

* * *

When I woke the next morning, I felt tired and uncertain. Maybe it was fear over what I'd said to Zel, or maybe it was the dreams I had that night. I

41

couldn't remember much, but I had a faint memory of being barefoot and scared, running through the forest. Something was chasing me. I could almost recall a creature, wolf-like with long fangs and yellowish fur, but the image was there and then gone.

That night, I got to the coffee shop at my usual time and waited for Zel. Again, I felt nervous that I'd pushed too far too fast, but part of me didn't care. I wanted her to know how big my feelings were. And I was tired of us sneaking around.

I finished off my coffee and looked at my cell phone. It was 10:20 p.m.

Since that first night, she'd been here like clockwork at ten.

Now I felt a cramp in my belly. Where was she?

After fifteen more minutes, I headed out of the coffee shop and along East High Street. By the time I got to the Castle, my stomach was lurching, and my head had started to throb.

Something was wrong. Very wrong.

I looked up at the nearest tower, studying the single narrow window where I'd seen Zel wave every night after she got upstairs. It was dark. But the two windows next to it were bright behind their curtains.

I went to the base of the tower, staring up at the cold, dark brick. Zel's apartment was five stories high. No way I could climb up there. I considered barging into the building and knocking on the door of her apartment—based on where the windows were, I felt sure I could find it—but that was risky. If I showed up, her *Gothel* would know all about me.

I clenched my hands, anxiety squeezing my belly. I had to do something. But what?

I looked up at the tower again and had an idea.

Maybe I could reach her the old-fashioned way.

I dug around in the bushes at the base of the Castle's front wall and gathered a handful of pebbles. Taking a few steps back, I hurled one. It hit the wall a short way below the window. On my next try, I missed the window by about half a foot. The third time was the charm, the rock plinking against the glass. I threw half a dozen others and was just about to gather more ammunition when a light turned on behind the curtain. A moment later,

Zel's face appeared. Old wood shrieked as she raised the window.

"Stop," she said, her voice a loud hiss. "Please."

"What's going on?" I called out, looking up at the tower. "Are you all right?"

"I'm fine. Just go away."

A lump formed in my throat. "What do you mean? I want to see you."

"You can't." When Zel turned her head to the side as if checking for someone, I was startled. Instead of her long, gleaming blond hair, I saw only jagged tufts. "Now go. Please."

"What'd she do to you?" I asked. "Your *Gothel*?"

"Nothing." Zel had lowered her voice to a whisper, and her words barely reached me. "Now why don't you just—"

Before she could finish, Zel backed away. An older woman appeared, dark hair framing a face pinched with anger. She shook her head as if to dismiss me, then backed away. A moment later, the window slammed down, and the light went off.

I waited a moment for Zel to return, but she was gone.

After that, I didn't hesitate.

I flung open the front door leading into the vestibule, a cauldron of anger and fear rising within me. A second door that faced the lobby was locked. The checkered marble floor and wide oak desk were deserted. I turned to the keypad beside the door and began pressing random numbers. It was too late for a package delivery, but surely someone must've been expecting takeout.

After a dozen tries, I heard the door buzz.

I yanked the handle and ran for the elevator.

Waiting, I stared at the double brass doors, willing them to part. Overhead, the number on the digital readout was frozen at 3. I shifted from foot to foot. All I could think about was the old woman's angry face and Zel's sheared locks.

Moving past the elevator, I pushed through a doorway marked stairwell.

I took the stone steps two at a time until they ran out. The hallway I stepped into was narrow with worn green carpet and silvery wallpaper threaded with vines. I followed the well-worn carpet to the end of the hall to where I knew Zel's apartment must be.

I banged forcefully on the door, putting my whole arm into it, same as I had when I'd been hurling pebbles. At first, there was no response. I took a deep breath and rapped again, three times in close succession, the heavy wooden door rattling.

Faintly, I heard a voice. Not Zel, someone else.

Her *Gothel*.

"Go away." She spoke with a faint German accent, putting a guttural twist on the words. "You are not welcome here."

"Let me in. I want to see her."

Silence.

I started to raise my fist to bang again when the door swung open. A woman no more than five feet tall looked out. Her broad face was twisted into a sneer, lines crisscrossing every inch of her flesh. Her squat, thick body was covered by a heavy gray nightgown. When she turned her face to mine, her dark eyes were full of fury, a glint of pleasure underneath. At first, I didn't know why, but then I realized: she must've thought she could control me like she controlled Zel.

"You will disturb the neighbors," she said, scowling. "Now go away."

"If you're worried about the neighbors, you better let me in to talk."

"I have nothing to say to you."

Despite her words, she stepped back from the door, creating just enough room for me to step in. The foyer was dark and claustrophobic. An oil painting of a windmill hung inside the doorway. Off to the side was a living room full of heavy wooden furniture. A large-screen TV was on the wall, an old movie playing on it. Something in black-and-white where a young woman was wandering lost in the forest. I thought again of my dream, wondering vaguely if Zel's *Gothel* had been the wolf that was chasing me.

I looked past the TV but didn't see any sign of Zel, or even a sign that she lived here.

Closing the door behind me, I studied the old woman.

"What'd you do to Zel?" I asked.

"I show her what is to happen when she sneaks around behind my back."

Her eyes sparkled as she said it, as if cruelty delighted her. "Like a common whore."

"Don't say that."

"Why not? It is true, no?" Her lips twisted into what might have been a smile. "Of course, she doesn't look like that anymore. Now she is ugly."

Looking past the old woman, I saw Zel peeking out from down the hallway. Her lovely blond hair had been cut away. No, *hacked off* was more like it. There was a long tuft on the right side, the edges jagged, while on the left, it was almost cut down to the scalp. The shape of her face was more visible without all that lush hair to frame it. The steep angles of her cheeks, the slight curve along her chin, the gentle slope toward her neck.

"No," I said, looking at Zel rather than her *Gothel*. "She's not ugly. She's still the most beautiful woman I've ever seen."

The old woman let out a sound like a cough. "Nonsense. The way she is looking, no man will want her."

"I want her." I took a step forward so that the old woman and I were only inches apart. "Tonight, she's leaving with me. And she's never coming back."

"She belongs here!"

"Not anymore."

The old woman tried to block me, but I pushed past her. As I moved through the darkened living room, Zel rushed toward me.

"You have to go," she said as I pulled her against my chest. "She's dangerous."

"I'm not leaving without you."

I pulled away from Zel, sensing movement behind me. When I turned, the old woman stood only a few feet away, hands clutched into fists.

"Lust has made a fool of you. But I won't let you ruin my goddaughter."

"You're the one that's ruined her. Not me."

I looked defiantly at Zel's *Gothel*. Despite my clear size advantage, she showed no sign of backing down, and something about her defiance unnerved me. On a wooden table beside me, I saw a small bronze statue of a little girl reading. I picked it up by the head, wielding the heavy piece like a weapon.

"Come on, Zel, it's time for us to go."

"For you, maybe." The old woman nearly shook with anger, her fists like small bricks at the end of her arms. "Not for her."

She raised her fist, which had something in it—a tiny black canister.

I swung the statue, but it was too late. Liquid sprayed my face. Wincing, I dropped to my knees, the statue tumbling from my hand. I sucked in a breath, pressed my hands against my eyes, feeling the fire driving deeper into the sockets.

"What've you done?" Zel asked, her voice sharp, nearly panicked.

I forced my stinging eyes open, desperate to find her. But all I could see was a faint outline with a blond halo.

"He will be all right," the old woman said. "But he must go."

"When he leaves, I'm going with him."

"Nonsense. You will stay here with me."

Determined to leave with Zel, I pushed to my feet, eyes scorching, tears tumbling down my cheeks. But the pain was too much, and I collapsed again.

Zel and her *Gothel*, outlined orbs of light and hulking pieces of dark wood, circled each other now.

"I won't spend another night under your roof," Zel said.

"You will do as I say." The old woman's voice was thick with rage. "As you should have done before you lay down with this *saukerl*. Or else you must be punished."

Since the old woman had already cut Zel's hair off, I had no idea what other penalty she had in mind. But I didn't want to find out.

"He loves me, you know," Zel said. "And I love him."

I groped at the floor for the statue but couldn't find it. Still, I kept reaching.

"You really believe he is still wanting you? The way you look now? You are a bigger fool than I thought."

"You're the fool. If you think you can stop me from leaving," Zel said, her voice shifting from anger to ice.

"Please, darling…" For the first time, I heard fear in the old woman's voice. "I'm sorry…I didn't mean…"

"You kept me here against my will." Zel sounded closer.

I continued to blink, tears streaking my cheeks, the room slowly coming into view—Zel at the narrow windows, right arm raised, something brownish and curved extending from her hand—was it the statue? "You made me small, *Gothel*, just like this little girl. And you kept me that way."

"No, I…"

Turning to where I heard the old woman's voice, I saw a blur of motion as another shape launched itself at her. Then I heard a scream. Blinking, I tried to see more clearly, but all I could make out was a misshapen creature with eight legs and two heads, writhing. The two women, fighting each other. I closed my eyes and brought my hands to my ears, drowning out the sound of the old woman's cries and the squelch of the statue as it met soft flesh and hard bone.

I sat there, blinking, not moving, until finally I felt a gentle hand on my arm.

"Are you okay?" Zel asked.

I nodded slowly.

She helped me stand, my legs still unsteady, and I thought I'd need to sit again. Until her lips touched mine. I opened my eyes and finally saw her clearly: cheeks spattered with blood, blue eyes wide, shorn blond hair sticking out every which way.

"Did you really mean it?" she asked. "About us being together forever?"

I looked at the blood spots on her face and winced, remembering how the statue had sounded coming down on the old woman's head.

Zel started to pull away from me, but I grabbed her wrist and held her.

"Listen," I said, staring into her eyes. "Your *Gothel* was wrong. I'll always want to be with you. You're still as beautiful as ever."

She looked at me with disbelief, a flicker of hope, and then suspicion.

"You don't mean that."

"Yes, I do."

"Even after what I've done?"

I felt a little nauseous. Maybe it was from the pepper spray and the headache, or maybe it was the coppery smell of blood. But I didn't care. I pulled Zel close, smoothing jagged tufts of hair against her head, absorbing the weight of her body as she leaned against me.

"I love you, Zel."

Faintly, I heard voices in the hall, followed by someone banging on the door. Zel pulled away from me.

"The neighbors," she said. "Someone must've called the police."

I nodded. "It's okay. We'll tell them a story…and it'll be the truth. Your aunt kept you against your will. I tried to save you…she attacked me, then did the same to you…it was self-defense."

Zel nodded slowly, a smile breaking across her face. I smiled back, wiping blood from her cheek. That was when it dawned on me. The dream I'd had. Her *Gothel* wasn't the wolf. It was Zel.

And I wondered, could we ever live happily ever after?

I had no idea, and I didn't believe in fairy tales anyway. But for a moment, I had a vision of Zel in a rocking chair, cradling a blond-haired baby with creamy skin and blue eyes like hers, singing that German lullaby in her high, sweet voice, the image as clear to me as if they were right here in the apartment.

Zel kissed me lightly on the lips, then pulled back.

"It's okay, we'll do this together," I said.

She kissed me again, harder this time, her mouth tasting faintly like copper.

I took her fingers, feeling the stickiness of the blood like glue, binding us, and together we made our way to the front door.

# The Emperor's New Clothes

By Laura Oles

Daniel Hayes pulled his BMW Series 5 into the Embassy Suites parking lot and took note of the Hyundai Santa Fe next to him. He preferred to park by models that he deemed lesser than his own. He ran his hands along the textured steering wheel and sighed. He'd been dodging his dealer's calls for weeks now, and it was only a matter of time before they'd find him and repossess the car, a vehicle he was certain he'd be able to afford. His eyes glanced up at the lighted hotel sign. Maybe the cure for his money problems waited inside.

This time would be different.

The sliding doors parted. Small groups of people loitered in the lobby. Daniel noted the bright framed digital sign toward the left of the lobby. He checked it, then continued down the hallway. The battered carpet below his Gucci loafers had seen better days; the dark maroon and black marbled pattern no longer able to shield the wear of so many travelers.

From a distance, Daniel spotted a group of men and one woman standing outside an open conference room door. Two men wore collared shirts and jeans, while the third wore a T-shirt that showcased an obscure band paired with cargo shorts and battered trainers that Daniel was certain had never seen the inside of a gym. The woman in the group far outclassed her male peers. Her white blouse and black flare pants were draped in a way that signaled money. She turned her attention from the group to Daniel.

"Are you here for Jason's seminar?" she asked, extending a hand. Several gold bangles clanked on her wrist. "I'm Heather. Nice to meet you."

Daniel shook her hand. "Daniel Hayes. Nice to meet you, too." She gestured to the men around her. "Please join us," she said. The trio of men seemed less enthusiastic about Daniel's arrival, but he was accustomed to being sized up in such a way. He shook hands with each of them, offering a subtle smile and nod accompanied by full eye contact.

"You heard him speak before?" one of the men asked.

Daniel shook his head. "No. Just watched his online stuff."

The men nodded, and two peeled off into the conference room while the third attempted to chat him up. The last man said, "His Insta's impressive. I mean, three vacation homes by the time he's thirty?"

Daniel nodded. "Wouldn't mind having one of those myself." He failed to add that he wouldn't mind having anything other than the two-bedroom apartment he shared with his high-school buddy. He'd leave that out for now.

He stepped inside the unremarkable room with its rows of folded chairs and side tables. Daniel guessed fifty people in the room, almost all men. He studied the first row. Jason Frye groupies, anxious to emulate his lead in getting rich and flexing hard on the gram.

Daniel took a seat in a middle row, which had open seats on either side of him. He checked his phone's silent mode and returned it to his back pocket. He heard the loud metal clang of the doors closing. He glanced over to see a man taking a seat behind him, the last chair in the aisle. Daniel didn't stare but clocked the man's Ferragamos sticking out from crossed legs.

Soon, Jason Frye emerged from a side door and stepped onto a small, elevated stage. He represented full normcore in his Everlane polo, Levi's, and Adidas sneakers.

Frye seemed smaller in person.

He rubbed his hands together and moved a bit closer to the front of the platform. "What's the one thing you're searching for?"

Someone yelled "money," while another one yelled "dollars," and Frye smiled but shook his head.

"What does money buy?" Frye asked.

"Lamborghinis! Yachts! Travel!"

Frye stood as the litany of answers continued. Then a small pause of silence.

"Freedom." The voice came from behind him.

Daniel nodded. He, too, wanted freedom. If he could just hit it big, he would finally be free of judgment from his family, from his high school friends, from his social media feed.

Frye smiled wide. "This man knows," he said, pointing to the man behind Daniel. "He gets it. And after this class, maybe you will too. My unique system for day trading will give you the kind of insider understanding of the markets that very few people have."

Daniel listened and took notes, but worried he didn't completely understand Frye's presentation. He had a trading account, but being up one day often meant being down the next. Soon, the down days felt more familiar, and he was more in the hole than when he'd started.

After an hour of fast talking and taking notes that felt more like hieroglyphs than a plan, Daniel slipped the notebook into his Tom Ford messenger. Frye's free seminar had ended, and he was now in the corner pitching his exclusive mentoring program to the front-row crew. Daniel stood to leave and spotted Mr. Freedom in his Ferragamos behind him in the hallway, checking his phone.

"I liked your answer earlier," Daniel said. "About freedom."

"Yeah, it's true, but you aren't going to find it in there."

"I'm getting that feeling," Daniel replied.

"Day trading is just gambling trying to be respectable. Sure, you can hit some good days, but it's like betting in Vegas."

"The house always wins."

The man's eyes lit up. "You see it. So, why are you in there?"

Daniel shrugged. "His socials are amazing, and his success speaks for itself."

"You think Jason Frye built all that from scratch with his super special system that he's hawking in a tired conference room?" The man shook his head. "Nah, that's grandpa's money in there. Granddad cut him off, hence the new hustle."

Daniel cocked his head at the comment, his view of Frye now diminished. "So, why are you here?"

"Scouting."

"Scouting for what?"

"People who understand what a real opportunity looks like." He handed Daniel a card. Heavyweight cream cardstock with rounded corners, just his name and Instagram handle in raised black lettering.

*Oliver Banks.*

"Daniel Hayes."

"Let's go get a drink, Daniel. I know a place I think you might like."

* * *

Daniel checked the address Oliver had given him. High in the Northside Austin Hills, the trees seemed taller, the hills lusher. He was breathing rarified air.

Daniel would have sold his roommate for a chance to drive some of the cars in this lot. His BMW lost a bit of luster next to its new neighbors. In the distance, the black lacquer exterior reflected the outside lights. There was no obvious signage, nothing to indicate the name of the place. He double checked the address on his GPS. He was in the right place.

As he walked closer, a small glowing emblem on a plaque by the door: A script "E" encased in a circle. A tall man, dressed in all black, bald with an earpiece, nodded at Daniel as he walked up. The man held up his hand.

"Are you…a member, sir?" he asked. No smile, no greeting.

"Um, no," Daniel replied. "I was invited by a friend."

"It's okay, Jake. He's with me." Oliver walked toward them and addressed the doorman. "Daniel is my guest this evening."

"Mr. Hayes, of course, sir." The doorman stepped aside and held the door. A blast of cold air greeted them, along with a floral fragrance that Daniel couldn't quite place.

"Welcome to the Emperor's Club," Oliver said.

To the right, a bar lined with leather highback stools traveled from one end of the room to the other. The mirrored wall showcased shelves of decorative liquor bottles and stemware of all sizes. Circular booths lined the opposite wall, and low leather couches coupled with small lacquer and glass side tables filled the middle space.

"Let's find a place to talk," Oliver said.

As Daniel followed him through a small crowd, a well-dressed man, mid-thirties, with a slight paunch above his belt, stopped Oliver with a wave. "Hey, you see my email?"

Oliver reached over and shook the man's hand. "I did, but I just got back from the Valley. Will get back to you tomorrow."

"Jeff's waiting for an answer."

Oliver nodded. "I know he doesn't like to wait. I'm surprised he's not still on his yacht with Lauren."

Daniel stood for a moment, silently contemplating. *No, he couldn't be talking about that* Jeff—*not the Jeff who ran the world with his online business that all started with books.*

They continued walking to an open booth. Oliver claimed one side and gestured for Daniel to sit across from him.

"Who was that?" Daniel asked.

"Alex Yates. He handles investment negotiations for Amazon."

Daniel nodded. "Impressive."

"Less so after you're around it for a while. Lots of guys—and a gal or two—have that kind of pedigree here."

A cocktail waitress arrived, tray in hand. Daniel ordered an Old Fashioned, and Oliver chose Bulleit neat. Once their drinks arrived, Oliver said, "You know, with the right investment and the right connections, you could travel in these circles too."

"I've had a couple of…investments…the last one disappointing." A flash of hot shame traveled up his neck.

Oliver seemed nonplussed. He waved a hand in the air. "Every person in this room has made bets that didn't pan out. You've got to be in the arena to fight. Sometimes you lose." He leaned forward, whispering, "But sometimes an opportunity comes along, and that one big break catapults you to another level. The losses are nothing but a blip on the radar."

The possibilities danced in Daniel's mind. How he'd love to finally show his family that he was successful. Especially Isaac.

"Let me know if anything like that comes up," Daniel said. "I'd be interested."

Oliver stayed quiet for a moment, then glanced around the room before leaning across the table. "I have something that's going to dominate an entire industry. We've got some big financial backers, but save space for a few smaller investors to get in. It's our way of giving back. The titans do all the heavy lifting. You'd know some of their names if you follow tech—but I can't disclose them right now."

Daniel hung on Oliver's every word. "Do you think they'd let me invest? I mean, I'd have to check it out, of course."

Oliver smiled in the way a parent placates a child. "Of course," he said. "I can tell you if it's good enough for these guys, you'd be getting a winning lotto ticket. He held Daniel's attention. "And I'm not sure you'll be a fit. You'd need to meet the half-mil minimum." Oliver sat back in his chair. "You know, maybe I shouldn't have mentioned it."

Daniel straightened. "I can manage the minimum." He had no idea how, but he'd deal with that later.

Oliver picked up his glass and took a sip of whiskey. "You know what?" he finally said. "I've got a good feeling about you, but you need to keep this between us. It's an invitation-only kind of investment."

"Of course." A hint of a smile crossed Daniel's lips.

Finally—his opportunity to silence his doubters.

This time would be different.

* * *

Daniel arrived at his father's house just shy of seven. He walked up the front porch and noticed several of the potted plants needed care. *Somebody should do something about that.* His hand gripped the knob, and when he peeked through the beveled glass window in the door, he spotted his older brother.

"Good evening, all," Daniel called, entering with a bottle of pinot noir cradled in his arm.

His brother seemed to give him a once-over before responding. "Dressed pretty sharp today, Danny. Big day?"

Isaac was quick to call Daniel by his childhood name to remind him of his place. Daniel knew his place. It was far above anything Isaac could fathom, and soon he'd prove it.

He ignored the slight. "Where's Dad?"

His brother pointed over his shoulder to the kitchen, "He's with Megan. She figured that since you called a family meeting, we might as well enjoy some food from Old Thousand."

"I hope she remembered the smoked salmon rangoon," he said. His father and sister stood over the island pulling containers out of brown paper bags. "How's class, Isaac? Anything happening in higher education?"

"You mean, other than trying to train kids, whose attention spans rival a goldfish, to value anything that doesn't emanate from their cell phones?"

Daniel pursed his lips. "Didn't mean to strike a nerve."

Isaac huffed, "Well, at least I've got tenure and health insurance."

Daniel recognized the dig. Isaac's idea of taking a risk involved wearing shorts in the summer. It's surprising they shared the same DNA. Isaac had no stomach for anything that drove his heart rate above sixty.

Daniel made his way into the kitchen and put his arm around his father, who was busy plating brisket fried rice. "Hey, Dad. How are you feeling?"

Walter's eyes brightened. "Better now that you're here."

He offered his sister a less enthusiastic hug. "Hey, Megan. How's things?"

"Dad needs to eat more and worry less."

"Ignore your sister. She fusses over me too much."

"Dad, you know that you can move in with me and Rob and the kids," Megan said. "This is a big house for one person."

He shook his head. "Your mother loved this house."

They gathered at the dining room table, his father's smile beaming as he gazed at his children. Daniel reached for the pinot noir and popped the cork before offering it to the table.

"What's with the wine, Danny? It feels like a big announcement is coming."

Daniel poured wine for his family and then himself and placed the bottle back on the table. "I suppose this is a kind of celebration."

"A celebration?" his father asked.

"I have an amazing business opportunity. And the best part is that you all can be part of it."

Megan's smile left as quickly as it arrived, and Isaac's transformed into a smirk.

"Tell us more." His father's voice had lost some enthusiasm, but he seemed to be working hard not to let it show.

"Yes, let's hear it," Isaac said. "I'm sure it's going to be a much better opportunity than your last one. I mean, who would have believed crypto would be a bust?"

The criticism stung. "Big celebrities were promoting crypto, so it's not like I was the only one who lost money."

Megan took a sip of wine and then said, "You still owe me the money you lost on the NFT Bored Ape craze."

Walter raised his hands. "Let's hear him out, okay?"

"Dad, you don't have to keep sticking up for him," Isaac said. "At some point, he needs to figure out how to make a real living and not just chase all these get-rich-quick schemes."

"Danny, Isaac is right," Megan said. "What about going back and finishing college? Or finding a full-time job?"

Daniel waved them off. "You don't understand how big this company is going to be. Investors are saying it has the potential to be a unicorn."

"A unicorn?"

This was Daniel's opportunity to prove his prowess to his family. "A unicorn is a startup that achieves a billion-dollar valuation."

Isaac remained unimpressed. "They call it a unicorn because it's so rare, right?"

Daniel hesitated but responded in the affirmative.

"So, what makes you think that you, with your litany of failed get-rich-quick schemes trailing behind you like jilted ex-girlfriends, has somehow found an inside track into a unicorn investment?"

Daniel straightened in his chair. "I have a very highly placed investing colleague that works with some of the top names in tech. Jeff and Mark are just two of them."

Megan choked on her wine. "So, you're dropping names of tech titans like you had dinner with them or something?"

"Not them, but someone who represents a startup they're going to invest in." Daniel pulled up his phone and showed them Oliver's profile. They took turns looking at the photo of Oliver at a swanky New York City restaurant, with Isaac scrolling through Oliver's feed. He returned the phone. "I don't see him posing with any of these tech giants you mentioned." Isaac waved a hand in the air. "And anyone can look rich on social media. It's not that hard."

"Big hat, no cattle," Megan added.

His father turned his body toward his youngest son. "Why don't you tell us what this investment is first, so we can understand a bit more?"

Daniel had been on the ropes ever since he'd arrived. He wouldn't let them steal this moment from him. Not this time. He sipped his wine. "It's a new entry in the virtual vacation space." He beamed as the words left his lips.

"Virtual vacation space? What the hell is that?" Megan asked.

"I can't get into all the proprietary technology," Daniel said, his voice more authoritative now. "But it's going to use virtual reality to give people who are homebound or unable to travel a fully immersive vacation without leaving home."

"How does it work?" Megan asked, her doubt leaving room for curiosity.

"The tech interacts with your neural pathways to engage all of your senses. Your body will feel like it's walking and experiencing your environment even if you're sitting in a chair."

"Some people do mushrooms for that," Isaac joked. He turned to their father. "Not that I have any experience with that."

Daniel ignored his brother's jab. "There'll be all kinds of upsells on the packages. Premiums for special add-ons like luxury hotels, train travel, even restaurant experiences."

Megan's skepticism seemed to return. "You think people are going to pay a premium to pretend to eat food at a pretend fancy restaurant?"

Daniel replied, "I'm embarrassed by your lack of vision. Your brain will trick your senses into believing it." He excused himself from the dinner table and returned with a document.

"This is highly confidential," he said, a serious tone now attached to his words. "I had to sign an NDA so they could brief me, but I'm going to share it with you."

Isaac took the document. He scanned it, scowled, and then handed it to Megan, who mimicked her older brother's response. His father took his time reading and nodded on occasion. More wine was consumed by all.

"So?" Daniel asked. "Do you see why I'm so excited about this?"

Isaac shook his head. "It's a lot of techno business jargon. Don't tell me you understand everything that's in that document."

Daniel shrugged. "I understand most of it. Oliver walked me through it, so I know you lay people may not get it like I do."

Megan sipped her wine, sighed, and returned her empty glass to the table for a heavier pour. "Daniel, we've seen you get so excited about these..." she paused, seeming to consider her words, "opportunities before, but they always feel like you're being hustled by some invisible fancy suits."

Before Daniel could defend himself, Isaac added, "If you're so smart, I'm sure you'll figure out how to fund this thing on your own. And then you can hold it over our heads if you strike gold. But as Mark Cuban would say, 'For those reasons, I'm out.'"

Daniel turned to his father. "You believe in me, Dad, don't you?"

* * *

Daniel arrived at the Emperor's Club a few minutes shy of their eight p.m. meeting. He stood away from the doorman screening guests, feeling like a high school kid waiting for a first date. He busied himself by scrolling through Oliver's Instagram feed, filled with shiny people wearing shiny accessories vacationing in shiny places with other shiny people.

"Anything interesting?" Oliver asked, startling Daniel from his screen.

"Just checking my messages." He quickly slipped the phone into his pocket.

Oliver greeted the doorman by name, and Daniel followed him inside to a nearby booth.

"I can't tell you how exciting this last week has been," Oliver said. "So many incredible things happening in this VR space right now. We've got more financial heavy hitters on board. Looks like we're going to hit our deliverables, which is impressive for such an ambitious project." He took a breath before asking, "And you?"

Daniel smiled, a hint of hesitation behind it. "Things are good. I've been working on the investment side from my end…"

Oliver held up his hand. "No pressure. I've got a line of guys behind you willing to take that investment slot if you can't manage the funds."

"No, no," Daniel said. "I've got the funds."

Oliver lifted an eyebrow. "You do?"

"It required some investment from my father, but he knows a fantastic opportunity when he sees it."

Oliver offered a nod. "I'm impressed with you, Daniel." He leaned in closer. "If you're ready to transfer the funds, we can add you to the team and include you on all our proprietary investor communications."

Daniel's throat suddenly felt lined with sand. "You mean, send it now?"

"Of course. That's what the Emperor's Club is about. Making deals and making history." He signaled around the room. "This place is an exclusive and communal space for some of the best minds in tech. With your investment, you'll be one of us."

*One of us.* His breath caught. He liked the sound of that. He'd be on the inside at last.

Oliver slipped his phone from his pocket, opened an app, and then held it up for Daniel to review. "Just type in this information and routing number from your bank to ours, and once we receive confirmation, you'll be added to our investor list."

Daniel's hand sweated as he typed in a slew of numbers. The phone pinged confirming half a million dollars was absorbed into the digital ether.

After a few moments, Oliver nodded, returned his phone to his pocket, and waved to a server. "Bring a bottle of Dom and the package from the office, please."

She returned with a tray holding two glasses and a small onyx lacquer box. A second hostess arrived with the Dom in an ice bucket nestled on a gold stand. A third hostess returned with a larger black box. She poured champagne into the glasses and placed the two boxes in the center of the table. Oliver handed Daniel a glass. "Here's to your life never being the same."

Daniel downed half the drink as if he'd been at a fraternity mixer, his anxiety overriding his manners. Oliver presented the smaller box. Daniel found a black-and-gold Emperor's Club membership card nestled in the center of the black fabric interior. He grinned like a child opening his most wished for Christmas gift. "Your privileges will start in one week."

He nodded to the second box. "Inside is a set of VR goggles. Now, it's a prototype, so don't be surprised if the software doesn't work perfectly. We're still in the move-fast, break-things stage."

Daniel reached for the box. Its matte black surface and hefty weight signaled expense. He began to pull at the structured lid.

"Don't open it here." He glanced around the room. "We need to keep this investment quiet. I'm sure you know there are a lot of people who would love to be in your shoes."

Daniel sat back, champagne in hand. With this decision, he'd prove to his family that the mortgage on his father's house was money well invested. His dad was the only one who could see his vision. Maybe he'd even get them each a vacation home, but only if they admitted they were wrong for doubting him.

* * *

Daniel pulled up to the Emperor's Club and found the parking lot surprisingly empty. Beater cars littered the lot. Just the standard collection of Acuras, Hondas, and a few pickup trucks. Maybe the employees were now parking in the guest lot. It would be his first night visiting the Emperor's Club without Oliver's connections. He strode to the front door with his membership card in case he received pushback from the doorman.

But there was no doorman.

Puzzled, Daniel walked through the front door and was greeted by a cold blast of air conditioning but little else. It was surprisingly empty for nine in the evening. He glanced around, searching for a familiar face.

He walked up to the bar and smiled at the bartender, a bald man in a white tuxedo shirt that strained to cover his chest. He ordered an Old Fashioned and then asked about the doorman.

"What doorman?"

"To verify the members coming in," he said.

The bartender laughed. "You don't need a membership to come here," he said, pushing the rocks glass toward Daniel. "That'll be fifteen dollars."

Daniel gave him a twenty. He reached into his pocket and pulled out the membership club card. "What's this then?" he asked, placing the card on the bar.

"Oh, I remember these. We handed these out for promotions when the new owner took over. The hostesses hand them out sometimes."

Daniel took his drink and the membership card that offered nothing now but confusion and sat at the table he'd occupied with Oliver the previous week. He checked his phone.

Still nothing.

After the first email Oliver sent as part of the investment group, Daniel had asked for other investors' email addresses. Oliver refused, explaining the big names didn't want to be bothered by small investors. Daniel told him that five hundred k didn't feel small. Oliver replied that it was pocket change for the others and to be grateful to be on board.

As he glanced up, he recognized a hostess. He waved to her.

"Can I help you with something?" she asked.

"You were here last week when I was meeting with Oliver."

She frowned.

Daniel pulled up his phone and showed her a photo.

"Oh, right," she said. "He asked me to bring the boxes and champagne for you."

"Do you know him?"

She shook her head. "He's been in a few times over the last month. Heard he had some private event where he rented out the place. Tipped me a hundred each time to nod and play along with him. Wanted the place to feel exclusive." She looked at his glass. "You want me to bring you another?"

Daniel handed her his last twenty and nodded. At this point, what he had left in his wallet wouldn't help him deal with what was coming next.

* * *

Daniel entered his father's home to find him on the couch watching a football game. "What a nice surprise," he said. "I was just going to order some pizza. You hungry?"

He shook his head, his loose jeans a reminder he hadn't held down much food in weeks. He'd been putting off this conversation, hoping he'd been wrong. Hoping for some good news.

"No, Dad, I'm okay." He sat on the worn leather recliner next to his dad. "I need to talk to you."

His father leaned forward. "Are you okay?" He studied his son. "You're so pale."

Daniel buried his head in his hands. "I've run into a complication."

His father shifted in his seat. "What kind of complication?"

Daniel wiped his palms on his pants, sweat creeping along his brow and down his neck, heart pounding in his ears. "Dad, I haven't been able to reach Oliver about the investment. He might just be busy."

His father sat quietly, head down. "Did you give them everything?"

Daniel nodded.

"Is there any way to get it back?"

"I called the Austin Police Department, and they took my statement, but they aren't optimistic. The funds went to a Swiss bank account. Lots of privacy protections in place. And maybe Oliver's just tied up right now."

His father nodded, posture hunched, his furrowed brow betraying a feeble smile. "I'm sure you'll make it right, Son. I know you won't let me down." His father walked over to a nearby table, retrieved the VR glasses, and handed them to Daniel, who slipped them on.

After several moments, an image of a beach appeared in front of him. Decent graphics, but more like standing in front of a screensaver than being immersed in the space. After a few seconds—just long enough for Daniel to wish he could disappear into the scenery—the image went black.

Daniel slipped the goggles off and handed them to his father, the only tangible thing remaining of his half-million-dollar investment. He glanced around the living room, wondering how he'd be able to save this house. The house he'd grown up in, the house his mother had died in, the house that held all the memories of their childhoods.

He hugged his father and promised to see him again soon. As he stood to leave, he glanced over his shoulder. His father remained on the couch, the goggles in his lap. Daniel thought he heard a sob, but closed the door before he knew for sure.

It was time to find his next investment to save his father's house.

This time would be different.

# Three Billy Goats Gruff

By Michael Bracken

Hop Latent Viroid, aka HLVd, had spread throughout local cannabis crops, impacting the Gruff brothers' Three Billy Goats marijuana dispensary, as it had several of their competitors. The disease didn't kill their plants, but it did cause dudding. During the vegetative stage, infected plants were shorter, had smaller leaves, and had tighter node spacing. When flowering, the plants had smaller, looser buds and far fewer trichomes, resulting in half the cannabinoid content of healthy plants, and Three Billy Goats's overall crop yield had diminished more than thirty percent year over year. Having less product with lower potency resulted in a significant reduction in their revenue.

The Gruff brothers pointed fingers at one another, but they were equally to blame. Good sanitation practices might have prevented spread of the disease, but they didn't sterilize their tools, nor did they wear fresh gloves, hairnets, beard nets, and coveralls each time they entered their growing room. And they didn't realize what was happening until a competitor's plants tested positive for HLVd. By then, most of the small dispensaries in their community—especially those that grew their own product and were equally lax with sanitation efforts—had infected plants and *Closed* signs hanging in their front windows.

Only the cannabis plants at Troll Bridge Farm, located in a small valley accessible via a single one-lane bridge over the river, seemed immune to the disease. Twice weekly, fresh product from the farm replenished the Troll Bridge dispensary across the street from Three Billy Goats, and the Gruff brothers watched in dismay each day as their customers abandoned them for their competitor's higher quality cannabis and superior edibles.

Kid, the youngest Gruff brother, turned away from the window and ran his fingers through his long, greasy hair, the longest and greasiest of all the brothers'. He had been staring at the Troll Bridge Farm delivery van parked across the street and had decided it was time to do something. Excited, he bounced around the sales floor. "We need to talk to the old Troll. That's what we need to do."

"Ebenezer?" asked Billy, the middle Gruff brother. The Troll family had controlled their valley for several generations, and Ebenezer Troll, the patriarch, ran the farm with an iron fist. "He doesn't talk to anyone."

Buck, the oldest Gruff brother, snorted. "Least of all, us."

Bad blood between the Gruff family and the Troll family stretched all the way back to the founding of the town, and over time, the Trolls had gained a significant advantage.

"We need to convince him it's in his family's best interest to work with us," Kid said, still bouncing. "I can do that."

Both of his older brothers snorted. Buck stroked his beard thoughtfully and said, "Good luck."

* * *

Kid drove his Tesla west from town along the old highway, drumming nervously on the steering wheel the entire way. When the highway turned north to follow the river upstream, he exited onto a two-lane private road that led to the one-lane Troll Bridge and to Troll Valley on the far side of the river. As he approached the bridge, he was surprised to see a gate and a guard shack occupied by two men in uniform. From their short stature and stocky build, they were most certainly part of the Troll family.

He glided to a stop at the gate and powered down his window as a guard with a wire-stiff flat top exited the shack and approached. The guard examined the interior of the Tesla. "Yeah?"

"I'm here to see Ebenezer."

"Is he expecting you?"

"No, but he'll see me. Call him. Tell him it's Kid Gruff."

The guard stared at him for a moment and then said. "Wait here."

He disappeared into the guard shack, and Kid watched the two guards confer before the one with whom he'd spoken lifted a telephone handset. He couldn't hear what the guard said, but the conversation was brief. Soon, the guard returned.

"He doesn't want to see you," he said, "so you can turn your pansy-ass car around and go back where you came from."

Kid opened his door. Before he could swing his leg out, the guard slammed it shut.

Angrily, Kid asked, "Do you know who I am?"

"I do, and I don't care," the guard said. "Ebenezer doesn't want to see you. So, if you open that door again, I'll drag you out of that car and make it painfully obvious."

"Are you threatening me?"

"No, sir," he said. "I would never threaten one of the Gruff Brothers."

"That's right, you—"

"I'm just telling you what I was told to do."

* * *

Trolls littered the community. In addition to the marijuana grown at the Troll Bridge Farm and the dispensary at which they sold their product, members of the extended Troll family also manufactured Troll House Cookies and owned Troll Dolls, the town's only upscale strip club. Less publicly, they sharked loans, ran a sports book, and paid off local law enforcement to turn a blind eye to their less savory activities.

The Gruffs had not done as well. Despite being one of the town's founding families, several of their ancestors had spent time in the state pen for an assortment of low-level crimes, many of them related to drunkenness and crimes against persons. The Gruff brothers' Three Billy Goats marijuana dispensary was the only legitimate business any Gruff had operated since Jedidiah Gruff lost controlling interest in the Tri-County Bank and Trust back in the 1920s.

Though the family had done well during prohibition, bringing shine down from the mountains while the Troll family brought in Canadian whiskey, they had squandered all their money. When prohibition ended, the Gruff family had nothing to show for all their effort except several cases of alcoholism and a few tall tales to pass down to the next generation. The Trolls, on the other hand, had invested most of their illicit revenue into legitimate businesses.

The three Gruff brothers sat around their dispensary bemoaning the fact that they were the last of the lineage, with nothing to pass down to the next generation should any of them ever procreate.

"Our only hope is to marry Trolls," Billy said.

"I'd rather stab my eyes out," Kid said. He'd been subdued since his failure to meet with Ebenezer Troll.

"Besides," Buck added, "you know what happens any time a Gruff expresses interest in a Troll."

His two younger brothers went silent, remembering Uncle Wether.

"Well, I'm not interested in marrying a Troll," Billy said. "I just want a piece of their family business. If we could get some of the product coming out of that valley, we could rejuvenate this place."

"What do you propose we do?" Buck asked. "The old Troll won't see us. Kid proved that."

"We'll see about that." Billy hitched up his sagging jeans and crossed the street to the Troll Bridge dispensary.

He pushed through the front door and was surprised by how bright and inviting the store seemed compared to their place. If it weren't for the overwhelming aroma of cannabis, he would have sworn he was in a Baskin-Robbins.

A plump young woman with purple-dyed hair combed straight up greeted him with a broad smile. She wore pink bib overalls and held a sample tray featuring seven different flavors of gummies, all shaped like mystical animals.

"How may I help you?"

Billy grabbed a green unicorn off her sample tray and popped it into his mouth. "I'm from across the street."

Her smile faltered. "You're one of the Gruff brothers."

"Billy." As he chewed, the flavor of green apple exploded in his mouth.

"How—how can I help you?" She moved slowly to put a sales counter between them.

He pointed to his mouth. "This is pretty good."

"Best in the city," she said. "Why are you here? It's not just to sample our product—"

"Oh, no, not at all, but this is pretty good. Let me have that blue mermaid."

"Only one sample per—" He glared at her, and she handed him a blue mermaid gummy.

He popped it into his mouth and immediately tasted blueberries. "How do you guys do that? All our gummies taste like dried skunk crap."

"I don't make them," the young woman said. "I just sell them. Why are you here?"

"We need to talk to the old Troll."

"Great-grandfather? He won't meet with you."

"I think I know a way to convince him," Billy said. "Give me that red centaur."

She handed him the centaur. He popped it into his mouth and was rewarded with a burst of watermelon flavor.

"I'm thinking if I scoop up your plump little ass and take you with me, he might open the gate."

"I don't think he will."

In the entire time Billy had been in the Troll Bridge dispensary, no one had joined them, so he thought they might be alone. "Why not? What'd you do to offend him?"

"It's just that—"

Billy stepped around the counter, grabbed the young woman around the waist, and lifted her onto his shoulder. She yelped with surprise, and she began kicking her legs and pounding on his back with her fists.

"Cool your jets," Billy insisted. "I ain't going to hurt you."

He carried her out of the Troll Bridge dispensary and was halfway across the street before a trio of Trolls poured through the dispensary door behind them. The wore bib overalls, hairnets, and gloves.

"Put Xena down!" one of them commanded.

Billy turned. "Where the hell did you guys come from?"

Behind Billy, his brothers stepped out of the Three Billy Goats dispensary. Buck stood with his arms crossed, glaring across the street while Kid shuffled his feet nervously and danced around behind his eldest brother.

Xena shouted to the other Trolls. "He wants to talk to great-grandfather."

"That's all I want. You make it happen, I'll put her down."

The Trolls and the Gruffs stared at one another until one of the Trolls pulled a cell phone from the front pocket of his bib overalls. He dialed and turned away, walking back toward their dispensary as he spoke into the phone. A minute later, he returned.

"He'll see you if you put Xena down and go out to the farm right now."

"I don't think so," Billy said. "I'm taking this little gumball with me, and I'll let her go when I get there."

A moment later, Billy was in his Dodge Challenger, Xena belted securely into the seat beside him. "You got any more of those gummies?"

Xena reached into the front pocket of her overalls and handed him a yellow hippocampus, a pair of orange imps, and four large white yetis.

Billy popped them into his mouth, where the lemon, orange, and grapefruit flavors battled for supremacy, and he made the trip to the gated bridge in half the time his younger brother had taken in his Tesla.

"Open up," he told the guard who greeted him. "Ebenezer is expecting us."

"Us?"

He jerked a thumb at his passenger. "Me and little Xena here."

"You'll need to get out and walk across."

Driving after consuming several gummies had been a trip of a different kind, and Billy wasn't certain his legs would exit the car with him. But they did.

"Leave your keys. We'll need to move your car."

He handed his keyring to Xena, and she gave him half a dozen red dragons. The guard remaining inside the guardhouse opened the gate. Billy popped the cherry-flavored gummies into his mouth and headed across the bridge. The gate closed behind him. The gate on the far side remained closed.

Billy turned back. "Are they going to open the other gate when I get there?"

"You Gruffs are as dumb as everyone says you are," the guard said. "The only way off the bridge for you is into the river. Or we can shoot you for trespassing."

They stared at each other as Xena slipped behind the wheel of Billy's Challenger and drove away, her head barely visible over the steering wheel. The effect of all the gummies gave Billy an idea he might never have otherwise considered, and the next morning, he called his brothers from the next town downriver from the Troll Bridge. After they arrived in Buck's Dodge Ram Quad Cab to collect him from the convenience store where he waited, he told them about being trapped on the bridge.

"So, you jumped into the river?"

Billy shook his head and looked sheepishly at his brothers. "I thought I could fly," he admitted. "Those Troll Bridge gummies are some powerful shit."

* * *

"There's only one way into the valley," Buck told his younger brothers two weeks later as he stomped around the sales floor of their dispensary. "That's across the bridge."

"We already know *that*," Billy said. He had made it halfway across, and his younger brother hadn't even gotten that far.

"And what crosses that bridge twice a week?"

"What?" asked Kid.

Buck pointed out the window at the Troll Bridge Farm delivery van parked across the street. His younger brothers understood, and they began making plans. After each of the next several deliveries from the farm, Kid followed the delivery van out of the city, mapping the vehicle's never-variable route and verifying that there were never more than two Trolls in the van.

Three weeks after Buck suggested they hijack the delivery van and use it to cross the bridge into Troll Valley, the brothers were ready.  At 4:57 Thursday afternoon, as the driver stopped at the intersection of Gnome Street and Hobgoblin Avenue, Buck stepped in front of the van to prevent it from turning right.

As the driver honked the horn, Kid grabbed the door handle and gave it a tug. The door was locked.

"Open up," he shouted.  When the driver refused, Kid headbutted the window, spiderwebbing it. Then he headbutted it a second time, showering the driver with safety glass.  He reached inside, unlocked the door, and pushed the Troll across the bench seat as he climbed into the driver's seat. After Kid pressed the power unlock button, Buck slid into the passenger seat, crushing the driver between them, and Billy climbed into the back, where he silenced the other Troll with a glare that could crush tin cans.

As the van resumed its journey, Billy bound the second Troll's hands with duct tape and covered his mouth. Buck explained to the driver exactly what was going to happen. A mile from the highway exit, Kid pulled to the side of the highway, and they switched drivers.

"Remember," Buck reminded the driver, stomping his foot to emphasize the seriousness of his message. "You do anything you're not supposed to do, and your little friend back here gets it. You understand?"

The driver nodded vigorously.  Buck and Kid made themselves as inconspicuous as possible behind the front seat while Billy sat on the duct-taped Troll in the back.

Fifteen minutes later, the van slowed to a stop at the gate blocking access to the one-lane Troll Bridge. One of the uniformed men exited the guard shack and approached the van while the other opened the gate from inside the guard shack.  The driver slowly shook his head and motioned to the broken window.

The guard stopped. "What's wrong?"

Buck shoved his index finger into the back of the driver's head and whispered, "Nothing."

"Nothing," the driver squeaked.

The guard opened the van door and said, "Why don't you step out?"

"I—I can't."

Buck shoved the driver through the open door, where he crashed into the guard, and they both fell to the ground. He scrambled over the bench seat, shifted the van into gear, and jammed his foot against the accelerator. The van sped forward, and the door slammed shut. The Troll inside the guard shack hit the switch to close the gate, but too late. The van plowed through the opening, raced across the one-lane bridge, and crashed through the closed valley-side gate.

The van's engine sputtered and died, leaving the Gruff brothers almost a hundred yards downhill from the Troll Valley Farm's main office, a building that resembled a log cabin with a wide, covered porch the length of the building's front. Several steps led up to the porch, as did a steep handicap ramp.

The Gruff brothers piled out, dragging the trussed-up Troll with them.

Buck shouted, "Let us talk to Ebenezer, and nobody gets hurt!"

One of the guards from the other side of the river ran around the van. Billy headbutted the smaller man, knocking him unconscious. The second guard had been a dozen steps behind the first. When he saw what had happened to the first guard, he stopped.

"Back away," Buck commanded.

The second guard did as he was instructed.

"Now what?" Kid whispered to the others. The trussed-up Troll began thrashing about, so Kid ripped the duct tape from their hostage's mouth. "You got something you want to say?"

"Great-grandfather won't come to you. He never leaves the office. You must go to him. We all do."

"Okay, then," Buck said. "We'll need to hoof it from here."

Kid threw the trussed-up Troll over his shoulder, and the three brothers headed up the hill.

A shapely young Troll pushed a wheelchair containing an old Troll onto the porch. The old Troll's hair gray hung limply about his shoulders, and he squinted to watch their approach.

"That him?" Kid asked. The Troll on his shoulder mumbled something that sounded like an affirmative.

A dozen more Trolls streamed out of the building, joining the two already on the porch. A minute later, the Gruff brothers climbed the stairs to join them. Kid deposited the trussed-up Troll on the porch, and several family members helped unwrap him from the duct tape.

"You Ebenezer?" Buck asked as he stopped in front of the old Troll. Billy stood behind Buck while Kid shuffled about, unable to contain himself. Up close, they saw that Ebenezer was strapped into the chair, his gnarled hands folded in his lap.

The old Troll nodded. "You must be the Gruff brothers. What do you want?"

"We want to buy our supplies from you."

Ebenezer Troll's gaze swept the broken gate, the disabled delivery van, and the dazed guard climbing to his feet. "You did all this just—"

"You wouldn't meet with us."

"And why should I? You have nothing we want and nothing you can offer us."

"Money. We'll pay top dollar."

Ebenezer laughed. "The Gruffs have been nothing but a thorn in our side ever since we pushed Jedidiah Gruff off the board of the Tri-County Bank and Trust. You three are the last of a dying herd, and we'll all be better off to see you gone."

Nodding and tittering, the Trolls surrounding Ebenezer voiced their agreement.

Angry, Buck kicked out, knocking down the shapely young Troll who held Ebenezer's wheelchair in place. She fell, lost her grip on the wheelchair, and it rolled down the handicap ramp. The wheelchair headed down the hill, picking up speed, and a dozen stumpy-legged Trolls chased after it.

The wheelchair passed the two guards and the disabled van, bounced through the busted-open gate, started across the bridge, and then toppled over the side, into the river far below.

"Oh-oh," Kid said.

* * *

The three Guff brothers never returned to their dispensary or even to town. Instead, they ran through the Troll Valley Farm's cannabis fields, headed up into the hills, and were never seen or heard from again. The last three Gruffs did, however, leave a reminder of their presence. When they ran through the Troll's marijuana plants, they infected them with Hop Latent Viroid. Within a few years, even the Troll family couldn't produce significantly viable cannabis plants.

By then, though, Troll House Cookies had become popular nationwide, and the extended Troll family concentrated their resources on overtaking the Keebler family's cookie empire.

# Beauty and the Beast

By James A. Hearn

"I know this is sudden, my darling Belle, but you and Vincent must leave tonight," Gaston Chevalier said. The middle-aged politician raised a hand, bone-white in the moonlight, and stroked Belle's dimpled cheek. She leaned into her fiancée's palm, then kissed it.

Beside Gaston was the bodyguard Belle Dumas knew only as Vincent, a shaggy, hulking figure, his silence as tangible as the north wind that warned of an early winter. The conspirators stood in the driveway of Gaston's Manhattan mansion beneath a sky of gathering thunderheads. Belle felt the press of the quiet gloom as a physical weight on her shoulders.

"And not even my father will know where I am?" Belle asked with concern. "Gaston, he'll be worried sick."

Gaston cinched his velvet smoking jacket tighter against the cold. He had a Cuban cigar between his teeth, its glow pulsing with each breath. "Your father's getting older, Belle. Easily confused. He might say the wrong thing to the Feds about the whereabouts of their star witness."

"I've never lied to him before," Belle fretted.

Gaston's grin was a gash of gleaming teeth in his shadowy face. "When this political witch hunt is over, we'll go somewhere nice, your father included."

"I'll settle for somewhere warm," Belle said. She shivered, despite a woolen cap covering her pixie-cut blond hair and an overcoat that didn't quite hide her curves. She should be in her library by the fire, not stamping her boots against the cold.

Gaston looked down at her feet and scowled. He disliked these boots, Belle knew, because the heels brought her to his height. The New Jersey Senator championed women's rights, but only to a point below his eye level. Vincent towered over both of them, a brooding, silent mountain against a backdrop of skyscrapers.

"Belle, you're shivering," Gaston observed. Without asking, he began buttoning her coat. But the way he looked at her now, his dark eyes were peeling away her winter clothes layer by layer. Since their engagement, she'd held off his advances with a wink and a promise. Barely. Gaston was a boy who wished to open his Christmas presents early, and he'd occasionally shake the gifts, then sulk when Belle stopped him. If she could wait twenty-seven years, he could wait until their honeymoon.

Tonight, Belle caught a whiff of whiskey on this overgrown boy's breath. He was murmuring to himself in a distracted way, and she blushed at his drunken compliments. "You have a face that could launch a thousand ships," Gaston mused dreamily. "A modern-day Helen of Troy, that could inspire men to kill, or lay down their lives. Eh, Vincent?"

Vincent didn't answer as he surveyed the darkness and leaned against a Bentley Bentayga in the driveway. Nevertheless, he nodded in agreement, a faraway look on his face.

Men had always called her beautiful, though Belle didn't believe them. In a love poem, Gaston once described Belle's eyes as "the deep blue of an ocean just before the setting sun touches its waters," and her cheeks were "twin roses of fire that melted his heart." After one too many Old Fashioneds, Gaston confessed that he'd paid someone else to write his romantic missives, but he refused to say who.

Gaston finished his tender ministrations by tightening Belle's scarf; it felt like a noose around her neck. "There now. My pretty little prayer book won't catch a cold."

Belle started at his words. "I forgot to pack books!" Her passion was reading, especially Jane Austen and the English Romantics, and she was never without a book in her pocket. She moved toward the mansion's door, but Gaston caught her arm in an iron grip.

"No time," Gaston said levelly.

Belle bit back her protest when Gaston's fingers tightened. She looked past his oiled hair, haloed in moonlight like a fallen angel, to a window flickering with firelight. Her library lay beyond that windowpane, where a log still crackled in the fireplace. A mere ten minutes ago, she'd been curled up on a settee with a dog-eared copy of *Pride and Prejudice*, daydreaming of Mr. Fitzwilliam Darcy and country dances.

That was before the midnight call from Gaston's lawyers. Their informant at the Department of Justice had passed along the list of witnesses for Gaston's upcoming RICO trial…one of those names, to Belle's shock, was hers. Three hastily packed bags later, Belle stood in the freezing cold with no idea where Vincent was taking her, beyond Gaston's pat answer: Someplace safe.

Somehow, Belle couldn't associate *safe* with Vincent. Gaston's most trusted bodyguard had never given her a cross word or a reason to fear him. Not a rational reason, anyway. Something about the man's unassuming stare chilled Belle's blood, and she could never meet the green-gold eyes shining in his bearded face.

Belle chided herself. She gave no thought to volunteering in the soup kitchens on Skid Row or canvassing door-to-door for Gaston's re-election campaign in Brooklyn's toughest neighborhoods. It made no sense to fear the beastly Vincent, but she did.

Gaston frowned. "Having second thoughts?" He took her chin between his thumb and forefinger, tilting her head the way a horse trader might examine a filly he was reluctant to buy. "If Beautiful Belle doesn't become Brave Belle, my political enemies will destroy me with trumped-up charges of bribery and corruption."

There was a quiet menace in Gaston's voice that Belle had never heard before. She wondered what would happen if she refused to go. Would she be safe? Would her father?

"No second thoughts," Belle said. "If the Feds can't find me, they can't call me as a witness. Until your trial is over, disappearing is the only way I can protect you."

Gaston's eyes flicked to Vincent, and the big man visibly stiffened. In a heartbeat, something passed between them and just as quickly faded. Gaston said, "Both of you, give me a hug before you go."

During the group hug, Belle and Vincent came together. In the three years she'd known him, she'd never touched him, not even in a friendly handshake.

While Gaston had a softness to his burgeoning middle, the burly bodyguard seemed one rock-solid muscle. In demeanor, Gaston wore a constant smile that was usually genuine; other times, it was as oiled as his James Dean haircut. Vincent, in contrast, had an unruly mane of black hair and a bushy beard that hid any expression. Gaston, the politician, was handsome and charming. Civilized. Vincent was a grizzly bear who'd learned to walk on his hind legs like a man.

Before Gaston ended the three-way embrace, Belle felt Vincent do something strange. When her hand accidentally touched his, the walking, talking grizzly actually *flinched*.

Curious.

Gaston glanced at his Rolex. "You'd better go before we lose the night." He reached into a pocket and pulled out a key chain with a fob. "Belle, consider the Bentley Bentayga your going-away present for entering the Gaston Chevalier Witness Protection Program."

"Gaston, are you serious?" Belle asked. The luxury SUV parked beside them was worth a quarter of a million dollars if it were a dime.

"Certainly," Gaston said. But instead of handing Belle the fob, he dropped it in Vincent's meaty paw. "Take good care of her."

Belle didn't know if Gaston was talking about the Bentley or her. She was about to demand the fob when Vincent did something else odd.

He spoke. "I will, Gaston."

Vincent's voice was a deep rumble, the sound of a snow drift tumbling down a mountain in an avalanche. Crickets stopped their chirruping, and an owl took flight from a copse of oak trees.

*Three words*, Belle thought. That was probably his allotment for the day. What would they talk about during Gaston's long RICO trial? She had a vision of Christmas with Vincent and shivered. Talk about a silent night.

Then a terrible thought struck her. Starry-eyed girls from Gaston's campaign were always sniffing around his door, and if given half a chance, one of them might worm her way into his good graces. Or his bed. Belle resolved to call Gaston every night, not because she didn't trust him, but because she'd miss him too much.

*More lies.* Belle ignored the voice in her head, just as she ignored the warnings of danger in this hastily-made plan.

"One last thing," Gaston said. "Give me your phone."

"My ph-phone?" Belle stammered.

"You heard me." Gaston held out his hand imperiously.

Belle backed away and found herself tripping over Vincent's feet. In an instant, she was falling headfirst toward the SUV's bumper. She was going to break her fool neck, and Gaston's legal fortunes would improve with her death.

Then Vincent's bearded face filled Belle's vision, and he caught her, transforming her clumsy fall into the last dip of a tango. With no effort, he raised Belle up and gently set her on her feet.

"Thank you, Vincent," Belle said, breathless and flustered. "You can let go."

Vincent didn't move. In his arms, Belle felt a startling rush of electricity surge through her. He was a man to be feared, not someone who made her feel like—

"Vincent, let her go," Gaston said.

The way Vincent's eyes lingered on her, Belle knew he felt something different, too. He lowered his arms, his face returning to its former stony expression.

Belle turned to Gaston. "Why do you need my phone?"

"GPS." He pointed to the sky, as if they could see the orbiting network of global positioning system satellites above them. "We don't want the FBI, Elon Musk, or anyone else finding out where you are."

Belle heard an invisible prison door slamming shut the instant she handed over her cell phone. She was giving away her lifeline to the world and relinquishing control to a man she hardly knew. What if Vincent decided to make her temporary disappearance permanent, to protect Gaston?

"What about my father?" Belle asked. "Who'll look in on him if I leave?"

Gaston waved a hand dismissively. "I promise you, my people will take care of him as long as you're away."

Belle narrowed her eyes. Did he mean her father would be safe *while* she was gone, or *only if* she went with Vincent and stayed away?

"Meanwhile," Gaston said, "your phone and passport will be on a trip to Africa."

Belle swallowed. Some other "Belle" was taking a very long trip.

"As far as the Feds will know," Gaston continued, "you're traipsing around those villages you're always talking about, caring for refugees. They'll never find you."

*They'll never find you.* With these words echoing in her mind, Belle murmured goodbye to Gaston and slipped inside the Bentley. Through the window, she watched Gaston whisper something to Vincent, something she couldn't hear.

The last instructions given, Gaston started toward his mansion. Belle waved, but he shut the door without a backward glance. Behind the steering wheel, Vincent sat limned in the glow of the instrument panel. They were alone for the first time. "I wish I had my books," Belle said. In the face of tonight's events, it sounded like a childish wish in her own ears, but it was true.

Wordlessly, Vincent reached into a coat pocket and took something out.

"*Pride and Prejudice.*" Belle took the book from Vincent and flipped through the pages, her brows knitting together. This was her favorite edition—the official tie-in to the AE/BBC mini-series starring Jennifer Ehle and Colin Firth—but it wasn't her book. "Vincent, this isn't my copy. This one has handwritten notes in the margins."

"Oh?"

*Was there a smile playing beneath that beard?*

"That's my copy," Vincent said.

*His copy.* Gaston had never cracked a novel, as far as Belle knew. If it wasn't in *The Wall Street Journal* or the *Financial Times*, Gaston never read it.

"Thank you, Vincent," Belle said. Impulsively, she leaned over and kissed his cheek. His whiskers tickled her nose, but not in an unpleasant way. She was still scared of him, but the fear was mixing with another emotion she couldn't identify.

Vincent's smile was unmistakable now. He put the SUV in drive and pulled away from the mansion. Just before the security gates closed, Belle looked back to see a light beaming from Gaston's bedroom window. A silhouetted figure stood rigid and deathly still, and Belle felt the weight of his gaze. Then the lights flickered out.

* * *

Vincent knew he was a cursed man, and tonight's turn of events proved it. He didn't believe in fairy tale curses, of course. No enchantress had turned him into a monster, and no magic kiss would restore his humanity. But he did believe in the curses of being alone, unloved, and feared. Those were all too real.

He drove the Bentley northward, his thoughts as dark as the Maine forests rolling past the tinted windows. He studied his reflection in the rearview mirror and frowned. His hair was a mane of dark curls that matched his unkempt beard, and he looked like a glowering lion in a black Armani suit and matching trench coat.

Vincent's fierceness didn't stop him from feeling hurt when Gaston's staff whispered to themselves and called him The Beast, or when neighborhood kids turned tail and ran when he walked the streets. He inspired fear everywhere he went, like he always had. Even sweet, beautiful Belle Dumas was scared to death of him.

*And rightly so*, Vincent thought. *Until now.* Had a shared moment over their favorite novel changed her feelings? Nudged their fates in a new direction?

He tightened his grip on the steering wheel. *I am what I am, and that's all that I am.* The words belonged to a cartoon sailor, but they held a simple wisdom. Whenever any unpleasantness arose—Gaston's euphemism for anything threatening his campaign—Vincent handled it, without question and without remorse. The actions matched the appearance; he was The Beast, inside and out.

Absently, Vincent's hand strayed to the burner phone next to his shoulder-holstered Glock 17. He prayed the fateful call from Gaston would never come…because he wasn't sure he could follow through with it. He hoped the trial would pass, Gaston would be cleared, and Belle would be safe. Perhaps, in the months to come, Vincent would even catch a few moments of happiness.

Belle shifted in the passenger's seat, apparently in the middle of some dream. She *was* beautiful, more beautiful than any dream of beauty Vincent had ever known. He'd heard that phrase somewhere, or read it somewhere. Well, so what? If it wasn't in a poem already, Vincent would write it himself—just as he'd secretly written Gaston's.

Belle stirred, and Vincent guiltily averted his gaze.

"It looks stormy," he ventured. *Christ, I'm talking about the weather.*

Belle didn't respond. Her eyes were closed as she clutched Vincent's copy of *Pride and Prejudice* closer.

Vincent sighed. He had a vision of the secluded Airbnb he'd rented on a dummy credit card. The absentee owner had been all too happy to rent the house to him for three months, with the option to renew for three more.

They'd have a candlelit high tea and talk about Jane Austen, with cucumber sandwiches and a blazing fire. They'd start by analyzing Elizabeth Bennet's choice between Fitzwilliam Darcy and George Wickham, and finish with what? A kiss?

It was a useless fantasy, but Vincent indulged it, anyway. Without fantasy, what was life but a series of ever-increasing burdens punctuated by disappointment, betrayal, and sadness?

He drove on. The sun was up, but it had remained hidden since dawn. An overcast, wintry sky the color of a sunken battleship pressed down upon the forests, the road, and the Bentley. More snow lurked in those clouds, Vincent knew. Before making his way to New York, he'd grown up near here, in a forgotten logging town that ravaged the forest and died when the last tree was felled.

But the snowfall waited, biding its time. In the silence, the wind whispered, *Not yet*. The animals would hear the warning; Vincent imagined rabbits burrowing deeper into their warrens, squirrels sleeping upon their winter stores, and wolves fortifying their bellies with hot blood. Just beneath the clouds, birds hurried south.

*We're going the wrong way*, Vincent thought. But he kept driving in the opposite direction, toward darker skies.

* * *

Belle was dreaming of her father's house in Brooklyn, of a bright spring day. Her librarian mother hadn't yet succumbed to ovarian cancer, and their favorite books were stacked to the ceiling. Father had his pipe and Raymond Chandler, Mother hot tea and Hawthorne, and Belle had cocoa and Jane Austen. There was no Gaston. Oddly, Vincent was there, too, thumbing through *Pride and Prejudice*.

"We have all the time in the world," Belle said. Except it wasn't her voice, it was Louis Armstrong's.

Vincent put down his book and softly said, "We're here, my darling."

Belle could almost feel the touch of someone's fingers on her face, and she woke to see Vincent staring down at her, his hand on her cheek. The Bentley's engine was silent as snowflakes softly hit the windshield and melted. Wherever they were, it looked like the North Pole.

Vincent hastily withdrew his hand. "I, uh, couldn't wake you. I hope I didn't startle you."

"I was already awake."

Vincent murmured something about getting her bags and exited the vehicle. Beneath a leaden sky, he plodded through snow drifts toward the front door of a dreary, snow-capped mansion. Its frosted windows reminded Belle of eyes in a frozen face, forever closed in death. An army of dark trees surrounded them, as impenetrable as any forest in the folktales of the Brothers Grimm.

Belle stepped out to intense cold. As she stumbled through the snow, it melted right through her jeans. Vincent, seemingly impervious to the elements, was retrieving a key from a lock box on the doorknob.

"Where are we?" Belle asked.

"Maine." Vincent sounded almost happy.

Belle reached for her cell phone. Then, she remembered she didn't have it. "Where in Maine?"

"The nearest town is twenty miles," Vincent said. "Winterville."

"How appropriate." This wasn't some little vacation she was taking here. She was alone with a stranger, with no way to contact the outside world. And she was freezing.

Vincent frowned at her wet clothes. "Quick, get inside and take those pants off."

Belle took a step back. "I'll do no such thing."

"I only meant you should change out of your wet clothes," Vincent said. "I'll unload everything and bring your suitcases to the room you choose."

"We're sleeping in separate rooms," Belle declared. As she looked closer at the house, a single sunbeam burst through the clouds. It was two stories of red brick, with three chimneys and a courtyard that looked like it might be a charming garden in the spring. In the sunlight, the house was a page torn from a novel set in the English countryside, not a haunted house in the hinterlands of Stephen King's Maine. She felt Vincent's copy of *Pride & Prejudice* snug in her pocket.

When Vincent took out his phone and texted Gaston, Belle caught a glimpse of the gun under his coat. Then the clouds closed, the north wind howled, and the mansion was once again entombed in ice. Belle realized Vincent was there for one reason: to keep her quietly out of the way.

"I'll start a fire," Vincent said as he pocketed his phone. He took her elbow as if to lead her inside. "You'll be warm before you know it."

Belle shrugged off his arm. "Don't pretend you're my friend or my protector."

"We may not be friends, but we don't have to be enemies. And I will protect you, I swear."

Belle ignored the promise. "You have a phone."

"Yes."

"I don't. Is there Internet in this Godforsaken place?"

"Yes."

Belle folded her arms. "If I asked for access, may I have it? Would you let me send an email?"

Vincent didn't answer.

"You have the car fob, Vincent. If I wanted to leave, would you let me?"

Vincent looked away. "It's safer for you if you stay hidden during Gaston's trial."

Belle laughed. "You're not keeping *me* safe. You're keeping Gaston safe. And while I'm here, I'm keeping my father safe from Gaston. Vincent, you're my jailor. Nothing more. And this mansion is my prison."

* * *

The months of isolation passed slowly. Belle, with no phone or Internet, monitored the outside world via the Sunday edition of the *New York Times* that came on delivery trucks. She read the newspaper front to back, eager for coverage of Gaston's trial. The editorials were favorable, with scathing condemnations of the prosecution's lack of proof. The pool of witnesses had dried up, and Gaston's hired guns tore the remaining witnesses to shreds. In the obituaries, Belle recognized familiar names, shadowy figures connected to Gaston's businesses. Traffic accidents. Heart attacks. Belle wondered if Gaston had other people hidden away…or worse.

Gaston never called Vincent to check on her; while Belle found that upsetting, Vincent seemed relieved whenever she broached the subject. And if Gaston watched her via the security cameras Vincent installed soon after their arrival, Vincent wouldn't say.

On winter days, Belle walked through the snowy woods around the mansion. She grew adept at studying the birds and animals of the forest, and enjoyed hearing the woodpeckers or watching deer dip their heads to drink from a babbling brook, at least before it froze.

Vincent trailed her at a discreet distance, never venturing too close. It became a kind of game they played; could she slip away from him, if only for a few minutes? When she did elude him, when she no longer heard his heavy tread through the snow and leaves, she grew restive. Was he okay? Had he twisted an ankle?

In the evenings, Belle spent hours in a room she named the library. For his part, Vincent kept her supplied with firewood and new books. They'd arrived one day, boxes and boxes of them. Many were old favorites, but there were a few unfamiliar titles as well. After dinner, Vincent prepared her cocoa just as she liked it, with three marshmallows and a splash of cream, and left her to read in peace.

The mansion in the woods was still a prison, but it wasn't an unpleasant one. Through the magic of the Internet, Vincent provided for her every need and even her whims. Belle enjoyed testing the limits of Vincent's provision, dreaming up more and more exotic items for their menus. How he procured mangoes or chocolate truffles in the desolation of Maine, Belle didn't know.

Vincent would grin and shake his shaggy head at her requests. But he seemed to enjoy cooking their meals and the conversations they shared at the table. He was opening up to her, unfolding like a rose among thorns.

*He's happy,* Belle realized one day. *Maybe for the first time.*

It was Advent Sunday, and Vincent was literally decking the halls with boughs of holly. She found herself at the base of his ladder, handing him decorations before he asked for them. The brush of his hand against hers was an unspoken intimacy, as powerful as it was silent. When they finished, the mansion's melancholy interior was transformed into a Christmas wonderland.

To Belle's amazement, she realized she was happy too.

* * *

On Christmas Eve, Belle watched a Yule log crackle in the fireplace. It would last all night and into the morning, the product of Vincent's industrious ax. He chopped wood every day to feed the fires, and Belle sometimes watched his labors from the warmth of the house. The ax rose and fell, up and down, up and down, while a shirtless Vincent glistened and steamed. The memory was as warming as tonight's fire.

To the right of the hearth, a fully decorated Christmas tree twinkled merrily. She'd helped him hang the ornaments and tinsel, tie the ribbons, and string the lights. As a final touch, Vincent topped the ten-foot-tall Canaan Fir with a silver star. There were even wrapped presents beneath the boughs.

*All for me,* Belle thought. She had nothing for Vincent, of course, since she had no way of contacting the outside world. But somehow, that didn't make her feel less guilty. She could've found something, made him something. She sighed and returned to reading Charles Dickens's *A Christmas Carol.*

On cue, Vincent appeared with her cocoa in a chipped teacup. He placed it on the table and turned to leave when Belle took his hand.

"Stay," she said.

Vincent stopped. His expression was unreadable in the fire's dimness, though his eyes blazed with their own inner light. In the press of his hand, Belle felt the calluses from his ax.

A tableau of expectant silence held for several breaths, with only the sounds of the fire and a bitter wind whistling through the chimney. Outside, a blizzard was barreling down on them, but Vincent had gathered sufficient firewood and ordered extra provisions.

Belle knew she was safe here, with him. Safe from the storm, safe from wolves. Safe from Gaston.

"Sit with me," Belle said. "Please."

Vincent sat next to her, but far enough away to disengage his hand. He glanced at a security camera perched in the corner of the room, then back to her.

"What are you reading?" Vincent asked.

"*A Christmas Carol.*"

He eased himself onto the couch and stared at the fire. "I've often wondered at Scrooge's transformation. Do you think people can change, so quickly and completely?"

"I do," Belle said. She inched closer to him. "Anyone can change, if they only believe. Love can bloom in the stoniest heart."

Vincent cleared his throat. "Belle, you make me believe in miracles. You make me want to be a better man."

Belle took his hand again, and this time he did not take it away. Under the watchful eye of the security camera, they talked long into the night.

* * *

January and February came and went, each month colder than the last. March roared in like a lion, and with its coming, the winds shifted from north to south. The snows thawed, and nature awoke from her long sleep, cladding herself in verdant greens.

In the kitchen, Vincent watched Belle attempting to flip pancakes without a spatula. She kept tossing them into the air, and they kept landing on the stovetop. Her laughter was like music.

Since Christmas Eve, his heart had been filling itself with Belle. He felt loved. He felt accepted. Most of all, he felt at peace. He desperately hoped she felt the same way, too. "Belle, there's something I've been meaning to tell you."

"You hate my pancakes, I know."

Vincent touched her shoulder. Belle didn't flinch, but turned, her chin up, her lips parted. "I love your splattered, half-cooked pancakes. The way you burn the scrambled eggs. I love y—"

His phone chirped.

Vincent started. The burner, the one Gaston had given him the night of their departure. In all these months, Gaston had never called him. It could mean one of two things. Either the trial was over, and Belle was safe, or...the alternative was unthinkable.

Vincent read the message, then shifted the shoulder-holstered gun beneath his jacket.

"What's wrong?" Belle asked.

"We have to leave. Right now."

* * *

Gaston pocketed his phone and eased himself into a sitting position within the tree line. His car was parked down the road, and he'd come the final mile in patent leather shoes that weren't meant for walking. The house in the clearing looked comfortable, with smoke curling out of the chimneys.

*How quaint.*

Gaston checked his Beretta, then turned his attention to the front door. Any moment, Vincent and Belle would emerge.

What would happen? Would Vincent do his job, or would he try to take Belle away? And would she go with him willingly? That seemed doubtful. Laughable. She was a beautiful woman, and he was more animal than man. But then again, Gaston had watched through the security system, like a magic mirror into their little world, as they grew closer each passing day.

One way or another, Belle Dumas had to die. It was only a matter of time before the Feds picked up her trail, according to his DOJ sources. Then they'd put her on the stand, and Gaston would go to jail for the rest of his life.

The mansion's front door burst open.

* * *

"Vincent! Where are we going?"

Outside, all seemed as it should be to Belle. There was the Bentley, parked under the budding trees. Dappled sunlight spilled onto the grass, but no birds sang of spring. The forest was eerily quiet.

Vincent held her hand, his head on a swivel. "I don't know. Maybe the nearest Federal building."

Gaston emerged from behind the SUV.

"I don't think so, Vincent," Gaston said, gun raised. Belle's breath caught. Now she understood why Vincent wanted to leave so quickly. Gaston was on his way to kill her.

Belle raised her arms. "Why are you doing this, Gaston?"

"Because Vincent won't."

Vincent stepped into the line of fire, shielding Belle as he rushed forward.

His roar of rage was thunderous as his hand plunged for the Glock underneath his jacket.

Belle's scream was cut short by a single gunshot, and she couldn't tell which man had fired. Then Vincent staggered to the ground, clutching his bloodied left arm. Heedless of Gaston, Belle dropped to her knees and took Vincent in her arms. His eyes rolled back in his head, blood seeping through his jacket. His gun was nowhere to be seen.

"Vincent, can you hear me?" Belle put a finger to his neck. The pulse was there, but his breathing was shallow. She cradled his head and stroked his bearded cheeks.

"You're my Mr. Darcy," Belle said. She didn't know if he could hear her, but if he were dying, she needed to say what was in her heart. "I love you. It's been coming on so gradually, I didn't know until now." Like the villainous George Wickham in *Pride and Prejudice*, Gaston had only the appearance of goodness, nothing more.

Gaston dropped his aim and laughed. "You love this beast of a man, Belle? He's a nobody, a common hood I plucked from the streets."

"I do," Belle said defiantly. "Let me kiss him before he dies. Please, Gaston."

Gaston's gaze was pure venom. "Suit yourself, Belle. It'll be the last thing either of you do, so make it good."

Belle looked at Vincent. His gold-flecked green eyes were open, and tears streamed down his cheeks. He whispered, "Belle, your eyes are the deep blue of an ocean just before the setting sun touches its waters. Your cheeks are twin roses of fire that melt my heart."

Belle gasped. "The poems…it was you, Vincent? Oh my darling, of course it was you."

"Place your hand on my heart," Vincent said, and she did. "Do you feel that?"

Belle nodded.

"You've given it life. Kiss me, and I can die a happy man."

Belle bent down, her lips hovering an inch above Vincent's. Then he brought his head up. Their kiss was better than any fairy tale, the kiss of true love. If they lived or died, they were finally free, no longer cursed by their former lives and beholden to Gaston. When Belle stood, she raised Vincent's Glock directly at Gaston's chest. He froze, uncertainty on his face.

"*You* are the beast, Gaston, and a rabid one. It's past time you were put down."

Gaston's predatory grin chilled her to the bone. "Belle, darling, let's talk this over. If you'll lower the gun—"

Belle pulled the trigger as Gaston fired. His shot whizzed past her ear, but Belle's aim was true. Gaston dropped his gun and fell backward, his limbs giving a final, feeble twitch.

Belle helped Vincent up. He leaned against her, but she did not bend under his weight. She felt strong, as if she could cradle him in her arms and carry him a thousand miles.

"You saved me, Belle. And not just my life."

"We saved each other, my love."

# The Bremen Musicians

By Debra H. Goldstein

"Do you know what a tontine is?"

In the months since I've been the executive director of the Holocaust Education Center, I can't remember anyone asking a more bizarre question than the one just posed. Speechless, I failed to respond. The well-dressed middle-aged woman, who carried a wooden violin case that had seen better days, repeated her question.

In the aftermath of the horror of the October 7 massacre, most of our education center guests have asked historical questions about Israel and Hamas. Not one raised the specter of a tontine.

"Yes. It's an investment scheme where people own shares. Each time an investor dies, their share is distributed among those still living. The last one standing gets the entire pot. The same holds true with tontines tied to a specific bottle of good wine or another valuable object."

Smiling, she said, "I'm sorry. I forgot to introduce myself. My name is Sarah Bremen Schwartz."

I recognized the Bremen name immediately from my list of donors. Cat Bremen had been our largest until her death last week at the ripe old age of ninety-one. Her attorney had already informed us that the education center would receive a large bequest from her estate.

"Are you Cat Bremen's daughter?"

"Yes."

"My sincere condolences. May her memory be a blessing. She was a wonderful woman."

"That she was." Sarah pointed toward my nametag. "And you are Liucija Wright."

Since my nametag said it all, I waited for her to continue.

"I guess you're wondering why I'm here today with this violin case. A few months ago, when I was in town, Mother and I attended the L'Chaim Gala fundraiser where a young man, a protégé of Yitzhak Perlman, played a special violin gifted to him from the Violins of Hope collection."

Although I knew that during the Holocaust, violins were important in many ways for entertainment and survival, I wasn't sure how our education center and the case in Sarah's hand fit with the Violins of Hope's mission to restore Holocaust violins. "I'm sorry I didn't have the opportunity to meet you that evening. Being new, I was juggling a lot of things behind the scenes."

"It didn't show. Besides, we were only there for the first half of the program. Mother had me bring her because she wanted to hear the young man play. She was particularly sorry not to hear him play *Hatikvah* during the second half of the program, but she was so tired that we left at intermission. Despite only listening to part of his performance, the beauty of his music and the description of the Violins for Hope restoration program had a profound impact on my mother." She lifted the violin case, enabling me to get a better view of its well-worn wood.

"Mother thought highly of you, Liucija. She made me promise to bring this violin to you when she passed away. I'm honoring my word."

"How does understanding a tontine relate to this violin?"

"The violin is the tontine. Mother's friend, Red 'Rooster' Rosen, was murdered when the Be'eri kibbutz was raided during the Hamas massacre. Mother became the group's last one standing."

"Rooster Rosen, the Israeli singer who was a sensation in her younger days?"

"Yes. Rooster, Mother, and two others were the members of the tontine. Ironically, for all the years since their concentration camp imprisonment liberation, Mother was the physical keeper of the violin. She kept it hidden in the back of the master bedroom closet in every house we lived in. None of us kids were allowed to play with it. At some time, we each asked why. Her answer always was the same. 'It isn't mine. I'm only the caretaker of a memory.'"

"What did she mean by that?"

"None of us knew, and Mother refused to elaborate. The night we attended the Gala, Mother was overcome with emotion. Rather than sleep, she told me the story of this violin. It's a tale of death and survival."

The somber tone and determined look on Sarah's face made me wonder what tragedy befell the violin and Cat. Although I wasn't hired until she was in the last stages of her terminal illness, I was assured by everyone that she'd been a super worker and benefactor of the Jewish community organizations until becoming ill. "I know your mother was a Holocaust survivor and that she helped create our center because she believed 'We Must Remember.'"

"That's right. After Mother learned of Rooster's slaughter, she called to tell me that she was the tontine survivor. She said she'd always planned to destroy the violin if she was the last one standing. Instead, because of the horror of October 7 and the present political climate, she changed her mind. Mother made me promise that when she died, I'd seek your help convincing the Weinsteins this violin deserves to be restored."

"And that's why you're here?"

She nodded. "I'm willing to underwrite the cost. May I tell you the violin and my mother's story?"

"Of course. Instead of standing in the entry hall, why don't we sit in my office? Would you like some water or a soft drink?"

"Water would be fine."

Once I settled Sarah on my small couch, I went to the breakroom. From the refrigerator, I took a bottle of water for her and a can of classic Coca-Cola for me.

As I trekked back to my office, I reflected on what could have made Cat, Rooster, and two others create their tontine.

Apparently, Cat believed there was a tie between the tontine violin and the Violins of Hope project. According to the story told at the Gala,

Moshe Weinstein, a violin craftsman, moved his family from Lithuania to Palestine in 1938. His extended family remained in Lithuania. In 1941, communication between Moshe and his Lithuanian family abruptly stopped. After liberation, Moshe learned that he, his wife, and their children were the only family survivors. The other members, four hundred, had been killed. Despite the horrific loss of his family to the Nazis and no resale market for German violins, Moshe purchased German violins brought to him rather than letting them be destroyed.

Moshe's son, Amnon, also a master violin craftsman, continued the family business after his father's death in 1986. After ashes fell from the case of a violin once played in the camps, Amnon refused to work on that violin or any other related to the Holocaust. Ten years later, while training his son, Avshi—to follow in his footsteps—Amnon finally confronted his Holocaust memories and the history of the violins in his father's collection. The result was a compulsion to restore and tell each violin's story. At the time of the Gala, there were approximately one hundred twenty violins in the traveling collection.

Re-entering my office, I saw Sarah had opened the violin case and placed it on my coffee table. She'd removed the violin and set it across the case, strings down. An indented gash ran down the back. As I handed Sarah her water and joined her on the couch, I noticed a white envelope with my name also on the table. Rather than reach for the envelope, while she opened the bottle and took a sip, I stared at the damaged violin. In a world that had just seen more Jews killed in one day than any other since the Holocaust, I couldn't anticipate the tragic story behind this violin's history.

"You may not know," Sarah said, "that my mother was born in Vienna. Because of the respect her physician father had, her family was part of the upper class. That meant they had servants, a box at the opera house, owned an apartment building where her family occupied two of the flats, private schooling with violin lessons, and the belief that the family was so entrenched in Viennese society that being Jewish didn't matter. Once Hitler invaded Vienna, the life my mother knew changed drastically."

Sarah picked up the envelope and held it out. "Rather than me recounting my mother's story, she thought it best she told you herself."

I took the envelope. "May I read this now?"

"Please," Sarah said. She leaned back against the pillows of the couch.

I opened the envelope. It contained two sheets of lined paper. Every line on each side was filled with a spidery handwriting. Quietly, I read.

* * *

Dear Liucija,

If you are reading this, Sarah told you I was the last survivor in a tontine and "winner" of this violin. Although you and I never had the opportunity to know each other well, from what I've seen, you are the perfect person to get this violin, once used to take a life, into the hands of the Weinsteins.

There were four of us in the tontine. Before the war, we lived in apartments in a building owned by my parents. Our family failed to leave Vienna when we had the chance, and my parents remained in the building. We had two apartments, one we lived in as a family and the other my father used as his office. We were forced to turn over our family apartment to Nazi officers. Out of respect for my father and his willingness to provide medical care to all who needed it, including the invaders, we were permitted to live in a few rooms of the office apartment.

At times, we'd wake up to find tenants missing. Although we understood their probable fate when Nazi officers took over those units, we never learned the truth about their disappearances. My sister Dot's best friend, Rose, was in our apartment in 1942 when her parents were seized. Rose was like a daughter to my parents, and they let her stay with us. She shared the room with Dot and me, while a new group of Nazis occupied her apartment.

In February 1944, our parents were rousted from our home and taken away. We tried to go with them. Dot, Rose, and I were told not to worry. We'd be joining them within the next few weeks when there would be another train.

The Nazis were true to their word. Two weeks later, our threesome stood on the train platform, joined by my best friend in life, Elenor "Doggy" Benjamin. We met when we were six, and she tried to sneak a stray dog into class. He didn't get to stay, but because of him and all the other ones who tended to follow her home, someone nicknamed her Doggy Benjamin. I asked where her parents were. She shrugged.

We made a motley-looking foursome. I was a gawky, but precocious twelve-year-old. I've already told you about Elenor. The other two were my beautiful sixteen-year-old sister, Dot, and her flame-haired friend, Rose Rosen. As Sarah may have told you, the world later came to know her as the chanteuse Red "Rooster" Rosen. She was slaughtered during the October 7 massacre in Israel.

With our parents gone, we didn't have guidance on what possessions to take. Rose and Dot each packed their suitcases with a few pairs of pants and blouses, but mostly the dress-up gowns they'd bought for parties that season. To Rose, it was especially important, even if another thing could squeeze into her suitcase, that she also took a small bag that held only a form-fitting red dress. Because she'd never had the opportunity to wear it, she didn't want it to be crushed. Elenor and I took basic clothing, some toys, and my violin—the one Sarah brought you today.

When the train finally stopped, we were ordered to leave our luggage. They said it would be delivered to us later. I may have been young, but I wasn't naïve, and I refused to leave my violin. Rose grabbed her small bag. I saw other people hold on to things they cherished, too. One woman carefully balanced a delicate vase while clutching a bird cage with a live parrot in it.

When we left the train, we saw men in uniforms guiding passengers into two lines. The left one had mostly older people and children, many who looked the same age as Elenor and me. The right line had able-bodied young people.

At the point we exited the train, the person welcoming and directing passengers was a handsome man in a different uniform than many of the others. Whispers went around that he was the camp's commandant. When we reached him, he tried sending Elenor and me to the line on the left and Dot and Rose to the one on the right. Dot objected. She told him the four of us had to stay together. Dot could be a donkey sometimes, but she could also flutter her eyes and convince people to do what she wanted.

The commandant paused and took a good look at Dot and then, Rose. "Why should I keep you together? How does that benefit me?"

Dot fluttered her eyes and replied, "Entertainment. We are the Bremen Musicians."

"I've never heard of you."

"Sir, from your accent, I gather you are from Germany. Perhaps you haven't had an opportunity to be where we perform. Remember, it was a three-day train ride to get here."

"How do I know what you're telling me is true?"

"We can give you a small sample of our music," Dot said. I muttered something, but she grasped my shoulder. Dropping her voice to a low purr, she continued, "Of course, you won't get the full effect because we don't have all our instruments. My little sister and I play the violin. Rose is our lead singer. Even though she doesn't have accompaniment, you can hear how beautifully she sings." The look she gave Rose said, "sing for your supper."

Rose opened her mouth. Her pitch was perfect as the most delicate traditional German lullaby escaped her lips. From the way the lines in the man's face relaxed, it was obvious Rose enchanted him. He turned his attention to Elenor, "And what is it that you do as one of the Bremen Musicians?"

"I yodel."

He furrowed his brow. "You what?"

"Yodel," Elenor repeated.

Dot interrupted before Elenor could say anything else. "Rose's voice and our violins bring a sound of sweetness or a feeling of peace to our audiences, but every now and then we need to liven things up. Elenor's yodel is a staccato counterpoint to our smoothness."

Although I wasn't sure he was fully convinced, he allowed Elenor and me to go with Dot and Rose to the line on the right. Dot wasn't taking any chances, he'd change his mind. She pushed Elenor and me to quickly move forward.

I could write more about our dire existence until we were liberated. About how we lacked food, means to clean ourselves, warm clothing, shared one wooden slat bed, and didn't dare leave our possessions. The latter wasn't because we were afraid someone would take them. We knew they would.

The first night, the commandant had us brought to his living quarters. His two connected rooms at the end of the officer's barracks were far different than ours. One room was a combined office and living room with a couch, tables, a few chairs, and a desk. Between framed pictures on the walls and lovely knick-knacks throughout the room, I felt like I was back in my family's apartment instead of in a camp. At the end were two doors. One, which was cracked, was a bathroom. I assumed the other door led to his bedroom. As you can imagine, I had my violin with me. Rose had her bag with the red dress.

"So," the commandant said. "Let's hear the Bremen Musicians."

"But we are short a violin," Dot noted.

"Not a problem." He called for an aide. When he came, the commandant asked him to bring us a violin. The aide went and returned with one almost immediately. It wasn't as fine as mine, but it would do.

Dot opened that violin's case and began to tune it as best she could. I did the same with mine. It was obvious from the way the commandant shifted his legs, he was getting restless. Rose held up her bag. "While they prep their violins, would you like me to slip into one of the dresses I perform in?"

She took the grunting sound he'd made to be a "yes" and started for the bathroom, but the commandant blocked her way. He pointed to the closed door. "There is more room to change in there. Let me show you."

That night, they were only in his bedroom long enough for her to change while he watched. They came out of the room, and Rose, even with no make-up and a stubble of red hair, was absolutely stunning in that dress. Having lived with Dot and me, Rose knew the words to many of the songs we played, and we melded well. Even if she sang something that wasn't familiar to Dot and me, we quietly played chords so she could outpower us with her magnificent voice. At one point, the commandant pointed to Elenor. "What about her?"

"We save Elenor for a special number at the end," Rose said. "If you'd like us to do it now, we will."

He nodded.

"Fine, when I reach Elenor's yodeling part, I'll point to her."

Dot and I gazed at each other, unsure of what was going to happen. Without us accompanying her, Rose began singing a folk song about the Alps and a little mountain goat. Dot picked up her violin and added background chords. As the words of the song talked about how the little mountain goat jumped from mountain to mountain, Rose pointed at Elenor.

To my surprise, Elenor let out a perfect yodel as piercing as a distant dog howling at the moon. Rose grinned and then picked up the words of the song when Elenor finished. Dot and I exchanged glances but said nothing. We were so amazed neither Dot nor I picked up our violins again. Rose and Elenor worked in two more yodels before Rose ended the song. The commandant stood and applauded. He walked over to Elenor and patted her on the head. "You surprised me. Your yodel was the perfect ending for tonight. I must go now. You will all come again."

Once we were outside and began walking back to our barracks, Dot and I pounced on Elenor, asking how she'd learned to yodel. She pointed at Rose. "When my parents had her babysit me, Rose tried teaching me to sing."

"And she couldn't sing five notes in a row correctly," Rose said. "That's when I thought that learning to yodel might be easier, or at least more fun. Elenor was a natural."

The next week, we were summoned again to perform for an hour. The commandant had Rose leave her red dress in his closet. We pressed her about his room. She turned her head away from us and said, "Much like the living room, it's filled with artwork, crystal vases, and other beautiful things—all of which were probably brought here in the same way as Cat's violin and my red dress. The furniture is simple. There is a bed and dresser, but instead of nightstands, there are small metal locked filing cabinets. The room also has a private exit. He's able to go in and out on the dark side of the barracks without being seen."

During the next few months, he wanted Rose to sing, but there were also nights he had Dot and me only play the violins. To add to our repertoire, Rose taught Elenor different songs where we could add a yodel. Still, we never did more than one yodel song a night.

Other women who lived in our barracks made snide remarks about the four of us getting extra food because we were the commandant's pets. They were sure he was favoring us because we were given some of the easiest work tasks. Elenor and I were assigned kitchen duty. Dot and Rose had outdoor farm responsibilities. Dot was tasked with helping a prisoner, veterinarian Howard Bremen, care for the animals. She was strong physically and worked in the barn near the pig troughs. That wasn't for Rose.

So, Dot took on animal-related duties while Rose handled tasks that didn't require working directly with a live animal. Maybe letting Rose keep track of supplies or hide in the hayloft was a tradeoff for what she experienced once a week, or maybe it allowed Dot to spend more time working with Howard. As his last name indicated, his family was native to the area, and why Dot had picked it for our music group. Howard took a shine to Dot, and the guards allowed them to roam more freely in this part of the compound.

Each week, things went well as the commandant relaxed during the hour we spent with him. Except watching Rose change in and out of her dress, he was a perfect gentleman to us.

We lost our magic touch at the end of 1944. No matter what Rose sang, or what we played, the commandant seemed restless and distracted. We arrived one night to find him disheveled and drunk. As usual, he followed Rose into his bedroom when she went to change. Only this time, things were different. Rose screamed.

Reflexively, the three of us crashed through the unlocked bedroom door, instruments in hand, just as he wrestled Rose to the bed. She struggled, scratching at him with her nails, but he pushed her arms to the bed. I couldn't let him hurt her, so I choked up on my violin like a bat and swung at his head. There was a loud crack.

The commandant froze. As he turned toward me, Dot charged, kicking him hard behind his knee. He stumbled. Then, fell to the floor, striking his head on the corner point of the metal cabinet. There was no blood, but he didn't move.

While the rest of us watched, Dot checked his breathing. The panic in her eyes confirmed my instrument of beauty and joy had become a lethal weapon. I rose to my feet, shivering. Elenor tried to comfort me, but Dot didn't. She checked if Rose was hurt and then glanced at the clock on the wall. "We only have forty-five minutes left of our hour. Make things look normal, so when we leave, it seems like he was fine. Rose, sing as loud as you can. Cat, put your violin in its case. Play mine."

"What?" I stared wide-eyed.

"We will die if we don't. Elenor, help me wrap him in his top sheet. While Cat continues the concert, I'll get help to move him."

"Who?" I whispered.

"Howard. He was assigned to the farm area tonight because a horse is due to foal."

Rose went into the other room and began singing, but my feet stayed planted. "Don't go. The two of you will be caught."

"Not if we're lucky. Look, we just killed the commandant. If things work, we'll survive another day. If we don't do anything, we'll be tortured or mercifully shot. This is our only chance. Elenor, I need you to stand by the door that goes outside and let us in when I double-knock. Cat, get in there with Rose and play!"

Rose and I did three songs, but it felt like the hour's concert, before Dot returned with Howard and a wheelbarrow. While Rose and I began another number, Dot, Elenor, and Howard lifted the sheeted commandant and dumped him into the wheelbarrow. "Lock the door behind us," Dot said. "When the hour is over, leave the regular way, and take both violins with you."

Rose still sang, but I stopped playing and stood in the doorway to the bedroom, looking at my sister. "Dot—"

"When you go back to our barracks, I'll try to join you outside, or I'll meet you there."

I rushed to my sister and clung to her. "I love you, Dot."

She kissed the top of my head and shook me off. "I love you, too, but right now I need you to play."

As Elenor let Howard and Dot out and locked the door behind them, I played the extra violin as if our lives depended on it. When the hour ended, we made sure the bed looked made and left as we normally would. As we exited the building, Dot slipped out of the shadows and joined us.

For the second time in one night, I hugged her.

"It's done," she said.

"How?" I asked.

"Let's just say the pigs will be eating well tonight. They were delighted to find a new snack in their trough," she whispered.

"My violin?"

She took it from me, leaving me with the one she usually played. "We're going to have to hold on to it. Howard told me there are whispers that the Nazis have lost the war. If that's true, people may think the commandant ran for his own survival, but if they open the case and see the violin, they may realize what really happened. With a little luck, we'll be free to go home soon."

It must have been obvious that I was uncomfortable being forced to keep the violin because Dot stopped us before we reached the barracks and demanded we put our hands together. "We are going to survive! Let's make a tontine pact tonight."

"A what?" Elenor said.

"Cat's violin is the instrument of our survival, and nothing will ever have more value. Let's promise each other that it will be a symbol of living until the last one of us dies."

We all agreed.

In the next weeks, the camp changed. Guards left, and no new guards or people came. We were happy to be rid of the terrible beasts, but the camp was still deadly. The poor sanitation grew worse. People got sick. Someone said there was a typhus outbreak.

Dot was one of those stricken. It started with a bad headache. Then, fever, chills, and a rash that spread. I snuck extra food for her from the kitchen, but she wouldn't eat. So, my only recourse was cold cloths to try to bring her fever down.

As she got sicker, Howard, no longer being watched by the few remaining guards, snuck in to help me care for her. On the day the last guards disappeared, and the liberators came, Dot died. And the Bremen Musicians did too.

Rose insisted the tontine must continue. Keeping Dot's memory as a blessing, we eventually made new lives for ourselves. Rose and

Elenor traveled to Palestine and were part of the country becoming Israel. Howard and I came to America. Somewhere along the way, our shared experiences and grief turned into love, marriage, three children, and a business that gave us the means to be philanthropic. Many times, I started to destroy the violin, but Howard told me I couldn't because of the promise we'd made to my sister.

Elenor worked as a teacher in Israel. She married and had one daughter. She passed away when she was sixty-seven, leaving Rose and me in the tontine.

You probably know that when Rose emigrated, she moved to the Be'eri kibbutz. Although she became an international entertainer using the name Red "Rooster" Rosen, her happy place was on the kibbutz. She never married nor had children of her own, but every kibbutz child and then their children, were her children. After she retired from singing twenty years ago, the only time she left Be'eri kibbutz was when she came to comfort me after Howard died.

Only because of her insistence, I kept the violin when I downsized. Until October 7, I detested that violin. Now, although the hands of each Bremen Musician and my violin are stained by the life we took, I understand why Rose and Dot saw my violin as a symbol of survival.

We all tried to live in a way that affirmed life. Between the tragedy of Rose's needless death and the slaughter of those she loved, when I learned about the Violins of Hope project, I realized this violin fulfills the meaning of "L'Chaim" or "To Life."

Liucija, I pray you will either yourself, or by helping Sarah, convince the Weinsteins to restore the violin in the name of the Bremen Musicians.

Cat Bremen

* * *

I put the letter on the couch between Sarah and me and wiped a tear from my eye. "I'll help. This violin, these women's stories, need to be told."

"Thank you," Sarah said. "May I leave the violin with you?"

"The violin and letter, please. There's no question that night, your mother and the other Bremen Musicians dispatched an evil beast and created a way for others to live happily ever after. Considering the Holocaust and the tragedy of October 7, the violin's restoration and sharing these women's stories will honor the spirit of the tontine, and the violin will continue to be an instrument of hope for the future."

# Jack and the Beanstalk

By Andrew Welsh-Huggins

Two weeks in a row that February, Jack's father's boss snuck off with the new overnight produce girl at three a.m. on the dot, and the pair spent the next twenty minutes horizontal on the breakroom couch. No surprise, Jack's father's boss was so focused on the task at hand that he didn't notice the fisheye security camera in the corner just above the faded OHSA workers' rights declaration. The one the suits at headquarters downtown ordered installed during a spate of illicit vaping earlier in the year. The one that inadvertently captured the whole to-do each morning.

Jack's father's boss for sure didn't know the grocery store's eleven-to-seven skeleton crew called an unscheduled break at 3:01 each morning to gather around the monitor in the office at the front of the store and watch the proceedings. Nor did he know about the various bets placed: on disrobing time; positions—her on top, him behind, weird yoga moves; and of course, time to climax.

Jack's father joined the fun the first two nights, along the way winning five bucks on how long she kept her eyes open, staring at the tiled ceiling, as his boss humped away like a seal crossing the sand to the surf. But he quickly figured out there were better ways to spend his twenty minutes, especially with prying eyes on just the one camera.

He started with the eight-cartridge Gillette razor packs, which retailed for a crazy $29.99 and which multiple guys he knew would be happy to take off his hands for ten apiece. Another night, he lifted the key to the liquor shop and tiptoed to his car with five bottles of Angel's Envy, bound for the boot joint down the street. Two nights in a row, he loaded up a crate of avocados bound for a taqueria happy to do a little side business.

On the second to last night, right before some killjoy told his boss about the camera, Jack's father commandeered a shopping cart, loaded up a quarter side of Black Angus—frozen so solid you could crack rocks on it—and wrestled it into the back of his pickup.

"Wake up," he said later that morning, standing over Jack's bed.

"Mmph."

"I said, wake up. I gotta job needs done."

Jack slowly opened her eyes and looked at her father.

"What time is it?"

"It's get-the-fuck-up o'clock. Move. This is important."

Jack grunted and pulled the thin blanket over her head.

"I said, get up," Jack's father said, ripping the blanket off the bed and throwing it on the floor.

"Really?" Jack said, curling herself into a ball. It was cold in the room, as always. She didn't know how many months behind they were to the gas company, but pretty sure they were in double digits by now.

Her father said, "I need some shut-eye. While I'm sawing logs, I need you to drive to Carl's and give him the thing in the truck. Don't take less than two fifty. It's worth four times that retail, all right?"

Without changing position, Jack said, "What is it?"

He told her.

"Why in the world does Carl need a quarter cow?"

"His daughter's getting married, and he promised all-you-can-eat steaks at the reception."

"Why?"

Her father yawned. "His daughter's fiancé is out on parole, and otherwise no one's gonna come, all right?"

"Parole for what?"

"Parole for something people don't want to think about. Other than that, I hear he's a nice kid. Just do it."

"I've got school."

"At nine. It's 7:45. Plenty of time. Plus, we need the money."

That's for damn sure, Jack said. But only to herself.

* * *

Naturally, she only made it six blocks before the truck died.

"Shit. Shit. Shit," she said, turning the key in vain.

She checked the time on her phone. Eight twenty-five. Even starting to walk now, she'd never make the first bell. And as much as she complained about school, she didn't want to miss Biology. Ms. Moffat was a good teacher. And she said Jackie—what Jack went by any second her father wasn't around—had potential, especially when it came to understanding how plants worked. Jackie also secretly thought Ms. Moffat liked the way Jackie got into it over Noah's Ark with the "It's Adam-and-Eve-not-Adam-and-Steve" crowd. So yeah, she never missed Biology.

Except today. Today, she was a mile and a half from Carl's run-down trailer with a frozen side of beef under a green Army blanket in the back of her father's pickup and no way to get it there. Or to get home. Which was just about par for the course.

She cursed again and considered her options. Calling her father was a no-go, since he'd be fast asleep and would never hear the ring, assuming his phone wasn't dead because he'd forgotten to charge it again. So there was that.

She was trying to think of who else she could call—which of her friends gave a rat's ass about the first bell and might still be at home and inclined to lend a helping hand (a short list, she had to admit)—when she looked to her right and saw a small repair place she hadn't noticed before. Chuck's Garage. Set back from the street, sketchy-looking an understatement, but with two things going for it: a light on in the small office and movement inside the two-door bay.

What the hell, she thought.

"Battery, for sure," the grease monkey—William, it turned out—said five minutes later, peering under the hood and fiddling with something. Hands grimy and worn, but also muscular from actual labor, not like some men she could think of.

"Okay."

"Running a special. Battery and labor eighty-nine dollars out the door."

Which would be $87.40 she didn't have.

"We take credit cards," he offered, reading her face.

Those she'd heard of, at least.

She checked her phone: eight forty-five. Unlikely she'd make first bell, but second was still a possibility.

"Question for you," she said.

"Which is?"

"You like steak?"

* * *

The guy, William, was a stand-up sort. She could tell he knew the deal was as lopsided as they come. He was so apologetic, he handed her a paper bag after writing up a receipt.

"What's this?"

"Breakfast burritos. Place around the corner. Best refried beans in town."

"Aren't they yours?"

"It's fine. Hope you enjoy them. It's Jackie, you said, right? Good luck with the truck."

"Thanks," Jackie said doubtfully, though she liked the way her name sounded when he said it. At home, her father insisted on calling her Jack as a daily reminder he'd have preferred a son, and it was getting old.

Which feeling might be why Jackie ignored multiple calls and texts from her father all day—who would have guessed; his phone was charged—until the moment of reckoning when she walked in after school and he stood before her, disbelief on his face.

"You traded Carl's quarter side of beef for burritos?"

"Yeah, as a matter of fact. Especially since he threw in a battery after that piece of shit truck died on the way. What was I supposed to do?"

"I thought I raised you better than that," her father said, grabbing the paper bag and tossing it in the kitchen trash.

"Hey—I was going to eat those."

"Not now, you're not. Not after this fuck-up."

They got into it for a while, but then he had to get ready for his evening nap, which was the only way he made it through the overnight. That and the bottles of Fireball he snuck into his lunch pail when he thought she wasn't looking.

"Don't forget to take the trash out," he said before face-planting.

"Trash this," she said to herself, adding a middle finger for good measure. Finally, right before bed, she grabbed the garbage bag, shivering against the cold as she marched through the falling snow, and tipped it into the dumpster. Fuming at her father and Carl and the rusted-out pickup truck the whole time. All of which meant she didn't sleep great until after four when she fell into a deep slumber. Which meant it took her a minute early the next morning to wake up and realize her phone was buzzing.

"Hullo?"

"Jackie?"

"Who's this?"

"It's William. From the garage? I put in the new battery? For the, um, cow thing?"

"How'd you get my number?"

"I took your info, remember? Anyway, listen, that bag of burritos? Do you still have it?"

"Not exactly," she said. "Why?"

"I made a mistake. I gave you the wrong bag. There was something in there my brother needs. Chuck, he's the owner."

"Something like what?"

William's voice caught. "Something he owes somebody. I really need it back."

Oh, for fuck's sake, Jackie thought. But what she said, because she liked the way her name sounded when William spoke it, was: "Hang on."

She pulled a pair of her loosest jeans over her pajamas, grabbed her parka, stuck her feet into her boots, and stumped over to the dumpster. Shaking with cold, cursing the bite of snow on her fingers, she lifted the lid and stared inside. To her surprise, the plastic garbage bag was torn open. An animal? She balanced herself on the bin's ledge, leaned over, and carefully looked around. Nope—no rabid raccoon ready to charge. But also, no paper bag of not-breakfast burritos, either. Weird. What kind of animal leaves gnawed pork chop bones and takes a bag of whatever?

She dropped to the asphalt and looked around. That's when she saw them. Shoeprints, leading away from the dumpster. Beside the prints, a scattered trail of coffee grounds and Winston butts—her father's breakfast of choice—leaving little question that someone had rooted around in their kitchen trash. The question was, why?

*Hang on*, she texted William, and followed the prints across the apartment parking lot.

I shouldn't be doing this, she thought. It was colder than she expected. It was also a shower morning, assuming there was any hot water, which would cost her ten extra minutes, and she didn't want to be late two days in a row. But William sounded desperate, and she figured she owed him a favor. A small favor—a two-thousand-dollar side of beef for an eighty-nine-dollar battery wasn't exactly fair dealing. But still.

The shoeprints led to a line of scraggly firs atop a rounded berm that separated the apartment building from the property around the corner. She nearly stopped there, deciding to call it a day, when she spied a print in the snow between two of the trees and in it, something she didn't expect to see. A twenty-dollar bill. She knelt and examined it, then tucked it into the parka's right pocket. Five yards farther on, she found another. She pocketed that one as well. Intrigued, she kept going against her better judgment, following the tracks—and two more bills—through the trees, across a small service road, and up an alley.

The trail ended at a pair of double metal doors at the basement level of a building smack in her path. She looked at the doors, and then up. And up.

She realized that for all the times she'd driven past this huge, abandoned food-processing facility, she'd never been around back. Which explained why she'd also never seen the huge, faded mural of the guy you saw on all the green bean cans looming over the abandoned loading docks, a representation that had to be at least ten—no, eleven, no, twelve—stories high. Which was interesting, sure, but no way in hell—

Her phone buzzed. William.

*Any luck?*

*No*, she wrote, and then happened to look down.

Another $20 bill lay just outside the double doors.

Naturally, the elevator wasn't working. And naturally, whoever took the torn paper bag filled with cash had ascended to the very top, according to the damp shoeprints she tracked concrete landing by concrete landing.

Six minutes later, struggling to catch her breath, she reached the top. Checking that her phone had a signal, she slowly opened the door. And found herself staring at a double-barreled shotgun pointed directly at her chest.

* * *

"Don't move," whispered the woman standing before Jackie. Behind her stretched a warren of offices and abandoned tables and chairs and metal desks. It was a mess, like a small tornado had come through, but that's not what caught Jackie's attention outside of the gun.

Something smelled really bad up here.

"I—" Jackie stammered.

"Who are you? We're not expecting anyone." She was so thin, Jackie wondered if she had cancer, or jogged a whole hell of a lot, except you probably didn't jog with so many bruises on your face, or with what looked like clumps of stringy blond hair missing, or wearing such a deeply stained pair of gray sweats.

"I'm, um, Jack. I mean, Jackie. I was just—"

She didn't get a chance to finish. A groan sounded on the other side of the room. A look of terror crossed the face of the woman holding the gun. Jackie shrank into herself, fearing the woman was about to fire. Instead, to her surprise, the woman gestured at a door behind her and jabbed a finger several times in its direction. Jackie didn't need an invitation; she scurried to the door and slipped inside, finding herself in a tiny closet with scarcely room to stand, let alone sit.

"What's going on?" a masculine voice said.

"Nothing."

Silence. Then: "What's that smell?"

"Smell?"

"I smell something." A pause. "Someone."

Another pause.

"Is someone here?" the man demanded.

Jackie's heart stopped while she waited for the woman's reply. Finally, she heard her say, "No one's here."

"No one?"

"No one, other than—"

"Is he still alive? Is that what I'm smelling?"

A chill crawled up Jackie's spine.

"No," the woman whispered after a moment. "How—"

"How what?"

"How could he be?"

* * *

Time didn't just stop; it congealed into a pile of frozen slush that Jackie slowly sank into, immobilized, unable to move despite the ache in her back and the fear in her heart. When her phone buzzed, she nearly wet herself and scrambled to silence it, heart hammering as if she'd climbed twelve stories again. But that had been at least a quarter of an hour ago, and she'd heard nothing else other than the woman's insistent patter in a dry, exhausted voice: "No one's here."

Jackie stood for so long in the dark that her eyes began to droop. Her chin bobbed to her chest for just a second before she snapped her head up as the door opened.

Oh God, she said to herself. Aloud, eyes adjusting to the light, she croaked, "Please don't hurt me."

The woman stared at her through bloodshot eyes.

"Hurry," she said. "He's asleep."

Jackie stumbled out of the closet, willing herself to stay upright despite the pins and needles burning her numb legs back to life. Casting a glance at the bedraggled woman, she wobbled uncertainly toward the exit. She was almost there when she glanced at a folding table shoved against the wall beside the entryway, its top covered with papers, an assortment of random tools such as pliers and handsaws, and a jumble of greasy junk-food bags and empty bottles of beer with unfamiliar green labels. At the far end sat the paper bag whose contents William the Grease Monkey needed back so desperately.

She stopped, debating, eyes flicking to the far side of the floor and back. Was it worth the risk, despite how needy William sounded? On the other hand, he had saved her butt by fixing the truck. Okay—one try. She edged toward the bag. Closer, closer—

The sound like a roar from an office across the way, the top half of its frosted windows smashed, the shattered bottom-half remainder forming a ragged up-and-down pattern like the world's deadliest mountain range overlooking the world's most dysfunctional kingdom.

"Who's here?"

"Run," the woman whispered.

"Shit," Jackie squeaked, deciding no way was the bag worth it. She spun in the opposite direction but at the last moment glanced again at the table. Rising above the fast-food debris sat a half-empty bucket of Kentucky Fried Chicken. Peering closer, she saw something out of place. Jutting from beneath the bucket's bottom was a gold-colored credit card. The kind you saw on TV being used in places like five-star hotels and Caribbean resorts that might as well have been on the moon for all the access she'd ever have to them. Why not, she thought, snatching the card and sprinting for the door.

* * *

"Where'd you get this?" her father demanded that night, thrusting the gold card at her.

"I found it."

"Where?"

"In the trash."

"Bullshit."

"I'm telling the truth."

She wasn't surprised her father was angry. She knew Carl was royally pissed about the steaks he'd promised his guests after his daughter's marriage to the guy out on parole for the thing (she'd looked it up; her father was right, it was super icky). Nevertheless, she thought an American Express Gold Card might cheer him up. He looked happy enough as he pocketed it before heading to work. Turns out she was on the money, so to speak, but her timing was off.

"Any more of those out there?" her father said the next morning.

"Any more of what?" she said, dunking a stale Pop-Tart into a glass of water.

"Those cards. The gold ones."

"Why?"

"No reason."

Jackie rolled her eyes.

"Okay. Maybe this guy at work."

"Maybe this guy at work, what?"

Her father sighed. "He gave me $100 for it."

"You got $100 for that card?"

"Just told you that."

"What about me?"

"What about you?"

"How much do I get?"

"How about a roof over your head and food on the table?"

Jackie glanced at the crack in the wall by the toaster, which she was pretty sure was wider today than yesterday, then looked down at the crumbs of Pop-Tart settling to the bottom of her water glass.

"Fifty bucks," she said.

* * *

In the end, her father gave her twenty, which was ten more than she figured on, so she called it a win. Even though he said he'd give her thirty if she brought home another card from "the trash," an offer she flat-out refused because there was no way in hell she was returning to the twelfth floor of the Green Guy Building to face the crazy woman with the shotgun and the scary as shit man and the weird smell permeating the place like someone tossed a road-kill possum into a porta-potty and three days passed before anyone noticed.

Then, she heard her phone ringing and saw she had a FaceTime call.

"Jesus. What happened to you?" She stared at William the Grease Monkey.

He stared back through two black eyes she knew instinctively he didn't get from changing somebody's oil.

"I'm sorry to bug you," he said softly. She realized he was having trouble speaking. "It's just, I really need that bag back."

* * *

She was going to go first thing because she kind of liked William. But the fact was, she liked Biology more. It was the right decision since Ms. Moffat did a whole thing about the reason why some sunflowers grew so freaking tall, like halfway to the sky, because of their internal vascular bundles, which was something Jackie had always wondered about. By contrast, she did not wonder a whole lot about trigonometry and was out the door and headed down the street by five minutes to ten.

She took her time ascending the stairs, creeping slowly step by step. She paused halfway up, spying something shiny in the corner. Bending over, she picked up a diamond earring with a gem the size of a corn pop. She thought back to the day before, to the $20 bills she found that must have fallen from William's paper bag. She thought briefly of the chilling question the scary-as-shit man asked the woman with the shotgun: "Is he still alive?"

And the woman's even more chilling response: "How could he be?"

Swallowing hard, Jackie pocketed the earring and continued up the stairs. Wondering as she did: where was the earring's match? Not to mention the person who delivered it?

Entering the remains of the office space on the twelfth floor undetected was a crap shoot. At least this time she was prepared. She stood for five minutes outside the door, pressing her ear against it to detect movement. At last, not exactly satisfied, but summoning up an image of William's black eyes and knowing she had no choice, she slowly tugged the door open and stepped inside.

* * *

For one blissful moment, she thought she was alone.

She wrinkled her nose, the smell even stronger than the day before. But eyes darting here and there, she didn't immediately see anyone. Especially a certain someone leveling a shotgun at her chest. She took a step forward, then another, and stopped.

There. A sound.

She strained to listen. At last, she made it out. A man snoring. The sound like a truck rolling down a mountain of cinder blocks. Louder, if that were possible, than the ruckus that blasted from her father's bedroom two minutes after he fell onto his mattress each morning. The man—that guy. Asleep in the office with shattered windows. Thank God.

She tiptoed across the floor, pausing once when she felt something beneath her sneaker. She went to her knees and stared at the object. A cracked cell phone case. She looked around and saw another. And another. First, a purloined bag of twenty-dollar bills. An American Express Gold Card. A diamond earring. Now cell phone cases. What was going on up here, anyway?

No time to dwell on it. She rose and crept toward the folding table. To her relief, the paper bag was still there, next to the jumble of fast-food trash and the empty beer bottles with the green labels. She didn't bother checking for other gold cards. Her father should be so lucky. Closer and closer. Almost there…

*Holy fuck.*

She stopped, fixed in place like a butterfly with a pin through its heart.

Against the wall beside the table, head slumped over, chest slowly rising and falling, the woman was fast asleep, shotgun in her lap. And on closer inspection, an arm beside the gun.

Not the woman's.

The next few seconds were a blur. Suppressing an urge to vomit, Jackie stumbled toward the table, hand reaching for the paper bag. Just before she grasped it, her boot landed on yet another cell phone case, and she skidded forward, losing her balance. Arms windmilling to stay upright, she almost made it, but instead of regaining her equilibrium, she fell forward, sweeping one of the beer bottles onto the floor with a loud, splintering crash. Up close to the table, she barely had time to register the brand—Harp—when she heard the woman groan.

Followed by a voice from the office.

"Who's there?"

The woman roused herself, looked around, and stilled, eyes on Jackie.

"Who's there?" the man repeated.

"No one," the woman said, gesturing at Jackie to flee. "No one's here."

"Then who's that?" the man said, emerging from the office and staring at Jackie.

She stared back, unable to move.

He was smaller than she guessed based on the sound of his voice and the fear he instilled in the woman—his wife? Girlfriend? Accomplice? Not that much taller than her, not exactly schlumpy but not exactly not schlumpy. Dressed in white painter's pants, an oversized San Francisco Giants jersey, and wearing on his head—was she seeing this right?—a short order cook's white chef hat.

"Go," the woman said, just as the man darted from his office, quick as a spider detecting a fly, heading straight for Jackie.

Jackie went. Because even across the room, she could see that the man's mouth was stained dark red.

She grabbed the paper bag in her right hand and a second empty bottle of Harp in her left. Without looking she flung the bottle in the man's direction and was rewarded with the sound of him crying out in pain. The feeling of accomplishment was quickly replaced by more fear when he yelled, "Thief," his feet thundering behind her.

Heart jackhammering, Jackie powered through the door and took the stairs three at a time. Then four. She heard him yelling behind her halfway down, at first gaining ground—"Crap, crap, crap"—and then, miraculously, falling behind, his voice fading in volume if not rage. She leaped down the final five steps, staggered, regained her footing, and sprinted for the back doors of the building and ran for her life.

* * *

"You've got to be kidding me."

Except, winded as Jackie was, it didn't come out that way. What she said, hands on her knees, staring at the scene that greeted her inside Chuck's Garage, was: "Huh huh huh huh huh-huh huh."

William the Grease Monkey, sporting a broken nose in addition to his black eyes, sat hunched on a metal chair, hands tied behind his back. Next to him sat a slightly older man with a face that looked like it had just emerged from a bag full of wasps. Had to be William's brother Chuck. Two men loomed over them, big as weightlifters, sane-looking as clowns, handsome as scarecrows, who might have been twins in their matching, sharp-creased dark suits.

"Don't hurt them," Jackie gasped, thrusting the paper bag at the twin on the right.

The man stared at her as if she'd just stepped through a mirror.

"The fuck are you?"

"The"—gasp—"missing"—wheeze—"money"—groan. "It's all there."

The first twin handed the bag to the second twin, who reached inside, pulled out a bundle of green bills, and frowned.

"Not all of it," he said.

"Most of it," Jackie said, starting to recover.

"Most ain't all," the second twin said. "We only deal with all." He nodded at the first twin, who bunched his right hand into a fist and leaned toward Chuck.

"Diamonds," Jackie said.

The first twin looked at her.

"What?"

"Diamonds," she said. "Credit cards—the gold kind. And cell phones. And the rest of your money. And, um, other stuff. So much stuff. I can show you."

"What are you talking about?"

"There's a place. Over there." She pointed in what she hoped was the direction of the Green Guy Building. "A man. He steals stuff. At least, I think. Or somebody steals for him." She thought about the smell, the arm in the woman's lap, and the tracks she followed up the stairs that she just now realized didn't track back down.

"Your point is?" the second twin said.

"I'll take you there. It'll be worth it," she added. "I promise."

"Why in the world should we trust you?"

"Because when you see what's inside, you won't be able to leave."

* * *

It took all the powers of persuasion Jackie had, but in the end, she convinced them that both twins had to come. Turns out the skills she learned debating the Bible thumpers in Biology class paid off, not to mention the techniques she'd gained over the years bargaining with her father. She wasn't thrilled about the twins' insistence on gagging William and his brother and re-tightening their bindings, but at least they were alive.

It also took all the courage she could muster to agree to a ride in the back seat of the twins' enormous black SUV, but it was obvious they weren't going to walk to the abandoned factory in the cold and snow with the kind of dress shoes they were wearing.

At first, hitting the steps, guns drawn, they insisted on her leading the way, obviously convinced it was a trap of some kind. But Jackie dragged her ass so much—half faked, and half because she was exhausted from her all-out sprint to the garage—that they lost their patience by the sixth floor and barged ahead.

She picked it up as they approached the twelfth floor, however, making sure she arrived on the landing the same time they did, one behind the other.

"Through there," she said. She waited until the first twin pulled the door open, took a breath, summoned the last of her strength, and charged into the second twin, causing both to fall inside, yelling and cursing.

She ran for the stairs. And didn't look back. And wasn't three floors down when she heard the first scream.

* * *

"You believe this shit?"

Her father commented the next day, walking in from his overnight shift, eyes glued to his phone. He sank into the chair beside Jackie and picked up her Pop-Tart.

"What shit?"

"This," he said, angling his phone at her. She glanced at a Channel 7 headline.

*Police Suspect Robbery Mastermind Cannibalized Unwitting Partners.*

"Whoa," Jackie said, feigning surprise.

Yet, she listened intently as her father recounted the gory details. Police responding to the report of a body outside the city's former frozen food factory found a hellish crime scene—scenes—they were still trying to unravel. Scattered in various rooms on the twelfth floor of the factory, formerly the site of the company's business offices, lay a treasure trove of stolen goods: jewelry, high-end purses; cell phones and other electronics; bundles of cash; and dozens of silver, gold, and even platinum-level credit cards. Strewn among these goods were grisly remains of several individuals who appeared to be errand men—and women—for the still unidentified perpetrator of a city-wide theft and fencing operation.

Somewhat incongruously, among those remains were mangled bodies of two men preliminarily identified as ringleaders of a protection and rackets operation that had terrorized several local businesses.

Complicating the investigation: the fact that the monster behind the operation, who apparently dispatched his errand runners in gruesome fashion as soon as their usefulness ended, was also dead, his body on the ground. Speculation that he'd jumped twelve stories. Or was pushed, since a woman was found in the man's hidey-hole staring out the window he fell through muttering, "No one's here, no one's here," over and over again.

"Credit cards," her father said with a frown, staring at his phone before looking at Jackie. "Anything I should know?"

"Probably not." She kept her head down, responding to a text William sent, thanking her again for returning the money. She still had a twinge in her arm from hurling a brick through the window of the twins' SUV as she fled the building. But retrieving the bag of cash belonging to the brothers in the front passenger seat had been worth it.

"Why should I believe you?" her father said.

Jackie thought about it, then pulled out the diamond ring the size of a corn pop and laid it on the table.

"Where'd you get that?" her father said, eyes suddenly the size of saucers.

"In the trash. Worth a lot, don't you think?"

"Duh. Answer the question."

Instead of responding, Jackie placed her phone on the table, pressed 911, waiting to hit the green call button.

"Jack?"

"Here's how I see it," she said. "You can keep the ring—*we* can keep it—but some things are going to change around here. Or I can call the police, and you, not me, can explain where you got it."

He cocked his head. "What kind of things?"

"Big things."

"Like what?"

"Like a lot. Starting with the most important one."

"Which is?"

She reached over and took her Pop-Tart out of his hand.

"My name isn't Jack."

# Cinderella

By Donna Andrews

My car was in the shop—again—so when I got off work, I had to walk all the way across the mall to the bus stop. Hate doing that—passing dozens of store windows full of stuff I can't afford. Plus, that day my boss at the pretzel place said something about how I needed to be nicer to the customers. Was he just having a rotten day and taking it out on me or was he working up to firing me? It was a crappy place to work, but I hated the idea of job hunting again. My job history basically sucked, so it was getting harder and harder to get a job, even at a crappy place. And besides—

Then I saw them. I'd glanced over at the window of one of the fanciest stores, and there they were. Glass slippers, like Cinderella would wear. Only these were real.

The store was closed, but they left spotlights on in the window to show off the merchandise. The glass gleamed and sparkled in the lights, and the diamonds set all over the shoes sent flashes of light all around. The heel was either made of silver or maybe covered with something silver colored, and the sole was bright red and shiny, like patent leather.

I stood there staring at them until one of the mall security guards came along and gave me a suspicious look. They don't like store employees hanging around after the mall closes. So, I pretended to answer my phone and talked into it really loudly. "About time! What door are you at? Okay, on my way."

And then I set off fast for the exit closest to the bus stop.

I came in early the next day. I got an ice cream cone from the food court and sat on one of the benches to eat it. A bench that was right across from the window with the glass slippers. I played it cool, pretending to be watching the crowds and texting with someone on my phone, only occasionally stealing a glance at the slippers. I'd already decided I had to have the slippers, and no way I could ever afford to buy them. I'd have to steal them, which meant I probably shouldn't let anyone see me mooning over the store window too much.

I figured even if my boss wasn't getting ready to fire me, it was time to end my pretzel-making career. I knew where I wanted to work next. At midnight, when the mall closed, the cleaning staff showed up to spend the next eight hours mopping and vacuuming and polishing. And I figured the security guards couldn't possibly watch all the cleaners all night long. So, the first step was to get hired as a cleaner.

A lot of businesses use a service, which would have been a pain, because those services clean dozens of places, and it might take forever to get assigned to the mall. But I lucked out. The mall hired its own cleaners. And didn't pay as well as the services. That sucked, but at least it meant they were always recruiting. I figured if the pretzel place gave me a bad reference, I could explain that I wasn't good at customer service and wanted a job where I could work by myself. Just me and my mop. Turned out they didn't even ask for references—just how soon could I start. The pretzel place was happy to let me go—bet I was right that the manager was working up to firing me. By the end of the week, I was officially a cleaner, with a stupid uniform and an ID badge that doubled as a key card to let me into the break room and the supply closet.

I laid low at first. Got to know the routines—mine and the guards'. Cleaning was hard work, but I didn't mind it so much. Maybe because I had a reason to be working—a bigger reason than just a lousy paycheck.

Or maybe I should have tried working as a cleaner a long time ago. I was good at it, thanks to all the scut work my crazy, neat-freak stepmother always used to make me do. I liked not having anyone hanging over me every minute. Okay, the mall security cameras were always there, at least out in the main part of the mall, but I got used to that. And at least they weren't nagging me. Or telling tales on me, like my stepsisters used to. I liked not having to deal with customers. Not even having to deal with people at all, most of the time. I even liked the cleaning itself. There was something really satisfying about it. Wiping fingerprints and nose prints off so the glass store fronts sparkled. Emptying out trash cans and relining them with fresh, empty liners. Mopping and polishing the floors until they gleamed. Wet days and snowy days, that was my favorite part. You'd think it would bother me that as soon as I left, people came swarming in to undo everything I'd done, but it didn't. There was something kind of reassuring, knowing that the same familiar routine would be waiting for me every night. And it turned out I was pretty good at cleaning. Who knew? I just figured my place always stayed in good shape because it was so small, and I had so little stuff.

It was going to take time, first getting to know the mall's overnight routine, and then figuring out a plan to get into the store that sold the glass slippers. A plan that wouldn't just get me in, of course. I also needed to get out again without being detected. Because I wanted to stay around. Not just for the fun of seeing what happened when they noticed the slippers were gone. I wanted to stay around as a cleaner for…well, for the time being. Until I figured out something I liked even more. Like maybe applying to one of the cleaning services that paid better.

But for now, I was happy. I had a job I liked. A job I was good at. The pay sucked, but no more than any of the other jobs I'd had. And I had a plan. A goal.

Little by little, I figured out how I was going to pull it off. I managed to get assigned to the section of the mall with the glass slipper store. I knew which guards covered that section, and I'd figured out that one of them sneaked outside a couple of times a night to grab a smoke.

I figured out the guards didn't carry a key that would let them into individual stores. There was a master key that did that, but it was locked up in the security office. Fat chance of using that.

I started studying how security worked with individual stores. In addition to their front entrance, for the customers, they all had a back door leading out into the service corridor.

And that was going to be useful. Out in the public areas, the security cameras got you coming and going, but mall management hadn't bothered with all that in the service corridors. Apart from a single camera covering each outside door, there weren't any cameras to watch out for.

Most of my fellow cleaners just gave a lick and a promise to the service corridors in their sections, but I made sure mine was as clean and tidy as the public areas. I think I'd have done it anyway, just because I couldn't stand having something I was responsible for being a mess.

I started taking a bus that got me to the mall earlier—before it closed. If anyone asked, I'd say I was just making sure I was there on time. Not something I'd worried about before the slippers. And since we weren't supposed to go out in the public areas with our cleaning gear until all the customers had left, I'd start by cleaning the service corridor. That gave me a chance to learn what the store employees did at closing and what, if anything, went on inside the stores when the mall was closed.

A few of the stores had their own cleaning services, but most just dumped the cleanup on the staff who did the closing. The store with the glass slippers did that. And most nights, all their employees did was dump the trash into a big receptacle around the corner at the far end of the service corridor. They didn't even dust the stuff in the window. It made me sad, the day I realized the glass slippers were starting to get dusty. Sad, and then anxious. I'd worried at first that someone would buy the shoes before I could grab them. Then I started worrying that the store might get rid of them. Send them back or put them on sale or whatever they did when something had been around too long.

I had to do something.

I'm not much on socializing, but I was always polite to the guards. Especially the one who usually worked my section of the mall. We struck up…well, you couldn't exactly call it a friendship. Just a nodding acquaintance, really, and that was all either of us wanted. I'm no looker, and he was no Prince Charming. But we'd wish each other good night and good morning, exchange bits of mall gossip, and sometimes he'd bum a cigarette.

Same with the store employees. I wished them a good night if I passed them. If I was standing near a back door when one of them came through with the trash, I stopped and held it for them. They liked that. The doors were set to lock automatically when they closed, and the security guards gave the store employees hell if they found a door unlocked or propped open, so mostly the staff took their keys with them. And having me hold the door open saved them from having to fish out their keys—or maybe even from getting locked out if they forgot the keys. It was a long way around to the front of the stores to get back in that way.

And most of them liked having me there when they dumped the trash because they were a little scared of the service corridors. Not surprising. The corridors weren't pretty—concrete floors and painted cinderblock walls, and on top of the lack of security cameras, they were badly lit and kind of creepy. I didn't start the rumors about people being robbed or assaulted in the service corridors, but I made sure to pass them along. When the employees left, most of them seemed to prefer going out the front door of their stores—out into the mall. That was good. It meant if I could figure out a way to keep the lock from catching when whoever dumped the glass slipper store's trash went back inside, the clerk might leave without even noticing it was unlocked.

And eventually, what I was waiting for happened. I had just started work in the service corridor, scrubbing scuff marks off the bottom foot of the cinderblock walls. One of the glass slipper store's employees came out into the service corridor carrying two enormous bags of trash. When she stepped outside, she patted her pockets, then grabbed the door before it closed. She set the bags down and went back inside. She returned with a broom and propped the door open with the handle before trudging down the corridor. I watched out of the corner of my eye until she disappeared around the corner.

I ran to the door, opened it, and peered in. No one in sight. I flipped the lock to open and then went back to work. The store employee returned in a minute or so. We wished each other a good evening, and she went back inside, taking the broom with her.

I came back a couple of hours later, after I'd seen the guard go out for his first smoke break of the night. If their security was good, the store employee would have checked the door before she left, and when she found it open, relocked it. But if I were lucky, she'd assume the door was locked—after all, it always was.

And the door was open.

I slipped inside. My first impulse was to run for the front window, grab the glass slippers, and run out again. But if I did that, the employee might remember that I'd been alone in the corridor when she'd propped the door open. I reminded myself to be patient.

Instead, I searched the employees-only area. It was so cluttered and filthy I almost gave in to the temptation to do something about it. My fingers itched to tidy. But I resisted and focused on searching. Eventually, I found a wooden rack with a couple of hooks on it. One hook held a key whose tag said "Door." It looked like the one I'd seen the employees use.

I pocketed it and slipped back out into the service corridor. I glanced around and then tried the key. It was the right one.

I had a copy made that morning on my way home. And that night, when the guard was on his cigarette break, I tested my new key to make sure it worked, replaced the original, and locked the door again.

Now all I had to do was wait. I decided to let some time go by before I claimed my glass slippers. Time enough for the employee to forget I'd had access to the unlocked door. For the guy in the hardware store to make a few hundred other keys and forget my face. For the security guards to forget they'd ever seen me staring at the glass slippers.

I kept the key on my key ring. I even labeled it with a bit of white tape that said "Cindy." My little inside joke.

Then I started watching for a time when the security guards were busy with what they called an incident. They always called for backup whenever they had an incident, which meant most of the guards would be in one place, and if the incident was at the other side of the mall, I'd be safe using my key. And most weeks, we'd get at least one incident. Car alarms going off in the parking lot were so common they almost didn't count as incidents, but they might give me the time I needed. Once we'd had a drunk peeing on one of the glass entrance doors. There was that time a kid crawled into the fake igloo in the middle of the Santa village and fell asleep, and his parents thought he'd been kidnapped. And the time a dog got loose from the pet shop and kept the guards hopping for an hour and a half, until one of them finally dug into a trash can in the food court and found a half-eaten burger to use as bait. Sooner or later, an incident would come along.

My chance finally came one night when the guards figured out they had some stowaways—high school kids who had dared each other to hide in one of the stores and stay in the mall partying all night. They always got caught and kicked out, but it took all the guards to do it, and it kept them busy for a while.

When I was sure the guards were at one end of the mall trying to corner the stowaways, I let myself into the glass slipper store. It was dark except for the front, where the spotlights shone on the fancy shoes in the window. Red leather stilettos with four-inch heels that came to a point about the size of the eraser on the end of a pencil. Pink pumps with heels that were almost as tall and pointy, and two fluffy black pom-poms stuck to the toes.

And the glass slippers.

I waited while my eyes adjusted to the dark inside the store, and then I crept to the front. I had my knapsack with me, empty except for a sweater to cover the shoes. All I had to do was grab them, stuff them in the knapsack, and get out.

I was reaching for one of the slippers when—

"Freeze! Put your hands up!"

I froze, but I didn't put my hands up. I turned just enough to see the security guard behind me. Not one I'd ever seen before. Why wasn't he chasing the stowaways? Where was the guard who knew me? I might be able to convince him that I was playing a prank.

I decided to try that anyway.

"Okay, you caught me," I said. "I've been dying to see what a thousand-dollar pair of shoes feels like. Guess I should've asked the salesclerks to let me try them on in the daytime. Only I knew they'd laugh and—"

"Just shut up." He was pulling out his radio. Damn! He was calling the police.

"Please." I began inching away. "I didn't mean any harm. I only—"

"I said, shut up." He took a step closer as if to make sure I couldn't get away.

I reached behind me into the window display, grabbed one of the red stilettos, and swung.

It hit him in the eye, the left one, and the heel went in, all four inches of it. He made a weird kind of gurgling noise and keeled over.

I stood there looking at him for what seemed like a couple of centuries, watching blood come out of his eye and pool onto the floor.

And then I saw a flash of movement outside. A couple of teenage girls ran by, giggling, a security guard chasing them.

Time to move.

I grabbed the glass slippers, stuffed them in my knapsack, and headed for the exit, reminding myself to walk, not run.

I stepped into the service corridor, looking around. It was empty. I walked (not ran) to the break room. Also empty. I stowed the knapsack in my locker and went back to work polishing the floor in a corridor that led to one of the exits. Every so often, I'd see one or two of the stowaways sprinting past in the main part of the mall. Or one of the remaining security guards escorting captured stowaways to wherever they were keeping them. The police showed up eventually. They came to the door near where I was polishing, so I let them in and told them where to find security. They apologized for walking on my freshly polished floor.

If it sounds like I was cool, calm, and collected. I wasn't. More like dazed.

It could be worse, I kept reminding myself. They'd blame the stowaways for the dead security guard, right?

It seemed like at least another century until my shift was over. Longest night of my life. I trudged back to the break room, changed into my own clothes, hoisted the knapsack onto my back, and headed for the bus stop.

I started feeling more like myself on the long bus ride home. The cold air helped. And the sheer overwhelming ordinariness of the day. Nightshift workers like me slumped tiredly in our seats as we headed home. Sleepy office workers sneaked sips of coffee from their travel cups.

Something hit me. Most of the office-bound women wore sneakers or comfortable flats. I figured most of them had shoes in their desks or tucked away in their purses or tote bags—classier shoes that they'd change into when they got to their offices.

If they could only see what I had in my knapsack.

Most days, I fell into bed as soon as I got home. Not today. I set the knapsack on the card table that served as my dining room. I took a shower. I didn't seem to have any blood on me or my clothes, but you never knew. I stowed the clothes I'd been wearing in a black garbage bag. Later, I could take the bag someplace and get rid of it.

Later. For now, I was going to enjoy my loot. My treasure. My prize.

I reached into the knapsack and pulled out one of the slippers.

It didn't look the same. Maybe it was because I only had one not very bright light on, but it didn't sparkle the way it had under the spotlights.

And I had imagined tapping it with one of my nails and hearing a sweet, silvery ringing sound, like a fancy glass would make. But it didn't ring.

It wasn't glass. It was some kind of see-through plastic. And the diamonds weren't diamonds. They were rhinestones.

"It's just a piece of junk," I whispered. "Tacky, overpriced junk."

I sat there for a while, staring at the shoe, trying to figure out how I felt. Sad, maybe. But not sad because the shoe turned out to be a fake. Sad because I'd just blown everything. I'd been happy the whole time I'd been planning to steal the slippers. Carrying out my plan had led me to finding a job I liked and could do well. And as long as I had the slippers to look forward to, I was…I don't know. Content. Even on days when I couldn't do anything to move the plan forward, I would still feel okay about it, because I knew a certain amount of waiting was part of the plan.

If only I still had the slippers to look forward to.

Maybe if I'd waited longer, I'd have found a chance to get a closer look at the slippers and figured out they were junk before I made my move. Or found a time when the security guard wouldn't have caught me.

I glanced at the clock. Ten thirty. They'd have found the body by now. I wondered how long it would be before they found me. Maybe I was lucky and hadn't left behind any evidence.

I didn't feel lucky. And I didn't think much of my chances of fooling them if they interrogated me.

Maybe I should try the slippers on now while I had the chance. If I'd left any incriminating evidence, the cops would show up soon. I looked down, and that's when I saw the size.

You've got to be kidding me. The damned thing was too small. Why hadn't the size ever occurred to me? I finally managed to wedge my foot in, but it hurt like hell. And I realized the slippers were only going to look good on someone with tiny, beautiful, perfectly manicured feet.

Still, I'd put them on, just this once, and walk across the room. I had time for that, didn't I?

I reached into my knapsack.

The other slipper wasn't there.

I turned the knapsack inside out. No luck. And the slipper wasn't anywhere in my studio apartment. I didn't even have to get up off the sofa bed to see that.

I remembered the top of the knapsack had been flapping loose. I hadn't thought it mattered, since there was nothing in it but the two slippers with the sweater on top.

So where had I dropped the other shoe? In the store, while I was running from the dead security guard? In the service corridor? In my locker? On the bus?

Did it really matter? Sooner or later, they'd find it.

And then me.

I pulled the slipper off and resisted the temptation to throw it across the room. Instead, I set it carefully on the card table.

"I should get rid of you," I told it. "You're incriminating evidence."

But I knew I wouldn't do it. I had nothing left. I'd probably just sit here staring at the fake slipper until the cops showed up with the other glass slipper and knocked on my door.

# The Frog Prince

By Josh Pachter

Bill Fogg—no, sorry, no relation to Phileas—was an *ugly* fucker.

To make things worse, Bill knew he was a troll.

And to make things *worst*, he was crazy in love with a woman who was so far out of his league she wasn't even playing the same sport.

Molly Driver, the subject of Bill's affection, was a solid ten, a stone fox: five foot twelve, face of a goddess, long golden hair, all the right curves in all the right places…you get the picture. And no, sorry, the word "subject" earlier in this paragraph is not a typo. Molly was no inanimate *object*—she was a human being, damn it, and she deserved to be treated with respect.

Ironically, what she did for a living was sit behind the wheel of the getaway car when Jimmy Thompson and his gang robbed banks, which they did all over the Pacific Northwest—well, all over the Portland metropolitan area, anyway—and had been doing successfully for several months.

Poor ugly Bill was in the gang but just barely. He was Jimmy's stepbrother—Bill's mom had married Jimmy's dad years after their first marriages had ended in divorce—so they brought him along on their jobs and gave him a cut of the take.

While Jimmy and Jamal and Gino were inside, waving guns around and scooping up cash, Bill stood watch out in the street. The idea was, if the cops showed, he'd pound on the bank's front door, which would signal the gang to abort the mission and zip out the back. Except, Jimmy's strong suit was casing the banks and their neighborhoods beforehand, so he knew when the coast was most likely to be clear, and the cops never *did* show up until well after the four of them had piled into their heistmobile *du jour* and Molly had got them the hell away from there. Which means Bill never really did anything that helped—but he was Jimmy's kid brother, so he was an official member of the gang and collected his share of the proceeds…and dreamt his hopeless dreams of Molly Driver.

Truth be told, Jimmy and Jamal and Gino all had the hots for Molly, too—if you got one look at her, you'd understand—but she was apparently uninterested in playing Bonnie to a bunch of latter-day Clydes. Unlike the rest of them, who lived entirely in the moment, Molly had her eyes on the future. She rented a cheap third-floor walkup in St. Johns, with a view across SERVPRO's massive parking lot to the Willamette River, and saved every possible penny for a down payment on a decent 2B/1B closer to downtown, maybe even in Goose Hollow, near the Japanese Garden, if she could ever find something in her price range that wasn't a total shithole.

The boys in the gang hung out together outside of robbing hours, and of course, there was a standing invitation for Molly to join them in their revels, but she wasn't interested in throwing away her ill-gotten gains on guzzling booze or gambling on the quarter horses out at the Meadows. She'd rather stay home and watch TV or read a library book. Her only extravagance was yarn. Molly was a knitter, and once a month she dropped off a load of scarves—wheat, arbor, honeycomb, rosewood—at one of the CityTeam shelters, rotating between the men's and the women's.

When I said just now that the boys hung out together, what I meant was Jimmy, Jamal, and Gino. Bill would sometimes tag along, but the truth is he didn't really care for the taste of alcohol, and he thought horse racing was cruel, so as time passed, he found himself less interested in spending his off-hours with the rest of the gang. And, frankly, they were happier without him than with him. You get right down to it, Bill was kind of a drag. Not to mention, he was not a fellow you wanted to be seen with, given his unsightly mug and all.

One unseasonably warm morning last October, the five of them met for breakfast at Fried Egg I'm in Love on SE Hawthorne—the guys all had the signature Yolko Ono sandwich, and Molly ate half of a Smells Like Protein Spirit with vegan sausage and took the rest to go. Then they pulled off their twelfth consecutive successful job, thanks to anti-facial recognition masks that thwarted the security cameras, cleaning out the Umpqua Bank right next door. They piled into the Hyundai Elantra Molly had boosted before sunrise in Hazelwood and peeled away from the curb, then abandoned the car across the river in the lot next to the Washington Park and Zoo Railway.

Bill suggested riding the train, since they were there, and Jimmy, Jamal, and Gino thought that sounded just dopey enough to be fun. Molly demurred, though, and took her half a sandwich and disappeared. Nobody had any idea how she planned to get home from there, or even if home was where she was going, but that was Molly Driver for you, girl had a mind and a life of her own.

Anyway, the guys were disappointed to find out the Zooliner only ran on a half-mile loop, and although they'd just taken more than seventeen thousand dollars from the Umpqua Bank's tellers, they were not about to pay twenty-four bucks a head for admission to the Oregon Zoo *plus* an extra five clams apiece for the train when they could be spending that money on beer, so they grabbed an Uber to McMenamins Crystal Brewery, slid into a booth, and ordered a couple of pitchers of Abbot's Habit Tripel—plus a Coke for Bill.

Deep into the second pitcher, the conversation turned to the absent Molly Driver.

"Where'd you find her, Jimmy?" asked Jamal Aarne.

"I was looking for a wheelman," Jimmy Thompson replied, "and she came highly recommended. She can drive like nobody's business, amiright?"

"You can say that again," Gino Uther nodded. "And the *looks* on her! Man, oh, man."

"That blond hair," Jamal sighed, emptying his glass and setting it down on the scarred wooden table with a thump. "I could nestle my face into *that*."

Jimmy refilled his own glass, ignoring Jamal's, and signaled to the tattooed hulk behind the bar for another pitcher. "What do you think, little brother?"

he addressed Bill, who was tucked into a corner of the booth and nursing his Coke. "What do you think she's got under the hood?"

Bill was unused to being included in the gang's conversations, and he looked nervously around the brewpub. "Under the hood?" he mumbled, figuring he must have missed something important.

"He's talkin' about Miz Molly, dummy." Gino laughed.

"Hey!" said Jimmy sharply. "Billy ain't the sharpest knife in the drawer, but he's *family*, shitbag. Don't go calling him names."

Gino stared sheepishly into his empty glass.

"What your brother's asking about," Jamal explained with exaggerated patience, "is what Molly's like when her engine's revved. Bet you'd like to take her for a drive, wouldn't you? Do you think she'd let you take the wheel?"

Bill's eyes widened as he realized what they were discussing. "You guys are *gross*," he said. "You shouldn't talk about Molly that way. She's a *lady*, not some—some *hooker* or something."

He shoved Gino out of the booth and slid out himself, bumping into the hulk with the tattoos and sloshing beer from the gang's fresh pitcher as he stormed out of the brewpub.

Behind him, he heard Jimmy and Jamal and even Gino explode into laughter.

* * *

It took Bill more than an hour to walk off his anger. Muttering to himself, he headed up Burnside, past Powell's City of Books and Voodoo Donut and across the bridge, all the way east to SE Floral and down through Laurelhurst Park. He would have stopped to feed the ducks on Firwood Lake—he liked feeding the ducks—only he didn't have any bread. He should've gone into the Whole Paycheck and bought a loaf, only he hadn't thought of it. He was still too pissed off. When he finally reached the little house he and Jimmy shared on SE Salmon, he went into his bedroom and straight for his collection.

When Bill was a kid, his mom had bought him the complete set of Shelly Duvall's *Faerie Tale Theatre* on DVD: all twenty-seven episodes. His favorite was *The Tale of the Frog Prince*, the very first show in the series, with Michael Richards and René Auberjonois and Candy Clark, plus Teri Garr as the haughty princess and, of course, the incomparable Robin Williams as both the frog and, at the end, Prince Robin. He had watched that movie dozens of times over the years, probably close to a hundred, and he knew the voiceover narration and dialogue by heart.

He reached for *The Tale of the Frog Prince* now, carefully removed the silver disk from its keep case, and slid it into his DVD player. He settled himself on his bed with his stuffed penguin, wrapped his fluffy comforter around him, and pressed *Play* on his remote control.

Truth be told, Bill was probably somewhere on the autism spectrum. I mean, if the spectrum is a straight line—which nowadays most experts agree it isn't, but more like a set of concentric circles—Bill was probably right around Level 2, "needs some support," although he'd never been diagnosed and wasn't getting any help.

"Hello, I'm Shelly Duvall," the skinny lady with the curly red hair and the crown of flowers on her head told him. "Welcome to *Faerie Tale Theatre*."

When she finished talking, the screen went black for a moment, and then the invisible narrator said, "Once upon a time, a long, long time ago," and Bill was inside King Geoffrey and Queen Gwynneth's castle and completely enthralled by the old crone Grizelda's magical potion and the birth of the prince, the queen's decision not to invite Grizelda to the christening even though "a promise is a promise" and Grizelda's revenge…

But the *real* fun began about a third of the way through the program, when Robin Williams made his first appearance as the frog.

Bill smiled when, accused by the vain princess of being a toad, the green creature sneered, "I am not a toad. I am a frog, and *fiercely* proud of it."

Bill hugged his penguin to his chest and grinned when, offered a beautiful dress in exchange for rescuing the princess's golden ball from the well, the amphibian scoffed, "We frogs have no use for fabric."

He nodded appreciatively and mouthed the words himself when King Geoffrey responded to the princess's "But, Daddy, he's ugly" by chiding, "Ah-ah-ah, my dear girl, you mustn't associate beauty with virtue—that's a common error."

He laughed with delight as the frog entertained the King and Queen's dinner guests, saying: "I was on the way here, and I met a female frog. She said, 'Spawn? We haven't even had dinner yet!' I said, 'Ri-deet,' and she said, 'Wi-*dat?*'"

And poor Bill's heart soared when, after the frog bested a deadly scorpion in battle, the princess finally had a change of heart and gave him the kiss he'd been promised—and Froggie shimmered and ballooned into the handsome, human, *naked* Prince Robin.

You know, maybe Bill *wasn't* autistic, just a little bit crazy. Because, by the time the princess's fairy godmother made her final promise that "that would be the very last of her frog tricks," an idea had blossomed somewhere in the depths of his brain.

If he could win the heart of a fair maiden and get Molly Driver—a princess, if ever there was one—to bestow a kiss upon him, *he* would miraculously and instantaneously change from being ugly to, if not necessarily *handsome*, at least no longer a troll.

It would work, Bill thought. It *had* to work.

The trick was to find a way to earn—or beg, borrow, or steal—that kiss.

He went into his bathroom and took a good, long look at himself in the mirror.

What he saw was the right *number* of everything—two eyes, two ears, a nose, a mouth—and all of it in the right places. The problem was that the various parts were individually flawed—the nose was swollen and twisted from being broken in a fight with a grade-school bully, the ears were cauliflowered from the year he spent wrestling before dropping out of high school, two teeth were missing and the rest were yellowed, his cheeks were hollow and pocked with acne scars—and the combined effect was like something out of a horror movie.

His best feature—okay, fine, his *only* half-decent feature—was his eyes. They were gentle and kind, but even *they* were an issue, since one of them was watery gray and the other changed color between pale blue and hazel, depending on the light.

Bill looked at himself in the mirror and shook his head sadly. He was *fugly*. There was no way around it, and Molly Driver wouldn't *ever* kiss a guy who looked as repulsive as he did.

And at that moment, just as one of the bulbs in the light fixture above the bathroom mirror sizzled and went out, a light bulb went on over Bill Fogg's head.

*  *  *

"Voilà!" M'chel Conklin whipped off the sheet protecting Bill's clothing and spun the chair around so he could get a look at himself in the mirror.

Bill gasped.

"I," he said, and found that he had no idea how to continue the sentence.

M'chel was one of the best hair, wig, and makeup artists in Portland, with more than fifteen years of experience in television, film, and runway work, and she had outdone herself this time.

Bill had surfed the interweb, came up with her name and contact information, and made an appointment. When he showed up at her studio the first time for a consultation, she sat him down in her chair and studied his face, not with disgust, but thoughtfully. "A ton of bronzer, for sure, and maybe prosthetics and bondo to build up the cheekbones," she murmured, making notes in a spiral-bound book. "Airbrushing to smooth out the skin, obviously whitening strips for the teeth, and blue-toned lipstick to boost the white…or else just go with a dental appliance. Maybe contacts for the eyes—although the heterochromia's almost sexy. The hair's not awful, but a weft wouldn't hurt…."

The price she quoted Bill would have made most men reconsider—a thousand smackers. Even though Bill didn't have a lot of smarts, one thing he *did* have was money, given that he lived rent-free with his stepbrother and barely spent any of his share of the bank-job takings. So, they'd made a second appointment, this time for four solid hours to finish the work begun during his first visit, at the end of which M'chel again said "Voilà!" and Bill gasped, barely recognizing himself in her studio's illuminated mirror.

* * *

His plan was to follow Molly around until she dropped something, like Teri Garr dropping that golden ball down the well in *The Tale of the Frog Prince*, and then he would pick it up and hand it to her, and she would reward him with the kiss that would magically turn him from Frankenstein's monster to a dreamboat.

Well, the following-her-around part went okay. After his session with M'chel Conklin, he put on the fedora he'd bought to further conceal his identity and went straight to Molly's neighborhood. He ducked into the alley between her building and the sister structure next door *just* as she came out the front door carrying a gym bag and an oversized purse and walked down the five wooden stairs to the sidewalk. He dogged her footsteps to West Coast Fitness, where she worked out for forty-five minutes and showered. He hung around outside Cathedral Coffee and watched through the plate-glass window while she drank a cappuccino, then trailed twenty feet behind her from there to the Safeway. When she came out with a brown paper bag of groceries in addition to the other things she carried, his hopes of her dropping something skyrocketed.

The problem was that she turned out to be—Bill knew that "sure-footed" was a word, so maybe there was also such a thing as "sure-*handed*." Whether that was a word or not, it *ought* to be, because sure-handed was what Molly Driver was, not only behind the wheel of a getaway car but also managing everything while navigating the narrow sidewalks and busy intersections that led back to her apartment.

When they turned the corner onto North Leavitt and came within sight of her place, Bill panicked. He had another two minutes, tops, before she disappeared up the steps and through the door, so he quickly closed the gap between them and, just as she reached the mouth of the alley, he bumped her from behind.

Molly staggered and barely stopped herself from falling. Her gym bag and purse strap remained slung across her shoulder, but her groceries went flying. Apologizing profusely, Bill scooped cans of tuna and boxes of mac 'n' cheese and loaf of seeded rye bread from the ground and tucked it all back into the brown paper sack that had somehow not gotten torn to shit in the "accident" and returned it to her.

Maybe she was flustered from the impact, but she didn't seem all that grateful for the help. She snatched the bag from Bill's hands and turned away.

"Yeah, well, you're welcome," he said, pitching his voice low so she wouldn't recognize it.

She turned back and examined him from head to toe, and Bill knew that what she saw beneath the hat was a thousand bucks worth of handsome. He stood there and let her look.

"You practically knocked me down," Molly said at last, more beautiful in her anger than Bill had ever seen her. "What do you want, me to *thank* you?"

"What I want," he said, keeping the words low-pitched and steady despite the adrenaline and cortisol seeping out of his adrenal glands, "is a kiss."

Her eyes widened. "A *kiss?* Are you nuts? It's a good thing I got eggs in the apartment. If I had eggs in that bag, they'd be all broke to hell and gone."

"If anything is broken or damaged," Bill said, "I'll be happy to replace it. All I ask in return, fair lady, is a simple kiss."

"*Fair lady?*" Molly snorted. "What are you, a Knight of the Round Table?"

Bill made a little bow. "My name is Prince," he said. "Robin Prince. And I'd be honored if you would—"

"Oh, fuck off," Molly said, turning away again.

And Bill, seeing his last chance about to evaporate, grabbed her by the arm and pulled her into the alley.

Molly jerked free, dropped her bag of groceries on purpose this time, and fumbled with the clasp of her handbag.

"One kiss," Bill said, less sure of himself now, almost pleading. "Come on, Molly, one kiss won't hurt you none."

At the sound of her name, Molly Driver froze. She stared at the handsome stranger in the dim light of the alley and blinked. "You know who I am? Have you been stalking me, you asshole?"

Bill could have punched himself right in his thousand-dollar face for the slip. He held up his hands, palms toward her. "I'm not going to hurt you, honest, I'm not. I just need you to kiss me, so I can—"

He took a step toward her, and she yanked one of the eleven-inch stainless-steel single-point knitting needles from her bag and lunged.

The point went through and through Bill Fogg, center mass, and flung him back against the alley's brick wall. As he slid to the ground, blood and gore from the exit wound smeared the bricks, and his hat and hairpiece came off and landed on the asphalt beside his body.

Molly approached him carefully and nudged his leg with the toe of her gray Hoka Arahi size six running shoe, but that was a reflex. She knew the moment she stabbed him, she had killed him.

When, sure enough, he didn't move, she hunkered down beside him and turned his head so she could see his face in the faint light from the nearest streetlamp. Her eyes widened in shock, and she worked a finger into the dead guy's mouth and fished out the silicon cheek pads and fake teeth.

"Bill?" she said, softly, trying hard not to believe it. She wiped the lifeless face with her sleeve and watched the makeup rub off, revealing the ugly mug of the only member of the gang who had never had the balls to hit on her. "Billy? Oh, God, no!"

She collapsed to the ground and pulled his head onto her lap, murmuring, "Billy, oh, Bill, oh, Jesus."

She was still sitting there in the dim light of the alley, her back against the blood-smeared brick wall, stroking Bill Fogg's ugly face mechanically with her pink lacquered fingernails, when she heard the approaching wail of the sirens.

# Little Red Riding Hood

By Barb Goffman

Friendship Heights, Maryland. May 1997.

And they lived happily ever after.

Maisie sighed as she flipped through photos her best friend, Violet, had mailed her. Violet laughing as she and Paul ate their yellow wedding cake. Violet wearing a goofy grin as she and Paul did the chicken dance. Violet throwing her bouquet—over Maisie's head, just out of reach. Violet and Paul glowed in all of them. Maisie had no doubt their marriage would last.

If only Maisie could find someone who made her that happy, too, who made her feel complete. Maybe tonight's blind date would be the one. She rarely dated. Had a hard time finding a man she felt comfortable with. One she could trust. But hope remained eternal.

The phone on her bedside table rang. Maisie turned off the *Pretty Woman* soundtrack playing on her stereo and answered.

"Hi," a tinny voice said. "It's Connor. I'm downstairs."

Was it four o'clock already? She checked her watch. Ten to. He was early. Courteous. A good sign. She buzzed him into her apartment building and ran to the bathroom to double-check her makeup and fluff her honey-blond hair.

Soon, a knock sounded, and she opened the door. *Oh.* Not quite the handsome guy Violet had promised, but still attractive. Connor's dark eyes were big, his eyebrows bushy, his brown hair shaggy. He had a long nose and an overbite that made his teeth look big. Maisie glanced down to take in the whole picture. He also had big hands. At least that was promising. Maybe a great personality would round out the package.

"Maisie? I'm Connor."

"Hi. It's nice to meet you. Come in for a second. I want to grab my jacket. It looks like rain."

She turned to her closet—in her studio apartment, everything was steps away—and when she twisted back, Connor was standing in her entryway, holding out a chocolate rose. A smile bloomed on her face. *How lovely.* Then he pulled a bottle of red wine from behind his back.

"For you," he said.

"Wow. Thank you." He was going all out, Maisie thought, especially considering they were heading to the movies, not hanging at her place. Another good sign. She left the wine and chocolate in her galley kitchen, shrugged on her red jacket, and they set off.

When they stepped from the elevator into the lobby of her apartment building, Connor swept his hand, like *The Price is Right* models do when presenting the Showcase Showdown prizes. "Couldn't help notice this when I arrived. It's…interesting."

Talk about an understatement. The building was called The Woods, and the lobby was designed to feel like a forest, with dozens of ferns, succulents, and potted trees set throughout the room. The wooden tables looked like stumps. The grainy leather chairs were a rich brown, reminding Maisie of bark. On days she felt nostalgic, she'd sit amongst the foliage, safely snuggled in one of the chairs, and breathe deeply. For a little while, she'd be a kid again, dipping her toes into the cold lake behind her grandmother's summer cabin in northern Vermont, gazing at the surrounding forest of sugar maples and eastern hemlocks while a cool breeze brushed her face. Other people felt the lobby's décor was a bit much, she knew, but to Maisie, it represented peace—carefree childhood days and a place she'd thought she'd never want to leave. Until she did.

"It's perfect," she said. "Like being outdoors without having to—"

"Be outdoors?"

"Exactly. I'm not much of an outdoor girl." Might as well get that out there in case this date went somewhere. "But I like nature. Looking at it, I mean. From afar. Or close up, if I'm sitting here in the lobby, which I do sometimes, with a book or just to enjoy the greenery because…I like nature. Indoor nature." *Indoor nature?* She sounded like a loon. But it was the truest statement she could make. She liked nature from the safety of inside.

Once upon a time, she'd liked outdoor nature too, but that was a long time ago.

"Are you a plant lady?" Connor asked, a hint of mirth in his voice as he opened the door to the vestibule and then the building's front door.

"A what?" Drizzle was falling as they stepped onto the sidewalk, so she tugged on her hood, hoping her hair wouldn't frizz.

"Like a cat lady, but instead of a load of cats, you have plants. It's not a bad idea. Sunlight's free, unlike Fancy Feast. And plants don't need to be licensed or have their litter changed or go to the vet or—"

"I'm not a plant lady." Maisie laughed and started walking toward the movie theater. "I just like—"

"Indoor nature. Got it." He winked.

Wow. This man could charm the socks off a tuxedo cat—not that she'd tell him that. Then he might think she was a cat lady, too. "The theater's a few blocks this way."

"Perfect. We'll pass my car so I can grab my umbrella. You're okay with walking there, right?"

"Sure. It's not far."

They were going to see *Jerry Maguire* at a two-screen theater in northwest DC. Maisie had been eager to see the film since its release six months ago, but she'd been waiting for it to come out on video. Watching at home didn't come with risks.

Halfway down the block, they stopped beside a black Audi. As Connor retrieved his umbrella, Maisie breathed in the refreshing scent of ozone in the air. She loved a warm rain.

Connor popped the umbrella open and held it over both of them, prompting her to walk closely beside him. His proximity set off her anxiety, but she counted slowly to five in her head, reminding herself she was safe, and she relaxed.

As he told her about his job as a sales rep for a pharmaceutical company, they crossed the road, going from Maryland into DC. They strolled down a tree-lined street, with Bloomingdale's to their left and Lord & Taylor straight ahead. Saks Fifth Avenue and Neiman Marcus were nearby too. Maisie couldn't afford to shop at any of them, but she loved to browse. Nothing bad could happen to her in a fancy department store, not with other customers around.

"You're a reporter, right?" Connor said. "How do you afford this neighborhood?"

"The Tooth Fairy was generous."

"I'm serious. Are you a trust-fund kid?"

"I wish. My apartment's tiny, and I rarely go out." She smiled, making a joke, even though it was true.

"I'm still serious."

"So am I. When I do venture out, I browse. It's fun—and free. Anyway, I'm glad you suggested this movie. I adore Tom Cruise."

"Me too."

"Which do you like better, *Top Gun* or *The Firm*? Ooh, or *A Few Good Men*? That scene where Jack Nicholson's on the stand—'I want the truth!' 'You can't handle the truth!'—that's what made Violet decide to go to law school."

"Really?" he asked. "Paul never told me that."

"You guys went to high school together, right?"

"Yeah. We were tight back then. Played the same sports. Partied together. Even pledged the same fraternity, though at different colleges. I knew Paul lucked out when I met Violet."

"She's great. A lot of fun."

"Exactly. A fun girl. Since you're both so close, I figured you'd be a fun girl too." Connor raised an eyebrow.

"I have my moments." She chuckled, enjoying their banter.

"Lucky me. I'm sorry I missed their wedding. It would've been nice to meet you there. Maybe get in a dance."

"That *would* have been nice." Maisie flashed him another smile. "So, what's your favorite Tom Cruise film?"

"I'm betting it'll be *Jerry Maguire*. How could it not be with you as my date?"

She pushed his arm. "Now *I'm* serious."

"*Top Gun* and *The Firm*. Of course."

"Any others?"

"Shooting down planes and shutting down law firms, what could be better than that?" He laughed. "Okay, but remember, you asked. I thought Cruise's layered performance in *Born on the Fourth of July* was stellar. I believed every second of his rage and the ultimate message of self-acceptance. He earned that Oscar nomination. And he should've received one for *A Few Good Men*, too. He held his own with Nicholson in the pivotal courtroom scene. His delivery was great, and I especially appreciated how he showed his thoughts through nuanced facial expressions. But a lot of good movies came out that year. The competition was stiff. I didn't think Pacino deserved the win, but I didn't get to vote."

Maisie's mouth fell open.

He shrugged. "I minored in film."

A grin stretched across Maisie's face. Connor was an interesting man indeed.

They reached the theater. He paid for their tickets, she declined his offer of popcorn, and they entered the auditorium. Maisie was glad to see all the groups of women. Safety in numbers.

In the center of the room, she and Connor shrugged off their damp jackets and settled into cushy chairs, waiting for the previews to start. Maisie checked her watch: 4:15 p.m. When Connor had suggested starting their date with this late-afternoon movie, the timing had made her uneasy. A memory she usually kept buried deep had tried to surface. But Maisie had pushed it away and told Connor yes.

*It was a long time ago*, she reminded herself.

"Do you not like popcorn?" he asked, pulling her back to the present.

"I do. Buttered, salted, kettle. If it's crunchy, I like it. But not so close to dinner. How about you?"

"Oh, yeah. I love nibbling on things."

*Was he flirting with her?* To her surprise, she hoped he was.

The lights dimmed, and the previews began. Connor wasn't one of those obnoxious people who talked during the previews. This date was getting better and better.

It was nearly seven when they left the theater. Huddled under his umbrella, they discussed the movie on the walk to the Cheesecake Factory. A perfect place for a first date, Maisie thought. They served practically everything. Even picky eaters could find something to order. Maisie wasn't picky, but Connor didn't know that. If this was how he planned a date, it boded well for their future.

"It'll be about an hour wait," the hostess said.

"This is why we should've had popcorn." Connor rubbed his stomach.

"Poor baby," Maisie said. "There's a California Pizza Kitchen upstairs. Why don't we see how long the wait is there?"

"Lead on, Macduff."

Connor might've minored in film, but he'd clearly never seen *Macbeth*. Otherwise, he'd know the correct phrase was "Lay on, Macduff." But Maisie kept that thought to herself.

They stepped onto the mini-mall's escalator, and Connor rested his hand on her back. She started, her skin tingling as if she'd touched a live wire. Her mind flashed to the summer she turned nineteen—the last one she spent in Vermont—the day her grandmother went to see a sick friend. Maisie invited a guy to come hang out at the cabin. It was late afternoon when Rolf arrived. They filled a picnic basket and ambled through the woods to a clearing on the other side of the lake. They chatted and ate. Flirted and laughed. Even kissed a couple of times. She wouldn't go further. It was a wonderful day until, on the way back to the cabin, in the thick of the forest, Rolf showed his true colors. He pressed his hand against her back and…

Maisie cringed, and she was back in the present with Connor. His hand fell away.

She made small talk about pop culture, trying to get things back on track. She even got him to admit he liked the Spice Girls, but he denied having a favorite one. (She suspected that was a lie.) She confessed she loved *The X Files* but insisted it was because of the stories, not David Duchovny's hotness. (And that was a lie.) Soon enough, they were seated for dinner and decided on red sangria and Thai chicken pizza to share. The drinks arrived quickly, and Connor raised his glass.

"To new friends, even if you *are* lying about David Duchovny."

"I am not." Giggling, she clinked her glass against his and took a sip. "Delicious."

He eyed her up and down as he swallowed. "Now that's no lie."

Maisie felt a moment of unease, remembering the way Rolf told her she looked "good enough to eat" during their picnic. But she shook it off. Yes, Connor was flirting with her, but they were in a crowded restaurant. And Connor was no Rolf. She took a large drink of her sangria, and their conversation returned to the movie.

"Hard to pick the best part," he said, "but you gotta love the 'Show me the money' scene."

"Wasn't Cuba Gooding Jr. hysterical when he danced?" Maisie laughed. "But what I enjoyed most was how Tom Cruise changed from a man who was using Renée Zellweger to a man who loved her."

A smile played on Connor's face. "When Violet told me about you, she didn't mention you were a romantic."

"It's not like I read bodice rippers," Maisie said. "But you have to admit, the movie's ending was pretty perfect."

"When Zellweger said, 'You had me at hello'?"

"Well, yes. But I was thinking about the part before that, when Cuba Gooding Jr. was on the phone with his wife, how happy he was to share his triumph with her. *That's* when Tom Cruise realized he couldn't truly enjoy the moment because his wife wasn't there to share it. That she was what he wanted, what he needed."

"That she completed him," he finished.

"Exactly." She appreciated that Connor paid attention to the romance in the movie and understood how important it was to find your other half. A lot of guys would remember only the sports scenes. *Violet, wherever you are, thanks for setting us up.*

"You're right. The end was pretty perfect." Connor covered her hand with his, and after a few seconds—after she didn't recoil from his touch this time—he grinned.

Letting Connor grasp her hand was a triumph for Maisie, considering her instinct to pull away. Since that terrible day with Rolf six years before, she'd needed to feel completely comfortable with a guy before even kissing him, which is why she'd had only one boyfriend in all that time. But this date was going amazingly well, except for that moment on the escalator. Now he was holding her hand. It was nice. She needed to be more open to things like this.

Their waiter appeared with more sangria. "Your dinners will be out shortly."

"Thanks," Connor said, as Maisie sipped from her glass. "So, you, Violet, and Paul went to college together?" he asked.

"Yeah. U Conn. Violet and I were roommates freshman year. We hit it off and stayed together until we graduated."

"Must've been fun. I hear it's a real party school. Paul met Violet at a fraternity keg party."

"In the fall of our senior year. She liked to burn off steam after midterms and finals."

He tilted his head. "But you didn't?"

"That wasn't my scene. I chose the school because it wasn't far from home and had a solid journalism program. Were you a big partier?"

"Well, yeah." He frowned as if her question mystified him.

Hmmm. Maisie drank some more. She didn't have anything against people having fun, but if partying was his thing, maybe they weren't well matched after all. Then again, they were talking about college. He could be a different person now—she hoped.

Their pizza arrived. Her mouth watered, and they dug in.

Connor told her about his job as a pharmaceutical sales rep. Maisie spoke about her features beat, how she relished writing happy stories, showing readers there were still good things in this world. The conversation was great, but as the meal went on, Maisie's head began to throb. Probably from the sangria, she realized. She'd had two glasses before the food arrived and another while they ate.

When they were nearly done with their entrees, Connor asked, "You want to hit a club next?"

It was a nice idea, even if clubs and bars weren't her scene. But Maisie's head was pounding. All she could think about was going to bed with a bottle of Advil. "I'm sorry, but the sangria has given me a bad headache. We should call it a night after this." At his narrowed eyes, she hurriedly said, "I really am enjoying the evening. It's just…" She tapped her brow.

"I get it. Sorry you're not feeling well."

Connor paid the check, and soon they were striding past Bloomingdale's, toward her building. The air still smelled of rain, but no drops were falling from the darkening sky. When they entered the tree-filled lobby, Maisie felt a sense of peace, despite her headache.

Behind her, the door opened. She turned to see her twentysomething next-door neighbor, Hunter, coming inside. His goatee had finally filled in. He'd been growing it for months.

"Hey, Maisie," he said. "Looks like your social life is way more exciting than mine." He held up two bags of groceries.

"Miracles do happen," she said with a laugh.

Maisie introduced Connor and Hunter as the elevator dinged. Hunter strode to it. When Maisie didn't follow him, he asked, "Want me to hold it for you?"

"No thanks," she said. "I'm not ready to come up yet. See you around."

Hunter was always helpful that way. He'd once suggested they trade spare keys for emergencies, but Maisie had declined, too put off by the fear that he might enter her apartment while she slept. As trustworthy as Hunter seemed, she wouldn't let herself be that vulnerable.

She returned her attention to Connor. "I had a good time. Thanks for walking me home."

"Of course. How's your head?"

"Nothing Advil won't fix."

He leaned in, and as her heart thumped harder than her head, he kissed her. His lips were soft and warm and wonderful. Just as he drew away, the pounding in her brain worsened, and she winced. From the look on his face, he'd noticed—and misunderstood.

She grabbed his arm. "It's not what you think. Just my head."

"No worries. I get it. I'll call you."

That didn't sound promising. As she tried to figure out what to say, he turned to leave but then wheeled back around.

"I'm sorry. Can I use your bathroom before I go home?"

"Uh, sure. Come on up." Her gut was screaming no, but she needed to stop seeing bogeymen around every corner. The date had been fantastic, and Violet and Paul had set them up, for heaven's sake. What better reference could there be?

In the elevator, Connor made jokes about Maisie's love of indoor nature, and she laughed, relieved they'd gotten past her gaffe.

"You don't really need to use the bathroom, do you?" she asked as they padded down the carpeted hallway to her place. "You just want to check I'm not a plant lady."

"Guilty as charged." He winked.

While Connor used the bathroom, Maisie hung up her red jacket and checked her answering machine. No messages. When Connor emerged, she hurried inside. She kept the Advil in her medicine cabinet. After downing a pill and trying in vain to tame her frizzy hair, she used the facilities too. That's when the music started up—the *Pretty Woman* soundtrack she'd been listening to that afternoon.

She returned to her main room to find Connor relaxed on the couch, his jacket tossed over one of its arms. The wine he'd brought sat open on the coffee table. Beside it lay the cork, her winged corkscrew, the stereo remote control, and two filled glasses. Connor was drinking from a third.

"I didn't know if you'd want wine or water, considering your headache, so I poured you one of each," he said. "I hope you don't mind. We've been having such a nice evening, I thought, why not talk some more?"

Maisie wasn't thrilled he'd made himself at home, but she did like him a lot, and she was hopeful the Advil would work its magic soon. In the meanwhile, more pleasant conversation sounded appealing. She settled on the couch and drank some of the water. Hydration would be her friend.

"You told the truth," Connor said, looking around. "No plants. Not a single one."

"It's a mercy. I have a green soul but a black thumb."

"You're very funny." He held up his glass, admiring it. "It's too bad you're not feeling up to trying the wine. It's smooth. Velvety."

"Maybe we could try what's left some other time." She drank more water.

"Sounds like a plan. So, what really made you decide to live here on the edge of the suburbs instead of downtown, where the action is? Don't tell me it's the forest downstairs."

"But it is. That, the affordable rent, and the thick walls. I never hear my neighbors."

"Good to know."

"You prefer downtown DC, I take it?"

"Oh yeah," he said. "Georgetown, Adams Morgan, Dupont Circle. I'll go anywhere I can party."

So he hadn't changed since college. Too bad. Between their conversation and the kiss, she'd hoped things would go somewhere with Connor. But it seemed they were too different in this important respect.

"I've been thinking about the movie," he said, "and how you think the relationship between Cruise and Zellweger is its heart. I don't agree."

"What do you mean?"

"It was Gooding's character who helped Cruise's Jerry to grow. Jerry sacrificed a lot for him, and in the end, they succeeded together, football star and agent. That was the most important relationship in the movie. The real one."

"More real than the love between Tom Cruise and Renée Zellweger?" she asked. "Even at the end?"

"Yeah." Connor refilled his glass and took a large sip. "Sure, he loved how she made him feel. He loved that she was a warm body at night. But, come on, he loved her kid way more than he loved her."

Maisie blinked, confused. "What about how he said she completed him. You agreed it was a perfect ending." She downed the rest of her water.

"Perfect overstates it. It was a good ending. Not a realistic ending, but a good one." Connor took the glass from her hand. "You feeling any better? You look woozy."

"I'm tired and a little dizzy." She didn't often drink sangria. "I'm sorry. I need to get some sleep."

"You want me to go?"

She nodded.

"You sure?" He gulped the rest of his wine, raised the volume on the stereo, and slid closer to her. "I feel like I should stick around and make sure you're okay."

"Not necessary."

He lifted her chin with his thumb. She stared up into his big eyes. "Oh, I think it is." He kissed her softly, and for a few seconds, she responded. But when she tried to pull away, he kissed her harder, pushing her down onto the cushion.

She twisted her head, struggling in vain against him. "Connor, stop. I don't feel well." But he mashed his lips onto hers once more. Again, she tried to push him off, but only succeeded in stopping the kiss. "I said no. You're going too fast."

He smirked. "Not when we're having so much fun." He forced his mouth back onto hers.

*No no no! This wasn't happening. Not again.* How could she have misjudged this man? She wrenched away and screamed for help. He reared back and slapped her.

As she lay there stunned, with the room spinning, Connor grabbed her chin. "Between the music and the thick walls, no one can hear you. So no one—not even your lame friend Hunter—is coming to your rescue. You brought this on yourself. I'd thought I was getting a fun girl, like Paul did. A party girl. But you're just a tease, letting me buy you dinner and a movie, then pleading the old headache routine. I don't like being used."

"It's not an act."

"Right."

"Please don't."

He rolled his eyes. "Relax. We're just gonna have a little fun. The pills I dissolved in your water haven't fully kicked in yet, but they will soon, and you'll be the willing girl I'd expected. You won't remember any of this anyway, so you might as well enjoy it." He crushed his lips against hers again and jammed his tongue into her mouth.

*Oh, God.* He'd roofied her. After all these years of being careful, she'd let this wolf into her apartment because Violet and Paul had vouched for him. He'd snowed them all.

She tried again to heave him off, but Connor was too strong. A feeling of helplessness washed over her, and she was in Vermont again, and Rolf was slamming her down into the dirt, flipping her over, and climbing on top, and the trees swayed and the birds cawed and his chapped lips covered hers, muffling her scream.

Maisie roused herself from the memory as her rage grew. *You're not in Vermont. You're not that defenseless teenager anymore.* Unable to push Connor away, she flailed her arms. Her fingers curled around something metal with wing-like handles and a sharp tip. She thrust it into him again and again and again, while he groaned and struggled and shuddered, until he slumped against her, and she could finally shove him off. Gurgling, with blood flowing from his mouth, Connor fell onto the floor, the corkscrew sticking out of his neck.

Maisie pitched herself off the couch, stumbling, knocking Connor's jacket to the floor. A baggie with pills slipped from a pocket. The roofies. The proof she'd need for the police.

She'd never called the police on Rolf, not wanting anyone to know he'd raped her in that dank forest. But she couldn't wish away this dead body on her floor. Wait…*was* he dead? Connor's chest wasn't rising. His vacant eyes lay open. That spelled dead to her. Still, she ran into the kitchen and grabbed a knife, just in case Connor sprang up and came after her, the way Glenn Close had at the end of *Fatal Attraction*. Then Maisie shut off the stereo, spoke to a 911 operator, and perched on her bed to wait.

Thanks to the roofies, she might not remember any of this. But she hoped she would. She didn't want to bottle up her memories anymore and let fear of wolfish men rule her life for one more day. She'd lived for six years on hyperalert. What good had it done? She'd still been played and found herself fighting a rapist, again. At least this time, she'd prevailed.

Assuming the police let her go—they'd have to believe her; she'd make them believe her—this summer, she'd use vacation time to visit her grandmother in Vermont. She'd even pack a picnic basket and stroll, not hurrying, not worrying, through the forest. No more limiting herself to safe indoor nature. She'd eat a sandwich in the clearing on the other side of the lake. And she'd do it alone. She didn't need a man to feel complete. Maisie was going to reclaim her life and live happily ever—just let someone try and stop her.

She stared at the knife in her hand and the blood staining her skin and shirt. Any man who attacked her again would learn he'd made a big mistake.

The predator never expects the prey to fight back.

# The Briar Patch

By Tom Milani

In all the time Rabbit had worked at Brothers Salvage, he'd never seen a customer like the man who'd just walked into the office. He wore penny loafers and wide-wale corduroy pants. His yellow turtleneck was topped by a thin, brown leather jacket.

Darrell, his boss, seemed amused at the man's clothes. Rabbit, more accustomed to being the butt of derision from people like Darrell, sympathized.

"I'm looking for a Nash Metropolitan," the man said.

Rabbit's ears perked up.

From behind the counter, Darrell pointed out the window. "Should be a couple up there."

Dirt trails wound like tributaries up the steep hill. Cars lined the banks on both sides. Scrub trees grew between the cars, and in some cases, they pierced the floorboards like spears.

"I'll show you where they are," Rabbit said.

Behind him, Darrell smirked. Once they were outside, Rabbit turned to the man.

"I'm Walter Maranville," he said, holding out his hand. "But everyone calls me Rabbit."

"John Fox," he said. When they shook hands, Rabbit felt iron in his grip.

Despite his shoes, Fox followed him up the slope without a problem. Rabbit didn't get many opportunities to show customers around. Most knew what they wanted and could get by with Darrell's grunted directions. Rabbit loved the apparent chaos of the yard, the cars and trucks seemingly placed at random, the underlying order there only if you knew where to look. The oldest cars were closest to the offices, the more recent arrivals at the top of the hill. The exceptions occurred when someone bought one of the cars outright and hauled it off. Then, whatever was brought in after was put in its place.

When the path leveled, Rabbit turned to Fox. "Are you looking to take off a specific part, or are you thinking of buying a whole car?"

Fox rubbed his chin. "That's an excellent question. I'll need to assess their condition before I decide."

Rabbit didn't know any people who spoke like English gentlemen, words clipped and proper. But like the iron he felt in Fox's handshake, Rabbit sensed controlled anger just below the surface of his reply.

To the right, the path steepened and narrowed. The cars facing the path were enucleated of headlights and splotched with rust, as if camouflaged to match the leaves of the sugar maples at the edge of the property line. Beyond them, the land fell away to the state road fronting the scrapyard.

"Are we close?" Fox asked.

Rabbit turned. Fox wasn't winded, but the lines between his eyebrows appeared cut, his face tight.

"Just a little farther," Rabbit said. He started up the path again. Ahead, the line of cars facing the path broke, but Rabbit knew the gap was an illusion. Two Packards had rested where the much smaller Nashes stood.

As they came into view, Rabbit pointed and turned, but Fox was already jogging past him. Rabbit idly wondered if Fox would take his disappointment out on him.

* * *

Darrell Porter did his drinking at The Briar Patch across the road from the scrapyard. Like the scrapyard, the bar had no view and no charm, and for that reason, he felt at home there.

Remus put a coaster on the bar and a draft beer on top of it. Darrell raised the glass in thanks.

The bartender leaned to the side, squinting out the picture window by the front door. "Is that an E-Type?" he asked.

Darrell nodded. "A fully restored seventy-four. British racing green paint, tan leather interior."

"Don't see many of those at the scrapyard."

Darrell drained some of his beer and rolled his shoulders. "Guy who owns the Jag waltzed into the office like he was dressed for a fancy dinner."

"Where's Rabbit?"

"Showing him the Nashes we got in yesterday."

Remus blinked. "Is he some kind of collector?"

Darrell was used to Remus's questions. The bar didn't get much traffic, and Remus was lonely and an extrovert. He also liked to keep his finger on the pulse of the community. It was good for business, he told Darrell once. But the business he was asking about wasn't any of his.

"He didn't say." Remus took the hint and went to the other end of the bar.

Before the pandemic, Darrell managed a crew of eight. In addition to selling the junk cars, Brothers Salvage had thriving scrap-metal and used-parts sales. When the pandemic threw a giant wrench into the gears of the operation, the owners shut down the scrap-metal and used-parts portions of the business. They told Darrell he had to lay off everyone, but he convinced them to retain Rabbit, who was dim but reliable. The other employees were only too happy to take the generous severance offered by the owners and the generous American Rescue Plan dollars offered by the Feds.

Initially, there was zero business. Hardly anyone went out. The Canadian border just to the north was closed, offices shut their doors to all but essential personnel, and restaurants went from sit-down to takeout and delivery. Darrell couldn't work from home, and he knew the owners' benevolence had an expiration date.

During his years working at Brothers Salvage, he'd run into questionable characters bringing in copper too new to be scrap and learned to look the other way. The materials never stayed in their original form for long, anyway.

So, when one of the yard's pre-pandemic customers offered Darrell the opportunity to serve as a middleman in a smuggling operation, he jumped at it. The plan sounded straightforward enough. Steel boxes were welded to the junk cars, their contents drugs of one sort or another. The cars would be brought to the scrapyard, inventoried, and hauled out by "buyers" within a week. Putting them on the books provided cover for the parties involved and generated sales for Brothers Salvage, not to mention a cut for Darrell. According to his contact, the cops had stopped enforcing any kind of moving violations—with traffic so light and COVID infections so high, the cost-to-benefit ratio tilted the wrong way—so there was little chance of the drivers being pulled over.

He had Rabbit validate the inventory database against the physical contents of the scrapyard and soon learned that Rabbit's memory was near-photographic. Beyond knowing the make and model of every car and truck, and where they were located, his recall extended to the geography of the scrapyard itself, parts of which were facing dangerous erosion. Darrell still hadn't decided how to deal with that.

He swiveled a half-turn on his stool. The Jaguar was still parked on the lot, the car as incongruous as the owner's clothes. Most of the men who passed through the scrapyard dressed in muted colors. They arrived in gray Camrys and Accords, vehicles pictured in the dictionary next to the definition of anonymous.

The Jaguar and its owner were anything but.

That worried Darrell, as did how long the transaction was taking. Well, Rabbit could talk. He decided he'd have one more beer and turned back to the bar. If Rabbit and the man hadn't returned by then, he'd go across the street to investigate.

Remus grabbed his empty and set a fresh draft down in its place. Some days, Remus read his mind the way all of Darrell's old girlfriends had, except in Remus's case, the consequences usually worked out in Darrell's favor. With women, they never did.

Remus nodded toward the window. "How would you like to be driving that Jaguar?"

Darrell looked over his shoulder. "I'm too big for those seats. Pickup truck's more my speed."

"Betcha Rabbit would love to be behind the wheel of that."

"No doubt." Rabbit drove his VW the way he talked and walked—fast and without stopping.

"He's a good kid," Remus said.

Darrell didn't know where that was coming from, but he could see the worry in Remus's eyes.

"Rabbit can take care of himself," Darrell said.

"True," Remus said. "But every now and then he needs a little help."

This time, Darrell took the hint. He lumbered off his stool. "Keep my beer cold," he said, not looking back.

* * *

Rabbit kept his expression neutral as Fox leaned into the Nash through the passenger-side window. Both doors were rusted shut, something Rabbit could have told him. Like a jack-in-the-box, Fox emerged from the car only long enough to retrieve a Mini Maglite from the inside pocket of his jacket.

Fox emerged a second time from the Nash and went to its mate. The other car's interior was a shell, and he didn't bother putting his head inside.

Now he faced Rabbit, his smile tight. "I was told these Nashes had particular features I desired but, judging by the grinding marks on the firewalls of both vehicles, they appear to be recently removed."

"Who told you?" Rabbit asked.

Fox's face twisted in confusion. "Who told me what?"

"About the Nashes."

"That's none of your concern."

Rabbit didn't like the menace in his voice. "Is there anything else you'd like to look at?"

Fox rested his elbows on the roof of one of the Nashes. "How long have you worked here, Rabbit?"

"A while," he said. "There were more of us before the pandemic, but since then, it's just me and Darrell."

"Is that the gentleman whom I met inside the offices?"

Rabbit thought Darrell would laugh at the idea that he was any kind of gentleman.

"He manages things," Rabbit said.

"Perhaps I should speak to him."

"He's gone for the day. You should come back tomorrow."

The look on Fox's face mirrored that of his teachers throughout the years. Disappointment. Frustration. Rabbit was so used to those expressions, they hardly registered. What did register was the pistol now in Fox's hand, pointed at his chest. Whatever else he thought about the man—his way of speaking, his clothes—Rabbit could tell Fox knew how to handle a gun.

"I don't think so," Fox said.

To Rabbit, he sounded sad.

Fox went on. "The three of us are going to have a conversation to rectify this situation."

Rabbit always enjoyed a good conversation, especially when he got to do most of the talking, but he suspected that wasn't going to be the case this time. He started down the path.

"Oh, Rabbit?"

He turned.

"If you try to run, I'll shoot off your kneecap. I'm told it's excruciating, and it will cripple you for life."

Rabbit didn't appreciate being threatened, but it was another thing he'd gotten used to and mostly took in stride. Still, it rankled coming from Fox, who had started to rub him the wrong way.

* * *

As soon as Darrell pushed through the door, he saw Rabbit sitting in a chair by the service counter and knew there was a problem. Rabbit never stood still, much less sat. When the man behind the counter swung a pistol his way, it became apparent why.

"You must be Darrell," the man said. He motioned for Darrell to take the chair next to Rabbit's.

The man stepped to the front door and flipped the sign to CLOSED before lowering the blinds. The way Rabbit avoided Darrell's gaze suggested Rabbit wasn't as dim as he'd thought.

"I came here for the Nash Metropolitans," the man started. His lips twisted, as if he'd eaten something sour. "Upon my examination, they proved not to be as advertised."

Darrell leaned forward. "How so?"

"I won't be trifled with," the man said. He centered the pistol on Darrell's chest.

"I haven't touched those cars since they were delivered yesterday," Darrell said.

"And yet, both bore fresh marks from an angle grinder."

Darrell turned to Rabbit, who still wouldn't look at him, before facing the man again. "I don't know anything about that."

"But it appears Rabbit does."

Darrell bit down on his words, unable to decide who annoyed him more—Rabbit, for taking something that didn't belong to him, or this guy, with his fancy clothes and his fancy words and the gun pointed at him.

For once, Rabbit didn't have anything to say. As much as Darrell savored his silence, he sensed the gunman's patience was reaching its limit.

"You'd better tell him, Rabbit."

Rabbit opened his mouth to object, and Darrell grabbed him by the chin. He squeezed his cheeks until he looked like a bluegill.

"The truth," he said, hoping Rabbit had sense enough to delay the gunman until Darrell could get the drop on him.

He released Rabbit's jaw. Rabbit shook his head like a boxer who'd been surprised by an uppercut.

"I can take you to where it's at, Mr. Fox," he said. Rabbit started to rise from the chair.

"Sit," Fox said, as if Rabbit were a pet dog. Darrell's level of annoyance rose another notch.

"Just to be clear, tell me exactly what you took," Fox went on.

Rabbit described steel boxes, tack-welded to the firewalls of the Nashes. Darrell wondered how Rabbit figured out what was going on. The Nashes must have been his first time stealing the boxes, because there'd been no complaints up until now.

"Where are they?" Fox asked.

Rabbit pointed over his shoulder. "Under the Studebaker."

The Studebaker was impossible to move without a crane. Darrell didn't know what Rabbit was planning.

Fox stepped to one of the worktables and hefted a coil of tow rope. He flung it toward Rabbit. "Tie up the big fellow, and we'll go retrieve what's mine."

Rabbit made a show of looping the rope around Darrell, the loops too tight for Darrell's taste, but the bitter end was within reach of his fingers.

"Boy Scout?" Fox asked.

"*Eagle* Scout," Rabbit replied.

Fox killed the lights as they left.

* * *

Rabbit kept looking over his shoulder as they ascended the path, but Fox was always right behind him, his pistol unwavering. After they passed the Nashes, the path became steeper and narrower. For the first time, the distance between him and Fox widened.

The Studebaker Hawk was Rabbit's favorite car on the lot, despite its condition. He could see beyond the rust and dents and missing components to the car as it originally existed on the showroom floor. The Studebaker reminded Rabbit of an animal, something with fins and a snout. After all that rain, he'd braced it with four-by-fours to keep it from tumbling into the valley.

"This isn't a race, Rabbit."

Rabbit turned. Fox's face was red, and beads of sweat dotted his forehead and upper lip. Rabbit smiled to himself. Maybe Fox wasn't *all that* after all.

"I get lost in my head, thinking about all the cars here, what they must have looked like new," Rabbit said. "I bet they all have stories to tell, how some owners treated them well, while others never washed or waxed them."

"Enough."

Rabbit shrugged, thinking it was a shame Fox didn't have more imagination.

They rounded a final curve, where the Studebaker rested at the crest. The rear half of the car cantilevered over open air. Fox's breath caught. Rabbit stifled a grin.

"What happened here?" Fox asked.

"A big storm blew down from Canada," Rabbit started. "The weather lady said it set a record for most rainfall in an hour. It washed away most of the hill."

Rabbit noticed how Fox steered clear of the car, as if he were afraid if he got too close, it would tumble down the slope. When Rabbit patted the hood of the Studebaker for good luck, Fox flinched. He blotted his forehead with a striped handkerchief.

"Show me the boxes," he said.

Rabbit dropped to his belly and scurried under the Studebaker. "They're not here." He backed out from under the car. "The ground must have shifted overnight."

Fox leveled the gun at him. "You idiot."

"I'm sorry." Rabbit made his voice meek. "I didn't think anything would happen."

"That's the problem," Fox said. "You didn't think."

"Don't make me climb down that cliff."

Fox's eyes narrowed. "I'll give you a choice, Rabbit. You can bring me back what's mine, or I'll shoot you where you stand."

"Please don't make me, Mr. Fox," Rabbit's voice quavered. "That big car will crush me."

"It would serve you right."

"Please."

"I'm counting to three. One. Two."

Rabbit darted under the car again, pulling himself to the edge of the cliff. He kicked at the dirt, and rocks skittered down the slope. Using the handholds he'd dug, he pulled himself into the hollow he'd carved into the hillside. From there, he could see the timbers he'd braced the Studebaker with, but he was hidden from Fox.

The steel boxes and his portable angle grinder rested on a tarp. He had a cooler with a few cans of soda and some candy bars. He liked to come here whenever he needed to get away from Darrell.

"Rabbit, bring me my boxes." Fox's voice sounded far away.

Rabbit tossed more rocks down the slope. He considered yelling as if he'd fallen, but it was too much trouble. Closing his eyes, he rested his head against the dirt wall.

Scraping against the Studebaker's undercarriage stirred him. He poked his head around the corner in time to see Fox's gun hand.

"Over here," Rabbit called, before darting back.

Two shots rang out. Rabbit threw more rocks down the slope.

"My boxes," Fox shouted. "I won't miss next time."

"Come and get them," Rabbit taunted.

He heard scrabbling above him, followed by a yell. Fox must have missed the handholds Rabbit had carved, for now his feet were visible, dangling over the hillside.

Rabbit chanced a look. Fox hung from the undercarriage of the Studebaker, both hands gripping its axle.

"Help me," Fox croaked.

Rabbit slipped between the timbers supporting the Studebaker and glanced up at Fox. His face was redder than before.

"Get me down, and we can work this out," Fox said.

"You shot at me," Rabbit said.

"I was trying to scare you, not kill you," Fox said.

Rabbit didn't like being lied to. "I don't think so," he said. He reached into Fox's pants pocket.

Fox tried to twist away. "What are you doing?"

Rabbit pulled out a set of keys. The Jaguar emblem was embossed onto a leather fob.

"You can have the car," Fox said, but his words sounded strained.

Rabbit moved to the other side of the timber. "Thanks," he said.

"Let me down," Fox said.

To Rabbit, it sounded more like a command than a request. "Sure thing," he said. He pressed his foot against the timber. The Studebaker groaned. So did Fox. Rabbit shoved the timber away from the hill.

* * *

By the time Darrell freed himself, his shoulders felt as if they'd come loose from their sockets, and his wrists were raw. He decided if Fox hadn't shot Rabbit, he would. Yet when Rabbit sauntered through the door, spinning a key ring on one finger, Darrell was unexpectedly relieved. Rabbit didn't appear to notice.

"You want to tell me what happened?" Darrell asked.

Rabbit stopped spinning the keys. "There was an accident with the Studebaker. Mr. Fox was checking the rear axle, and the hill gave way."

"An accident?" Darrell asked.

"Sometimes they happen," Rabbit said.

Darrell decided he didn't want to know. "Are those his keys?"

"He said I could have his car."

Darrell thought Rabbit was really pushing it. He worried about how connected Fox was and what he'd told his contacts, before another thought took hold.

"What were you thinking, going into the Nashes?"

Rabbit's expression turned serious, which was something novel, as far as Darrell was concerned.

"You didn't think I'd catch onto those old cars coming and going every week, the buyers hardly bothering to look at them? It's like you thought I was stupid or something."

Darrell's eyes widened. Rabbit's feelings were hurt. He decided to give Rabbit a version of the truth.

"I didn't want you involved if things went south."

"You didn't want to share your cut is what you mean."

Darrell moved his shoulders. "I was assuming all the risks—and doing all the arranging."

When Rabbit started to speak, Darrell held up his hand. "But I should have told you."

That was as far toward an apology as he was willing to go, but it seemed to satisfy Rabbit, who'd gone back to spinning the key ring on his finger.

There was one question Darrell had to ask. "Where is Fox's body?"

"You know that gap that opened up in the hillside after the rains?"

To Darrell, it looked like someone wanted to slice off a piece of the hillside, then changed their mind halfway through. A local geologist said it would close after the next storm.

"Is Fox in there?"

"Him and the Studebaker."

Rain was forecast overnight.

"Seeing as how Fox gave you his car, why don't you take it out for a spin?" Darrell said. "Just park it in one of the bays when you're done."

Rabbit's face lit up like Christmas morning.

As Darrell crossed the road to The Briar Patch, the Jaguar rumbled to life behind him. Inside the bar, Remus poured Darrell a draft. For a moment, they cocked their ears toward the door, listening as Rabbit ran the Jaguar through the gears.

"That man let Rabbit drive his car?" Remus asked.

Darrell wiped foam from his lips with the back of his hand. "It turns out, he was so taken with Rabbit, he left him the Jaguar."

Remus drew back in surprise, but quickly recovered. "I never liked a man who called attention to himself."

Darrell agreed. Being that flashy was bad for business. He'd let Rabbit drive the Jag for a few days, then they'd part it out. The car was too conspicuous to keep, but the parts would net him a small fortune. Net *them* a small fortune, he amended.

Darrell turned to Remus. "You know, I think I've been underestimating

Rabbit." And you, too, he thought. "If anybody asks," he started before Remus cut him off with a wink.

"That man drove off in the Studebaker."

So he knew. Rabbit must have called him before he came back to the office. It turned out Darrell was the one in the dark. Well, he could rectify that straight away. The three of them made a better team than just Darrell trying to do everything by himself. And maybe Remus would know how to unload the contents of the boxes Rabbit took. As Remus walked to the far end of the bar to attend to a customer, Darrell decided to ask Rabbit what he thought Remus's cut should be.

In the distance, a siren sounded. Darrell turned. The Jag sped past and, a moment later, so did a cop, light bar flashing. They wouldn't catch Rabbit, he thought. But if they did, he'd surely talk his way out of a ticket again.

Darrell turned back to the bar, just as Remus set a fresh beer down.

# King O' the Cats

By David Dean

Charlie and his employer, Mr. Jacobs, arrived for the pickup around midnight. Though this was far from unusual in the undertaking business, it was a first for Charlie. This task was normally reserved for Mr. Jacobs and his son, Oliver.

They were greeted at the door of the spacious three-story country home by two large, dark-haired men wearing black suits and white shirts. Charlie thought they must be twins. Without a word, they led them to a ground-floor bedroom and the body of Mr. Marion Trencavel.

It seemed obvious to Charlie that this was not the deceased's room as it contained no items of a personal nature, nothing but the narrow hospital-style bed upon which he lay, and the few medical items required for his palliative care. Charlie also noticed a pillow lying next to the old man's head that appeared to contain the impression of a face.

He flinched at this but said nothing, as the two silent men who'd taken up positions at either end of the bed were watching him with identical green gazes. Mr. Jacobs had stressed that this was a special family with unique sensibilities, requiring a delicate touch.

Near the bed stood a tall, flinty woman dressed in black, to include a lace veil draped over her head, leaving her face exposed. Like the pillow, it struck him as odd, even sinister, that she should be dressed so. They'd only received the call an hour before.

"Are you ready, Mrs. Trencavel?" Mr. Jacobs asked.

Charlie started at the breaking of the velvety silence.

The woman stepped back, inclining her head, but the watchers remained, eyeing Charlie like two monstrous cats.

Mr. Jacobs advanced, and Charlie began to follow, but his employer made a quick, impatient gesture that stopped him in his tracks, but not before he noticed the flecks of blood on the pillow where the nostrils and mouth would have been.

"Gentlemen," Jacobs addressed the two men, "is Mr. Trencavel prepared?"

"He received the *consolamentum*," one replied, then added, "He welcomed death."

"He died a *perfecti*," said the other.

At least this was what Charlie thought he'd heard.

Now it was Mr. Jacobs's turn to nod, then signal for Charlie to roll the gurney alongside the bed, which he did. Before he could get into position to shift the body, Mr. Jacobs again shooed him away.

"Shall we?" he said to the two men.

They transferred the frail remains of the person who had once been the most feared power broker in the city with little effort.

Mr. Jacobs fastened the straps that would stabilize the corpse during transport. "Will you send a suit, Mrs. Trencavel?"

"Yes," she replied in her dry, dusty voice.

Mr. Jacobs indicated that Charlie should take the handle at the feet and lead the way out.

The two men watched them as they made their way, the only evidence of their visit the deep tracks left by the gurney in the lush carpet.

*** 

"That seemed weird," Charlie observed as the hearse purred along with its midnight burden. "Who were those guys, and what were they talking about?"

"Don't worry about it, Charlie," Mr. Jacobs replied.

In his early twenties, the pudgy Charlie, with his thick-framed glasses and neatly-combed hair, possessed enough good manners to do what was required of him but little more. His simple duties consisted of greeting mourners, directing them to the register book, and placing flowers and wreaths at the grave sites. When things were quiet, he tidied up the funeral parlor and answered the phone, while Mr. Jacobs and his son, Oliver, tended to the darker aspects of their profession.

"Did you see that pillow, Mr. Jacobs?"

"What about it?" his employer asked as they cruised along the dark county road past trees thrashed by restless autumn winds.

"It looked kind of...funny."

Streetlamps began to appear as they reached the outskirts of the city, their haloes casting soft light on a succession of empty intersections and deserted sidewalks.

Mr. Jacobs braked for a traffic light, as a cluster of indistinct figures shambled toward them from the shadows. He glanced up and down the cross street, then smoothly accelerated through the red light as one of them hurled a bottle at the hearse. Behind them, there was the sound of breaking glass and indistinct shouts.

"Zombies—they're like zombies—these crackheads and meth freaks," Mr. Jacobs remarked. "Every year, there're more and more of them." He looked over to Charlie again. "I saw the pillow, Charlie—a wadded-up pillow. Why?"

"It's just that everything was so neat—but that pillow."

Mr. Jacobs turned onto Kennedy Boulevard and drove them deeper into the city. "This is why I don't use you on these calls, Charlie—you're too imaginative. If Oliver hadn't come down with the flu, you wouldn't be here now."

Charlie didn't much like Oliver and seldom worked with the tall, sardonic younger Jacobs. Oliver had a way of poking fun at him while wearing just the hint of a smile. He'd made it clear on more than one occasion that he didn't like working with Charlie either. "I'm sorry, Mr. Jacobs. I didn't mean to be any trouble—it just caught my attention—and those guys kind of spooked me."

"Those guys were the Tildrum brothers—Tom and Tim—they work...

*worked* for Mr. Trencavel. They're not used to strangers being…well, never mind what they're not used to—we're here." The automatic garage door of the funeral home slid up, and they glided in.

Once they had the gurney and its sheeted passenger out, Charlie and Mr. Jacobs guided it inside the parlor and down a corridor, coming to a stop at the entry to the refrigeration and embalming room. "I'll take Mr. Trencavel from here. Thanks for your help tonight."

Charlie turned to leave, but was halted by Mr. Jacobs. "Charlie, listen, with Oliver unavailable, I'll need your help again tomorrow evening."

"Tomorrow evening?"

"Yeah. Don't come in until about six. Okay?"

"Okay," Charlie agreed, then turned once more for the exit.

"And remember—we don't talk about our work, or our clients, Charlie—not ever."

"I know, Mr. Jacobs. I won't. Good night."

"Good night, Charlie. Get some rest."

* * *

Charlie didn't.

He dreamt and thrashed in his lumpy sofa bed most of the night. When he awoke after ten that morning, groggy and confused, all he could remember of the dreams were the huge black cats that lay watching him from every corner of his studio apartment, their eyes glowing with inhuman attentiveness.

Charlie threw back the twisted blankets and staggered over to the sink, filling a glass and drinking its entire contents in two long gulps. Feeling more himself after this, he tore open a yogurt container and began to eat with the last of his clean spoons. "Cats don't like me," he murmured to the empty room.

* * *

When Charlie arrived at work that evening, he found that there was a simple wooden casket in the viewing room, eight rows of cushioned folding chairs arrayed before it. There were no flowers. The coffin was closed, the room empty of mourners.

Charlie had checked the obituaries earlier and found no funerals or viewings scheduled. The only information on Mr. Trencavel's arrangements was that the funeral would be family only, the time and date to be determined. He was puzzled by the odd hours he was requested to work, and the presence of the coffin only increased his confusion. He crossed the thick carpeting and lifted the lid.

Mr. Marion Trencavel's sunken-cheeked face greeted him, eyes half-open, the whites gone gray as cobwebs and stained with small star-like bursts of blood. The image imprinted on the pillow rushed back to Charlie and, with a gasp, he allowed the lid to fall.

"That you, Charlie?" he heard Mr. Jacobs's call faintly from the direction of the office.

"I'm here, Mr. Jacobs!" Charlie cried, as he hurried out of the parlor and down the hallway.

"On time, as usual," Mr. Jacobs greeted the younger man with a smile. He was seated in front of a counter upon which rested a phone and several folders containing death certificates, burial permits, and other paperwork attendant to his business.

"Mr. Jacobs, is there a viewing tonight? I saw Mr. Trencavel in the—"

"That's a closed coffin, Charlie—I've told you not to open those."

"Yessir…I just didn't know…"

"I'll tell you what you need to know, Charlie."

Charlie nodded.

"Now sit and listen to me—this is important."

Drawing up a chair, Charlie sat opposite his employer.

"We're a small family business, as you already know; a business where discretion is extremely important. Families in this neighborhood, and the whole city for that matter, trust us with their loved ones—we're the last stop for them on this earth. Having been in this business for three generations, we've developed long-term relationships with certain families—important families. Sometimes we do special requests, honor certain customs that may appear strange or unusual to other people—outsiders—*tonight* is one of those times."

"So, we're burying Mr. Trencavel at nighttime? Is that it?"

"That's it, Charlie. Oliver and I have done this before, but I've always tried to keep you out of it."

"Will the internment be at Greenbough, Mr. Jacobs?"

"No, it'll be at Magnolia Hill. Why?"

"It's just Mr. Trencavel's not embalmed, and we're only supposed to bury the unembalmed at—"

"Stop." Mr. Jacobs raised one of his spade-like hands. "You're not a mortician, Charlie, that's what Oliver and I do. Stay in your lane, keep your mouth closed, and everything'll be fine."

Charlie didn't know what to say to that, but he'd seen enough corpses—embalmed and otherwise—to tell the difference.

"When will the family arrive?"

"Mrs. Trencavel will arrive with her escorts just before ten. The Cathari will begin arriving after that."

"You mean the Trencavels, Mr. Jacobs."

Jacobs studied Charlie for a moment before replying, "The Trencavels are part of the Cathari Family. There will be a number of them, but I think the chairs set up will suffice."

"Okay," Charlie murmured, adding, "Cathari?—I don't think I know any. Have they come to us before?"

"Many, many times, Charlie, they're one of our oldest clients."

Charlie recalled the scene at the house where they'd collected Mr. Trencavel—the ghastly pillow—the two frightening men. "Are they like the Mafia, Mr. Jacobs?"

Jacobs took a breath. "Charlie," he began in a patient, soothing tone, "the Cathari Family is a lot of things. They're like many families in one big family—not always through blood, but through ties going back many, many centuries. They've survived by adhering to their religion, their traditions, and, well…secrecy, really. This has allowed them to prosper in a lot of different…umm…businesses and enterprises."

"Secrecy, Mr. Jacobs?"

"They trust us with the funerals because they could trust my dad and my grandfather before me. Like I've said before—discretion is at the heart of our business."

Fascinated despite a growing uneasiness, Charlie persisted, "What do they do when they get here? Is that secret?"

"It's just a viewing not open to the public," Mr. Jacobs answered. "The interment, though, is a different matter. We're not involved in that—we just bring Mr. Trencavel to the cemetery—they do the rest."

"What do *we* do?"

"You'll be dropped off at the gate when we arrive to ensure that it's closed and locked behind us and no one comes in. I'll wait at the hearse behind a stand of trees near the gravesite—they don't want any outsiders watching."

Charlie's mouth fell open. "What about the cemetery workers?"

"There won't be any workers. The Cathari bury their own."

"Creepy," Charlie muttered.

"We're not here to judge."

"What kind of religion are they?"

The older man seemed to think, then stood, replying, "They're Cathari. Now, let's go to the diner down the street and have a good meal—my treat. It's going to be a long night."

* * *

Full from his meal and sleepy, Charlie was startled by the doorbell. The viewing was late, and for security reasons, the doors to the funeral home were locked. The neighborhood had deteriorated over the years and could be dangerous after dark.

Charlie hurried to the lobby entrance. Through the frosted windows, Mrs. Trencavel's veiled slender outline was sharply drawn by the porch light. Two large male figures flanked her, and Charlie drew the bolt, took a breath, and threw the door open. Mr. Jacobs appeared at his elbow.

"This way, Mrs. Trencavel," Mr. Jacobs said, as the three swept in like wind-driven shadows. Charlie trailed in their wake. "I think you'll find everything arranged as you wished."

As they approached the casket, Mr. Jacobs glanced to Charlie and raised his left hand, stopping him from coming closer. The men Charlie recalled as being Tom and Tim Tildrum—he didn't know which was which—resumed the same posts they'd maintained at Mr. Trencavel's deathbed—one at the foot and the other at the head of the coffin, their startling green eyes sweeping over Charlie with a cool interest.

Charlie noticed that Mr. Jacobs had turned the temperature down on the thermostat, and there was a distinct chill in the room. *It's because of the body,* he thought.

"Are you ready, Mrs. Trencavel?" he heard Mr. Jacobs ask.

"Go on," came the dry, brittle voice of the widow.

The undertaker lifted the upper half of the coffin's lid to reveal its somber contents.

Drawing back with a slight grimace, the widow placed a nosegay of lavender onto the corpse's chest. "These will help," she said. "They were his favorite flowers—they reminded him of our ancient homeland."

"As you can see, ma'am, but for the suit, he's untouched, just as you wished," Mr. Jacobs responded.

"Yes," came her whispery reply, "he must be as he was—perfected—unsullied. A little more light," she said, "the others need to see him clearly."

Charlie hurried to the dimmer switch and raised the wattage a few notches.

"That's enough," she commanded, and Charlie yanked his hand away.

As if cued, the mourners began to arrive, entering the room in a column of black clothes and muffled tread. With little in the way of greetings or conversation, they approached the widow and the coffin, both singly and in pairs. The widow received a bow of the head from each; the dead man, a kiss upon the forehead. Soon they were all seated and silently regarding the dead man and his living wife.

Charlie noticed that somehow, during the time the casket had been screened by the flow of mourners, a purple cloth had been lain atop it, and astoundingly, what appeared to be a large gold band, filigreed with indistinct figures. *It's a crown!* he thought.

Then he remembered that he hadn't put out the register journal for the funeral.

He hurried over to Mr. Jacobs, who stood at the back of the eerily quiet room and whispered, "The register, Mr. Jacobs—we didn't put it out."

"I know, Charlie—they don't want it. She knows who's here."

Several faces turned toward them, then turned away again when they ceased speaking. Mrs. Trencavel maintained her place in front of the coffin, the Tildrum brothers continued their watch at either end. The mourners looked on in silence. The minutes ticked on.

When the grandfather clock in the entrance hall struck eleven, Mrs. Trencavel made an upward motion with her pale hands, and the Cathari rose to their feet as one. "Mr. Jacobs?"

Mr. Jacobs hurried forward, then turned and spoke in a soft voice that carried easily in the muffled chamber, "If I could have the pallbearers come forward, please. I will close the coffin now, and we'll place the casket in the hearse. The rest of you may follow, then, please go to your cars and wait. We'll form a motorcade to proceed to Magnolia Hill Cemetery."

With little traffic at that time of night, the convoy arrived at Magnolia Hill just before midnight. Slowing to a stop at the entrance, Mr. Jacobs said, "Here're the keys, Charlie, open the gates and after the last car enters, lock them up again. You remain here. No one else comes in. When you see us returning, open the gates again. Understood?"

Charlie stepped out and did as he was told. He didn't understand how Mr. Jacobs could have keys to the gates, but figured it was all part of the arrangement with the cemetery owners. The hearse eased past him with a soft purring sound as the other cars followed. When the last had gone by, Charlie closed and locked the gates, his only illumination the yellowed lanterns mounted to the stone walls at either side of the entrance. The street in front of the cemetery was deserted, autumn leaves blown along it like small flames.

He watched the convoy as the last of the taillights winked out atop a rise that was the historic section of the cemetery. Charlie had never been involved in a burial there, as it had been his understanding that no more were allowed, and he was baffled as to how a service could be conducted in the dark.

In answer, a distant flame leapt into existence…then another…and another. Soon, there was a forest of torches atop the hill. Charlie found himself taking small steps in that direction. He remembered Mr. Jacob's instructions, but the gates were locked, nobody could enter, so what did it matter if he stayed or not? More than that, he was curious…so very curious. A fragment of some old warning about curiosity rose unbidden into his mind.

He began threading his way through the gravestones, creeping past obelisks and family mausoleums, his familiarity with the terrain aiding him as did the flaming beacons that drew him on and on. Halting, at last, just beyond the nimbus of the flickering torches, he peered around the edge of an old vault, his round face pressed close to its cold, pitted surface.

Not ten yards away, the mourners stood on either side of the open grave, many holding their torches aloft. The pallbearers advanced upon them, their burden still draped with its purple cloth and crowned with the circlet of gold. Each mourner bowed, or curtsied, while Mrs. Trencavel followed with the Tildrum brothers side-by-side behind her. Charlie recognized Mr. Jacobs amongst the mourners and felt a sense of dislocation and shock.

The bearers lowered the casket onto two boards that spanned the waiting grave and stepped back. Mrs. Trencavel, her skin pale as parchment, stepped to the head of the casket and removed the crown as the Tildrum brothers folded the purple cloth into a small square.

"Our King received the sacrament of *consolamentum*," cried the widow, holding the circlet aloft. "He was delivered of his suffering, his perfected spirit freed from the flesh devised by Satan to confine it. Our King—our *Perfecti*—is dead!"

The Cathari answered as one, "Our King is dead!" Four men took hold of the lowering straps which lay across the grave next to the two boards and lifted the coffin high enough for the supports to be removed. The plain pine casket was lowered into the grave, and the straps pulled out from beneath it.

"He will not return," she cried, leaning down to grab a fistful of dirt from the pile next to the burial site and tossing it atop the coffin.

"He will not return," the others repeated as they paraded past the grave, adding their handful of soil—thump…thump…thump…atop the oblong box.

Charlie didn't know what to make of it all. He'd never seen anything like this and now wished he hadn't. He turned to make his way back.

"Stay!" Mrs. Trencavel commanded, causing Charlie to fall back against the vault with a gasp. It was only after a very long moment he realized he wasn't being addressed. "Bring forward the successor," she cried.

Charlie peeked around the edge of the tomb once more and received another shock. Mr. Jacob's son, Oliver—tall, curly-headed, and handsome— strode out of the darkness and presented himself to Mrs. Trencavel, Tom and Tim now shadowing him.

Here was the *real* reason they needed him for this night funeral, Charlie realized with a pang of betrayal.

"The spirit of this man is austere and yearns only for ascendance to heaven!" Mrs. Trencavel declared, raising the coronet and placing it gently atop Oliver's head as he knelt to receive it. "This is the one fit to lead us with the ferocity and ruthlessness necessary in this world of Satan's making! This is the one designated by the late king, and as witnessed by myself. This, then, is the King of the Cathari!"

Oliver stood.

The Cathari knelt before him. "This is our King! None shall ever say so!"

Their newly-crowned ruler delivered his first decree in the calm, scornful manner Charlie was well acquainted. "Bury the dead!"

His subjects rose to their feet, shovels were produced, and men began to fill the grave. Charlie crept from the shelter of the tomb and into the maze of monuments, fearing every moment that Tom and Tim would come gliding out of the darkness to seize him.

"Don't let them get me. Don't let them get me," he whispered over and over in a little puffs of silvered breath.

Like Lot's wife, he looked back and saw the flames of the torches begin to wink out one by one. He hastened his steps, tripping on unseen obstacles that seemed to have erupted since his previous journey. Ahead, he could make out the gate by the yellow pool of light emitted by its flanking lanterns. The headlamps of the hearse flared into life. "Oh my god…oh my god…," he chanted in a new litany of terror.

He made his way onto the paved drive and began to run for all he was worth, reaching the gate just in time to see the funeral procession begin its return journey. Unable to fit the right key into the lock, he fumbled and stabbed at the fitting with each one on the ring until, at last, he found the right one and it turned with a metallic snap. The mechanism released, and Charlie shoved the gates wide just as he was caught in the approaching beams of the snaking convoy.

"Thank you, God…," he muttered, glancing over his shoulder, "…thank you!"

The hearse stopped, and the driver's window slid down, revealing Mr. Jacobs. "Mrs. Trencavel is in the car behind me—some family members will be taking her home, and the rest following. I'll go out and pull over—when the last car is through, lock up, and we'll head back."

"Okay…okay…good…" Charlie stepped back.

Jacobs gave him a second look and asked, "Why're you sweating, Charlie, and how'd your pants get dirty?"

Charlie brushed his trousers with his hands.

"Stop that," Mr. Jacobs ordered him. "I've got to pull out so the rest can get through. We'll talk on the way back."

Mr. Jacobs turned the Lincoln to the right, drove a few yards, and parked against the curb, the exhaust puffing small gray clouds into the cool, moist air.

The second car to pass was driven by one of the Tildrum brothers. He favored Charlie with a quick appraising glance, his green eyes luminous in the twilight of the lanterns, then continued on. Charlie could make out the silhouette of Mrs. Trencavel and Oliver in the back seat. The younger Jacobs no longer wore the diadem. The rest followed, and minutes later, he was locking the gate from the outside.

Charlie climbed into the waiting hearse, heart buzzing with fear while struggling with the knowledge that Mr. Jacobs had lied to him about everything.

"So what?…you fall down?" Mr. Jacobs asked after Charlie had given him the keys back.

"Yeah," Charlie agreed with a sheepish smile. "I was walking back and forth to stay awake and tripped on something."

Pulling into the roadway, the older man smiled, asking with a chuckle, "I can't take you anywhere, can I?"

Charlie chuckled too.

* * *

"Still planting 'em, Charlie?" the police officer asked as he slid his broad rump onto the stool next to Charlie in the busy diner.

"Yessir," he managed around a mouthful of soggy pancake.

"You mind if I join you?" Sgt. McDermott had worked several traffic details for Jacobs Funeral Home when they had long motorcades.

"No, sir," Charlie said more clearly now that he'd managed to swallow the great doughy lump.

"Anybody special?" the policeman asked as he perused the diner's own specials.

Not having slept well again and bursting to tell someone something of his adventure, he blurted out, "Mr. Trencavel—we buried Mr. Trencavel." After all, his obituary said there would be a funeral, just not when—so that much wasn't really a secret. "That's somebody special."

The officer's head whipped around at this news, his spiky mustache twitching, and heavy-lidded eyes widening, the pupils dilating. "So, the King o' the Cats is finally dead," he murmured. "That *is* somebody all right."

"Cats?" Charlie repeated.

"The Cathari—just a little play on words, Charlie. The intel boys tell me that once upon a time, they were an outlawed religious sect in Europe. There was even a crusade to wipe them out. Seems some survived, hid out, and a few hundred years later made it here. I'm surprised we weren't contacted by Mr. Jacobs—gangsters usually have big funerals and long motorcades."

"He was a gangster?" Charlie asked, feeling ever more detached from reality.

"They all are—they believe their souls are trapped in a world created by Satan, and that justifies doing anything until their souls are released to God. As for Trencavel? Yeah—he was a brutal bastard, or so the organized crime guys claim—extortion, narcotics, blackmail, bribery, and a lot of 'disappeared people' to account for."

"Murdered, you mean?"

"He was never charged with murder. No bodies. But none of them ever showed up again after crossing him, so what would you think?"

"Murder," Charlie whispered, remembering the bloody, death-mask pillow. "I think *he* was murdered."

"Who? Who was murdered, Charlie?"

"Mr. Trencavel," Charlie breathed, recalling the death scene as clearly as a photograph, the bizarre burial rites in the dead of night, but mostly, the lies Mr. Jacob had told him or led him to believe—the keen hurt of betrayal.

Cocooned in the warm, noisy atmosphere of the diner, Charlie began to talk.

When he was done, the police sergeant looked at him with worried eyes. "Don't say a word to anybody," he cautioned, standing and patting the younger man on the shoulder. "Go on about your business like we never had this conversation. I'll be in touch. Don't worry—we'll take care of you." Then he was gone.

Charlie did worry. He worried the whole agonizing three blocks to the funeral home. He felt awful thinking of how the police would question Mr. Jacobs; of how he might go to jail as an accomplice to the gangsters and probably be killed there. He worried how he'd make a living when that happened, of what he'd do. Just like that, he'd cut himself adrift with no one to turn to but Sgt. McDermott.

When Charlie arrived at the funeral home, he found the back hallway dim and hushed as it always was, and continued toward the office.

"Charlie, that you?" Mr. Jacobs called out from the viewing room. "In here."

Charlie was so befuddled that he couldn't remember whether a viewing was scheduled or not. Stepping through into the large parlor, he found Mr. Jacobs waiting for him, Oliver at his side, while Sgt. McDermott slouched in a cushioned folding chair.

Mr. Jacobs said, "Why in God's name did you watch Charlie? I warned you not to!"

"You shouldn't have done that," Sgt. McDermott agreed with a solemn nod. "Not much we can do now."

Charlie couldn't grasp what was happening. He could see a cheap empty casket on the bier, the kind used for immolations, Tim at its foot and Tom at its head, or perhaps it was the other way around.

The new King of the Cathari acknowledged the coffin with a wink, explaining, "I'm afraid it's up the chimney for you, Charlie. You see, Magnolia Hill is reserved for the *credentes*—the believers. The others, well…they go up in smoke…never more to be seen."

With small, eager smiles and bright green eyes, the Tildrum brothers glided toward Charlie, while he stood spellbound, still as a mouse, wishing that he could grow smaller and smaller until he disappeared altogether, then, with a start of terror, realized that he most certainly would.

# The Gingerbread Man

By Stacy Woodson

"The cookies are burning."

Jack sits in the living room of his Cape Cod-style home and reads the sports section from *The Staten Island Gazette* while he waits to leave for the lanes.

At least that's his plan—unless his daughter burns the house down first.

"The cookies are fine, Dad," Claire yells belatedly from the kitchen.

"Well, something is on fire." Jack shakes out the newspaper, grumbling. "Sure as hell ain't the Yankees."

"The Wilsons are burning leaves." Claire walks past Jack, dishtowel flipped over her shoulder, slams the window closed, and surveys the room. "Do you have your bowling ball, Dad?"

"It's by the door, Claire." He glances over his newspaper at the ball bag—red leather, worn plastic handles, *The Burner* stitched on the tag.

"It's time for a new one, don't you think?" Claire folds her arms and eyes the bag now.

It will be a cold day in hell before he replaces that bag, but he doesn't tell her that. He just pretends he can't hear her.

A timer dings. "*Those* are the cookies." Claire returns to the kitchen.

"I don't know why you spoil him like that," Jack calls after her. "The man has gained ten pounds."

"So have you, Dad," Claire calls back.

He lowers the newspaper, looks at his stomach, and frowns. "Hogwash."

The oven door bangs closed. Buttons beep.

Jack scans the box scores again, swears under his breath, and tosses the sports section onto the coffee table next to a dish with peppermints.

"The cookies need another minute," Claire says, breezing past him. "Liam," she calls from the bottom of the stairs. "Come say goodnight to your grandfather."

A door slams. Footsteps jackhammer overhead. Liam appears at the top of the stairs, hair wet, book tucked under his arm. "Hi, Grandpa!" He flashes a gap-toothed grin. Then, bounds down, Evel Knievels the last few risers, and launches himself through the living room onto the couch.

"Good job sticking the landing, kid." Jack ruffles his hair.

"Don't encourage him, Dad." She turns to Liam. "Did you brush your teeth?"

"Yes, ma'am."

Claire narrows her eyes.

Liam looks like Mickey, the way he won't meet his mother's gaze, and Jack doesn't buy his answer either. But the timer beeps. Claire returns to the kitchen. And the universe gives Liam a reprieve just like it used to give Mickey.

"You sure about those teeth, kid?" Jack nudges Liam. "She'll smell your breath, you know. She's smart that one." He picks up the dish with peppermints and winks.

"Thanks, Grandpa." Liam takes a peppermint, slips it in his mouth, and crunches.

"When you go upstairs, you make it right. You hear me?"

"Yes, sir."

"Now enough teeth stuff," Jack says. "What's the book?"

"*The Gingerbread Man*." Liam shows him the cover. "He's fast like me, Grandpa."

"You're right." Jack nods, thoughtfully. "Hope your life ends better than his did."

"Dad!" His daughter is back. She swats him with a dishtowel.

"What?" Jack raises his hands. "It's a dark ending, Claire."

"When you put it that way."

"The fox bites his head off. There's no other way to put it."

"Liam, say goodnight to your grandfather before he gives you nightmares."

"But Grandpa and I haven't read my story yet."

"I think he's covered the highlights."

"Pleeeease." Liam steeples his hands.

"You know he's always late, Claire."

She looks at the clock on the mantel. Then at Jack, and sighs. "Just until Grandpa needs to leave for the lanes, okay?"

"Yay!" Liam thrusts the book at Jack.

He takes it and waits for Liam to wiggle into his perfect spot on the couch. "You good?"

Liam nods.

"Now—" Jack stares at the cover thoughtfully and rubs his chin. "I'm happy to read this story to you, kid. Or—" He shrugs. "I can tell you a story about The *real* Gingerbread Man."

Liam's eyes narrow. "Are you messing with me, Grandpa?"

"Hand to God," Jack says reverently. "Guy's name is Francesco 'The Gingerbread Man' Romano. He was a high-stakes action bowler and—"

"Bowling." Liam groans. "This is a *bowling* story?"

"Kid—back in the sixties, bowling wasn't just bowling. At night, when alleys were closed to the public, small-time gangsters made high-stakes bets on players, big money matches—payouts so big that thugs would stick a knife to you if—"

"Dad!" A pan crashes in the sink. Claire appears in the doorway and stares.

"What?" Jack stares back.

"You know what."

"I'm trying to tell the kid a story here—one with an ending that isn't dark."

"Not that one, Dad. He's only seven."

"Seven and three-quarters, Mom." Liam thumps his chest.

"That three-quarters makes a difference, Claire."

Liam nods solemnly.

"I'll keep it G-rated."

"You never keep anything G-rated. Stick to the book." She leaves again. And they both sigh.

"We can't read about a cookie now, Grandpa. It's so boring."

"Want to get another book?"

Liam shakes his head. A second passes. Then, his face brightens. "I have an idea." He climbs onto his knees, cups his mouth, and whispers into Jack's ear, "We can still read the book, Grandpa. Just read it *your* way."

Jack frowns and turns his head to look at Liam. "My way?"

"You know—*your* way." Liam winks. At least he tries. One eye is squeezed shut, and he fights to keep the other open.

"I don't know, kid. Your mom may be right. This one may need to wait a few years."

"Seven and *three-quarters*, Grandpa. Remember?"

"That three-quarters does make a difference." Jack nods solemnly.

"Go on, Grandpa." Liam settles into the couch again. "Once upon a time. That's how stories start."

"You're right, kid." He leans closer to Liam, opens the book to a random page, and clears his throat. "Once upon a time. In Brooklyn…"

* * *

"You Jack O'Conner?"

I just took a bite of my pastrami and rye and was reading about the Barnyard Gang's latest convenience store robbery in the newspaper, when two schmuck-a-tellies wearing suits saddle up next to me at Flo's Lunch Counter.

This isn't a suit-side-of-town or a suit-kind-of-place, and I should have known things were headed sideways. But I'd just worked a double at the docks, and all I cared about was that sandwich. The pastrami was cooked just perfect. The mustard slathered on just right.

So, I glare at the guy hassling me—the dumpy one—and keep chewing.

"It's him, Sully," the tall guy says, looking at a picture.

Then, the schmucks exchange glances, lift me off the stool, and carry me out the door still holding my sandwich. Outside, they drop me next to a bus bench while folks at Flo's stare through the window like we're a Times Square peepshow.

"What gives?" I ask.

They don't answer.

So, I toss my sandwich aside and knuckle up, ready to give Dumpy a good pop. Until he flashes a badge and shoves me at a sedan.

"Get in the car, Jack." Dumpy opens the brown doorway to hell.

After Pop died, my brother and I rode in a car like that to Saint Anne's. The orphanage was one of the worst experiences of my life. Only one thing will make me climb in there willingly, and Dumpy telling me ain't it.

"Do I need a lawyer or something?" I ask—not because I care. The Express bus is at the curb, and when the door opens, I plan to make a run for it.

"You don't need a lawyer," Dumpy tells me.

I nod, tense, watching bus passengers file out.

"But Mickey might."

I swear under my breath and climb into the car.

***

When I arrive at the police station, I think I'm headed to a holding cell or an interrogation area. But the tall guy leaves me with my brother in a breakroom.

No one is with us. It's just me and Mickey—the same way it's been since we were kids. And I join him at the table. He kneads the palm of his hand, miniature crosses branded into the skin, just like mine.

"What happened, Mickey?"

"It's stupid, Jackie."

My brother is the kind of guy who says too much and never lands on a point, or he clams up and says nothing.

"Tell me anyway," I press.

He shakes his head.

It looks like clams are on the menu today.

"Mickey—" I try again, irritation in my voice starting to rise.

"I thought I saw Ma on Broadway, okay? Pop said she took off for LA. That she wanted to make it as an actress. It makes sense she'd finally come back, right?"

I shake my head. Mickey does this once a year. He thinks he sees Ma, flies his stupid flag, winds up in jail. "What else?" I ask. The cops picked him up, and I know there's more.

There's always more with Mickey.

"I needed a ticket, you know, to see her. But I didn't have any cash. So, I pulled a dipper."

He won't look at me now. And I know it's bad. "Please tell me you didn't."

"He knuckled up on me, Jackie." Words rush from his mouth now. "Everything happened so fast. I just kept thinking about Ma, how I had to see her. Before I realized it, I was on top of the guy swinging and—"

"How bad?"

He glances away.

"Mickey—" I fight to keep my voice even. "How bad did you hurt the guy?"

"They took him to New York Presbyterian."

"Damn it." I slam my hand against the table.

"I know, Jackie," he stammers. "I know…"

"Ma's dead, Mickey."

"You don't know that."

The thing is, I do know. But the truth about Ma would hurt Mickey more than chasing ghosts. So, I let it go, like I've let it go countless times before, because I will always protect my brother.

It's silent now, except for the clock ticking on the wall, and we sit like that for a while.

"I'm sorry, Jackie," Mickey whispers.

"I know."

"Maybe the guy won't press charges."

"Maybe," I say, even though I know this isn't part of their plan.

* * *

After Dumpy walks Mickey away, the tall guy strolls into the breakroom, tosses a file on the table, and sits across from me.

"You owe me a pastrami and rye," I tell him.

"Sorry about that," the guy says like we're friends now. "I'd like to start over. I'm Detective Vine. You can call me Bo."

"What's Mickey being charged with?"

"That's up to you, Jack."

"I knew it was coming." I fold my arms and laugh.

"What's that?"

"The ask."

This was never about Mickey. It was about me.

I figured it out when I saw Mickey in the breakroom instead of a holding cell. The way Bo and Dumpy yanked me from Flo's, the spectacle they made. The lunch counter is a gossip mill, and they wanted word to get out that I had a brush with the cops. I just needed to know why.

"What do you want, Detective *Bo Vine*?"

"Francisco 'The Gingerbread Man' Romano."

I frown. I figured Bo would want a line on a shipment, something connected to my job at the docks. Not a bead on a man named after a cookie. I tell him I don't know the guy, but he's flipping through his file now and doesn't seem to care.

"Word is you used to be an action bowler?"

"I made some scratch chasing pins. Won a few pot games," I tell him, intentionally soft-pedaling it. Until Bo slides a Polaroid in front of me.

Then, I stop talking.

After the fire at Saint Anne's, Mickey and I lived on our own, and I worked the circuit to make ends meet, high-stakes bowling matches financed by small-time gangsters. I went straight years ago for Mickey. I couldn't look out for my brother from a jail cell.

"This is you with Flash Deacon, right?" Bo taps the picture Kat took at The Alley the night I beat Flash.

"That's not my life anymore."

"It needs to be." He replaces the Polaroid with the article about the convenience store robberies, the one I tried to read before he and Dumpy ruined my lunch. "Romano is the getaway driver for the Barnyard Gang, and he's an action bowler. We find Romano, we find his crew."

*The Gingerbread Man*—I should have known that name was a moniker. Every action bowler has one.

The nickname is usually a clue about how the guy ticks. Flash curled into a ball, tip-toed toward the lane, and exploded at the foul line. I'm curious about Romano. Does he throw a ripper? Or does he like to eat gingerbread cookies when he bowls?

"The way the circuit runs the lane lottery, we need an insider to find him. We want you to find Romano, Jack."

My attention snaps back to Bo, and I laugh. "You can't be serious."

"Romano for Mickey. That's the deal."

"I've been out of the circuit for years."

"I'm sure you'll figure something out."

I shake my head. "This isn't just a game. You get that, right? You get crosswise with these guys, the ones who run the lanes, they play for keeps, Bo."

"So do we, Jack."

"Not the forever kind."

* * *

Bo gives me a week to find Romano and call him with the location, or Mickey's deal disappears. Every minute matters. I need to figure out where the circuit meets tonight.

I need to be on the lanes after dark.

My first stop is a pro shop called Lucky Strikes. One of my old running buddies, Louie "Lucky Dog" Leoni, owns the place. Even though Louie says he went legit, I know he still dips his tail in the action scene, and if anyone has a pulse on the circuit, it's him.

I wait until the shop is empty and walk inside.

The place is the size of a shoebox. It's shaped the same way, too. Shirts and shoes line the wall to the left. Bowling balls line the wall to the right, except the ball that's in the display window. It's red and shimmery, just like the bag that's there.

And I've never seen anything like it.

Louie is in the back behind the counter, personalizing a bowling ball with an engraver, a cigarette bobbing from each corner of his mouth. He forgets the smokes and grins when he sees me, manages to rescue one, and leaves the other where it lands, burning on the counter.

"Jackie 'Crazy-like-a-Fox' O'Connor." He transfers the surviving cigarette to his left hand and extends his right to shake mine. "How the hell are ya?"

"Making it." I smile. "Trying, anyway."

"Aren't we all." He returns the cigarette to his mouth, takes a long drag, and says on the exhale, "Heard about the scuffle at Flo's."

"That was fast."

He shrugs. "You know Flo's. I thought you went straight, man."

"I thought you did too."

"And so it goes."

Louie grabs an ashtray from Rivertown Barber that somehow found its way here, finishes off the cigarette. Then, reaches for the one still burning on the counter.

"What brings you here, Jack?" Another drag. Another exhale. "Don't get me wrong, I love seeing you, man. But even when you were running the circuit, you never came in here."

"I need some scratch." It's a lie. But I can't tell Louie about Mickey. Not because I don't trust him. When I was running and gunning, he always had my back. It's just better for Louie that he doesn't know the truth. "Who's top billing these days?"

"Wow. That's a tough one." He taps a finger on the counter—the only finger without a Band-Aid—while he rolls through a roster in his head. "Joey-the-Rooster is hot right now and a guy called Clydesdale."

"What about Romano?"

"The Gingerbread Man." He looks at me now, brows raised. "You heard of him?"

I shrug. "Flo's."

He nods, seeming to accept the lie. "Guy is top-notch. Runs strikes most nights. Folks can't catch him. Best I've ever seen since you."

"Pot big?"

"Yeah. It's big. But the guys he runs with are intense. Not sure you want a piece of that."

"Can't be worse than Flash. How do I find him?"

"Things are different now, Jack. You can't just show up and challenge a guy. The circuit doesn't work that way anymore. Cops have been cracking down. Busted Kat's place a while back. If you want in, you need to be vetted. You need a nod from Hog."

"How do I get that?"

"You need to beat him on the lanes."

* * *

I arrive at Rivertown Barber at ten p.m. just like Louie said. He promised everything would make sense when I see the place. But, so far, I'm still confused.

A guy named Rick is supposed to meet me at the door, but I'm early. So, I occupy my time reading the special that's advertised in the window.

When he finally emerges from the back, my eyes go wide. The man looks like he can bench press a Cadillac, and I'm guessing he doesn't cut hair. I tell him The Fox is here for Hog. He seems satisfied and lets me inside. We walk through the shop, past rows of empty chairs to a storage closet in the back. Then, he opens the door, yanks on the light, and tells me to take the stairs.

I get that doorway-to-hell feeling, the one that reminds me of Saint Anne's. But I think about Mickey—the cost if I fail—and I walk inside anyway.

It's dark and dank and the descent feels like it takes forever. At the bottom there's a sign that says Hog's Alley, but the clarity Louie promised me still isn't here.

The bowling alleys I know are big and loud. And they have plastic furniture, beat-up ball returns, and rental shoes with broken laces.

Not this place.

It's small and quiet. The furniture is leather and lush and sits behind ball returns that look like art, not machinery. There's a bar stocked with liquor and cigars and crystal glasses. It has a phone too. And my stomach tightens when I see it. If this is the circuit, Louie is right. I may know the game, but I don't know the rules anymore.

"Don't let this place mess with your head, Jack." Louie hefts the bowling bag from the display window onto the bar. "Sorry, I'm late, man."

"Don't worry about it." I look past Louie at the empty couches and empty lanes. "Hog isn't here yet."

"Of course, he isn't. You didn't think I'd let you play cold, did you? You have an hour to find the pocket and figure out how the lanes break." He thrusts a pair of shoes at me. "Size ten, right?"

That's my size. But I can't take the shoes or the shimmery ball inside that shimmery bag Louie put on the bar. "I can't use your inventory, Louie."

"No gear. No game." He pushes the shoes at me again. "You can pay me back when you beat Romano."

Guilt needles me. Even if I manage to beat Romano before the cops show up, the only payout I'll get is Mickey's freedom. And Louie doesn't deserve this.

I thank him, take the shoes anyway, and it makes me feel worse.

* * *

"Quit squeezing the ball, Jack."

I stare at the split—seven and ten—and shake my head.

"You'll get it." Louie sounds confident.

I'm not.

I've been throwing junk for forty-five minutes.

The return spits out the ball—fiery red. It's good looking. I wish my game looked that way too.

I blow out a breath, find my grip, and stand in front of the lane. I need to gamble with the gutter if I want to strike the ten, take out the seven, and finish with a spare. I approach the foul line, nothing fancy, and release the ball. It holds for a few feet, stalls, then dumps into the gutter.

Louie calls out another critique. "Follow through."

I swear under my breath.

"I'm sorry, man." Not just for my performance but for lying to Mickey about Ma and dragging Louie unwittingly into this mess. To get this meeting, Louie vouched for me, and his rep is also on the line.

The pins reset. I pick up the ball again.

"Leave it." Louie lights up a cigarette. "Let's get a drink."

"That's not going to help."

"It can't hurt."

Louie's right. Not much can at this point.

I follow him to the bar even though it's still empty like the rest of the place. He grabs a bottle of whiskey, pours two tumblers, and hands me the glass. The way Louie moves, it's like he knows the place, and I wonder if he moonlights here. But I don't ask, and he doesn't offer.

We just sit, sip, stare.

Louie smokes.

Maybe it's Mickey—the pressure to win. Maybe it's this place—the speakeasy vibe. Whatever the reason, I can't find my game here. "I don't know what's wrong with me."

"I do," Louie says, cigarette poised for another drag. "You went straight. You're a working stiff now, and your game is stiff too."

"You're funny." I laugh.

He stares.

"You're serious?"

"Remember when we were coming up in the circuit? You cared less about money and more about bragging rights. You were called The Fox for a reason, Jack. You need to find that guy again."

* * *

Hog is everything I expected.

He's big and brash and more show than bowl. Despite his lane theatrics—the porkpie hat, the cigar clenched between his teeth—he's a decent bowler and manages a bagger out of the gate. I guess Louie's pep talk worked because I land a strike too.

We continue to play. Not talking. Just bowling.

Mechanics aren't a problem for me now. It's the sound.

Hog—the way he breaths.

Louie—the way he smokes.

Me—the way my heart thuds in my ears.

There's only three of us here. Everything is amplified. Any flicker or shift when I approach the lane, screws with my release, and I end most of my frames with a spare.

On the seventh frame, Hog leaves for a drink—his version of a seventh-inning stretch, I guess. He still hasn't said a word to me, and I'm not sure about the protocol here.

So, I wait at the lanes.

It's awkward standing there—especially with Rick at the stairs, arms folded, eyeballing me now. So, I go to the bathroom and splash water on my face. When I return, Louie calls my name and puts me out of my misery—some of it anyway. It's hard to feel real relief when Mickey's freedom and Louie's rep are hanging over my head.

I join them at the bar. Louie pours drinks again—another whiskey for me and a refill for Hog.

I expect Hog to say something, finally. What do you think about the place? How about those Yankees? Interesting weather we're having. Anything. But he doesn't.

And neither do I.

Because Louie said to me, before we started the game, "Don't speak to Hog."

The man finishes his drink, lights up a fresh cigar, and signals for Louie. It's subtle, a tap on the bar, and Louie brings him an ashtray. Then, something happens—something I didn't expect.

Louie starts signing with Hog.

It throws me at first when I see it—two guys moving their hands with smokes hanging from their mouths. Then, the clarity Louie promised—I finally see it, and the quiet here makes sense now.

"Good match, Fox." Hog signs, but it's Louie's voice I hear. "Not great. The way Louie went on about you, I expected more."

Louie and Hog start signing again, and I'm anxious now. There are three frames left in the game. But Hog talks like we're done. And I wonder where this leaves me with the circuit.

"Louie tells me you want to make a run at the Gingerbread Man," Hog starts again. "If you want to catch him, you need to bowl better than that." He looks at Louie, continues to sign; Louie continues to translate. "Run him through The Barn. If he bags Rooster, I'll see what I can do."

Louie nods, his face composed, but I can tell he fights a smile.

I fight one too. I don't know how this night ended here. But I'm grateful for it.

Hog reaches to shake my hand until I extend mine, and he sees the welts on my hands. He signs again. "You a Saint Anne's kid?"

My face flushes. I push my hands in my pockets and nod.

He shakes his head. "Crazy what that woman did. Glad more than one of you survived that fire." He signs something to Louie, tips his hat, and walks away. Rick falls in behind him, and they continue up the stairs.

"The Fox is back." Louie says like he's announcing a fight.

I grin—a smile that's not heartfelt. I'm one step closer to helping Mickey, and I should be happy. But Hog's comment about Saint Anne's still sits with me. "Hey Louie—what did Hog say on his way out?"

"Pack Band-Aids."

That's not what I expected.

* * *

Beer, cigarettes, and wax—I didn't know I missed those smells until I walk into The Bowling Barn in New Jersey. The alley balls, plastic furniture, and rental shoes are here, too. This is my kind of place, and I'm ready to play.

I still have Louie's gear and walk past the rental counter to the edge of the lanes.

"There's Rooster." Louie points to a guy who lands a strike, pumps his fist, and crows. I shake my head and wonder if the circuit is only filled with showboats these days.

At least I only need to worry about one.

I start toward Rooster, my plan to challenge the guy, like we used to back in the day.

Until Louie stops me mid-stride.

"What are you doing, Jack?"

"Putting my ball in the return."

"The circuit doesn't work that way anymore. Rooster runs the place. To play Rooster, you need to beat The Barn."

"The Barn?" I look at Louie wide-eyed. There are twenty-six lanes teaming with action. Hog said bring Band-Aids, and now I know why.

"It will be fine, Jack. Most of the guys didn't cut their teeth here. They're imports."

"How many does that leave me?"

"You're about to find out." Louie walks behind the rental counter, grabs the handset to the intercom. "Attention in the Barn." He looks at me and grins. "All Barnyard bowlers—The Fox is here to take a run."

Animal sounds erupt across the lanes.

I swallow. There's a lot of livestock in here.

"Clydesdale, Duck-Duck, Templeton, Bull, and Trumpet-like-the-Swan," Louie rattles off names of bowlers who stand in front of me now. Five bowlers. Rooster makes six.

It's still a lot in one night.

A lane opens, and I play Duck-Duck first. I goose him by a wide margin, advance to Clydesdale, and quickly corral him too. I continue like this, beating one barnyard player after another. I blow out my bowling thumb when I beat Rooster, and this is the only dramatic moment of the night.

"Nice barn burner." Louie grins, his customary cigarette bobbing from the corner of his mouth. He reaches out to shake my hand, sees my thumb—bloated and bleeding—winces, and points me to the restroom.

Normally, back in the day, after a string of games like this, I'd leave with a lot of cash. But tonight, I played for access, not money, and I'm not worried about some shark or shyster jumping me. My mind is on Mickey. And when Bo walks into the bathroom, I'm not ready for it.

"Hello, Jack, or should I call you The Fox?" He's dressed like a bowler, smells like booze, and still manages to stand out.

"What the hell, Bo?" I look in the mirror at the stalls reflected behind me. There's only a handful, and the doors are ajar, so I know they're empty. But it doesn't make me feel better. It only takes one of Hog's guys to see me talking to a cop, and Mickey's freedom will be the least of my worries. "Have you been following me?"

I don't need an answer. The smug look on his face gives it away. I've been so focused on Mickey's freedom, I let my guard down, and I hate myself for it.

"When's the meet with Romano?" Bo turns on the water at the sink next to mine.

"I don't know."

"What do you mean, you don't know?"

"The date hasn't been set."

"Call when you have it."

"No." The word slides out before I realize I've said it. I've had a good night at the lanes, and maybe I'm channeling that salty action bowler Louie remembers from the past—the guy that would rather die than give someone the upper hand.

"What do you mean, no?"

"You give me a letter signed by the district attorney guaranteeing Mickey's freedom in exchange for the circuit location. Then, I'll call you."

Bo turns off the faucet. "I don't think you understand—"

"No. I don't think you do. If I don't get that letter, the deal is off."

I leave Bo and join Louie at the bar. I may have figured out a way to protect Mickey. But before this is over, I need to find a way to protect my friend.

"How's the thumb?"

"It sucks."

He hands me a beer. "Maybe this will help."

I take a long drink. My thumb still throbs. But the beer tastes good. "Now what?"

"We wait for Rivertown Barber to post the special."

* * *

It takes two days for Bo to come through with the letter, five for Rivertown Barber to put the special in the window. And I'm at Hog's Alley, again.

The place is different this time. Gangsters and hustlers are here, and Louie isn't working the bar. But I'm just as nervous and stare out at the lanes the same way again.

"Don't let this place mess with your head, Jack."

"You need new material, Louie."

"I have some." He holds my gear and motions for me to follow him to the lanes. "Remember that night at The Barn?" He unzips the bowling bag and shows me the words he's engraved on the ball.

"The Burner." I grin.

"The tag on the bag matches, too. You're called The Fox for a reason, Jack. This is a reminder in case you forget."

I nod. My throat turns thick. "Thanks, man."

"And Jack, one more thing—" He squeezes my shoulder. "Don't screw up. I have a lot of money on you tonight."

"Asshole."

He grins and walks away.

I hope he's joking. Especially since I know how things will end.

I take a deep breath, steady my nerves, and place my ball in the return. When I look back at Hog's Alley, more people are here—a small group. They're clustered around a guy with horn-rimmed glasses, eating ginger-bread cookies from a paper bag.

That answers one of my burning questions about Romano.

I don't turn away now. I still watch him. There's something about his face. I've seen him before I just can't remember where.

"Jack." Louie yanks me back to the lanes. "Throw a few balls and warm up."

I approach the lane and try to focus. But now that I've seen Romano, all I can think about is Detective Bo Vine and his plan. Call during the seven-frame stretch, confirm Romano is here—at least that's what he wants me to do. Then, the cops will raid the place.

Then, Mickey goes free.

I blow out a breath, look down, see Louie's engraving, and ground myself.

Hog starts the match, and Romano and I take our lanes. Romano throws the ball with two hands and plays the gutter. His form looks completely wrong, and yet, his precision is completely right.

We go head-to-head, strike after strike. And each frame we clear, the sicker I feel.

Not because of the seven-frame stretch and the call I need to make. It's because of Louie—what I need to do to protect him.

When we hit the seventh, I don't go to the bar. I walk to the bathroom and slam my thumb in the door. It's still raw from The Barn, and the pain is some of the worst I've felt in my life. I return to the lanes, head spinning, and find Louie.

I show him my thumb, and his eyes go wide.

"Jesus, Jack." He turns my hand, shaking his head.

"I can't get my thumb in that ball, Lou."

"It wouldn't come out if you did." He blows out a breath. "How's your left? Think you can throw a two-hander?"

"I won't win that way."

He lights up, takes a drag, eyes lingering on my thumb. "I'll talk to Hog and tell him if he drags out the seventh, I'll work the bar for free over the weekend. Then, I'll run back to the shop and grab a ball with a wider thumb hole. Some tape too."

"Appreciate it, man."

He walks over to Hog at the bar. They sign back and forth. Louie gives me a thumbs up and heads for the stairs. I wait two more minutes. Then, I ask the bartender for the phone and make the call. When I hang up, I expect to feel relief. I've secured Mickey's freedom.

But I don't.

These are my people. And I feel like a traitor.

The bartender pours Romano a whiskey, and I find myself still trying to place his face. When he reaches for his drink, I see the crosses branded into the skin, and I hate myself even more. Only three boys survived the fire that night: my brother, me, and Frankie. The way Hog mentioned the orphanage, I should have known Frankie would be here.

I walk over to him, and just like I did that night at Saint Anne's, I tell him to run.

****

"Dad!"

Jack blinks.

"Don't you hear the door?" Claire sets a plate of gingerbread cookies on the coffee table and leaves to answer it.

"What happened, Grandpa?" Liam whispers. "What happened to the Gingerbread Man?"

Jack glances past his grandson at the man in the horn-rimmed glasses who Claire hugs now.

"Hello, Liam."

"Hey, Uncle Frankie! Grandpa was just telling me a story about the Gingerbread—" He stops, just as Frankie reaches for a cookie, and his eyes go wide.

"You told him, didn't you, Jack?"

"He's seven and three-quarters. That three-quarters makes a difference." He winks at Liam. Then, stands, picks up his bowling bag, and walks to the door.

"Have fun tonight, boys," Claire calls.

"Thanks for the cookies." Frankie holds up the plate.

"You're taking the plate. Really?" Jack shakes his head. "You plan on sharing those with Louie?"

Frankie laughs. "Not a chance."

# Contributors

**Donna Andrews** (www.donnaandrews.com) is the *New York Times*-bestselling author of the Agatha-, Anthony-, and Lefty-winning Meg Langslow series from Minotaur. Her latest books are *Birder She Wrote* and *Let It Crow, Let It Crow, Let It Crow*—soon to be followed by *Between a Flock and a Hard Place* and *Rockin' Around the Chickadee*. She's a longtime member of Mystery Writers of America and Sisters in Crime and, strange to say, an inveterate punster.

**David Dean**'s short fiction has appeared regularly in *Ellery Queen's Mystery Magazine* since 1990 and garnered three Ellery Queen Readers Awards. His work has also been featured in many anthologies, including *The Best American Mystery Stories,* and earned nominations for the Shamus, Barry, Derringer, and Edgar Awards. David's novels and collected short stories are available through Genius Books and Amazon.

**John M. Floyd** (www.johnmfloyd.com) is the Edgar Award-nominated author of more than a thousand short stories in publications such as *Alfred Hitchcock's Mystery Magazine, Ellery Queen's Mystery Magazine, Strand Magazine, The Saturday Evening Post, The Best American Mystery Stories,* and *The Best Mystery Stories of the Year*. A former Air Force captain and IBM systems engineer, John is also a Shamus Award winner, a five-time Derringer Award winner, and the 2018 recipient of the Edward D. Hoch Memorial Golden Derringer for lifetime achievement in short mystery fiction.

Judge **Debra H. Goldstein** (www.DebraHGoldstein.com) is the author of Kensington's Sarah Blair mystery series (*Five Belles Too Many, Four Cuts*

*Too Many, Three Treats Too Many, Two Bites Too Many,* and *One Taste Too Many*) and two standalones: *Maze in Blue* and *Should Have Played Poker.* Her novels and short stories have been named Agatha, Anthony, Derringer, and Claymore finalists and received Silver Falchion, IPPY, AWC, and BWR awards.

**Barb Goffman** (www.barbgoffman.com) is the Agatha, Anthony, Macavity, and Ellery Queen Readers Award-winning author of nearly sixty crime short stories. She's been a finalist for major short-story crime awards forty-one times, including eighteen Agatha nominations, a category record. Her stories range from noir to cozy, and she's known for writing humor. Barb's an associate editor of *Black Cat Weekly,* an editor/coeditor of sixteen published and forthcoming anthologies, and a freelance editor, often focusing on traditional and cozy mysteries.

**James A. Hearn** (www.jamesahearn.com) is an Edgar Award nominee for best short story and his work has appeared in *The Best American Mystery and Suspense.* His stories have been published in *Alfred Hitchcock's Mystery Magazine, Black Cat Mystery Magazine,* and numerous anthologies, including *Monsters, Movies & Mayhem* and *The Eyes of Texas.* James is a two-time finalist for Writers of the Future, a contest honoring new authors in science fiction and fantasy.

**Adam Meyer** (www.adammeyerwriter.com) writes fiction and screenplays. His short stories have won the Derringer Award, been nominated for the Shamus Award, and appeared in *The Best American Mystery and Suspense Stories 2023.* He is the author of the novel *The Last Domino,* and the editor of the anthology *In Too Deep: Crime Stories Inspired by the Songs of Genesis.* He also writes TV movies and series for Lifetime, Discovery, National Geographic, and more.

**Tom Milani**'s (www.tommilani.com) short fiction has appeared in *Groovy Gumshoes: Private Eyes in the Psychedelic Sixties, Black Cat Weekly, Illicit*

*Motions,* and *Urban Pigs Press.* His novella *Barracuda Backfire,* Book 4 of the *Chop Shop* series, was published in April 2024.

**Laura Oles** (www.lauraoles.com) is the award-winning author of the Jamie Rush mystery series. Her debut mystery, *Daughters of Bad Men*, was an Agatha nominee, a Claymore Award finalist, and a Writers' League of Texas Award finalist. *Depths of Deceit*, her second novel, was named Best Mystery of 2022 by Indies Today. Her work has appeared in crime fiction anthologies, consumer magazines, and business publications. She lives in the Texas Hill Country with her family.

**Josh Pachter** (www.joshpachter.com) is a writer, editor, and translator. His short stories have been appearing in *Ellery Queen's Mystery Magazine* and elsewhere for more than half a century; in 2020, he received the Short Mystery Fiction Society's Golden Derringer for Lifetime Achievement. In 2024, *Dutch Threat* (Genius Book Publishing) was named a finalist for Left Coast Crime's Lefty Award for Best Debut Mystery Novel and Malice Domestic's Agatha Award for Best First Novel.

**Joseph S. Walker** (www.jswalkerauthor.com) is an Edgar Award and Derringer Award nominee whose short fiction has appeared in *Alfred Hitchcock's Mystery Magazine, Ellery Queen's Mystery Magazine, Mystery Weekly, Tough, The Best American Mystery and Suspense*, and three consecutive editions of *The Best Mystery Stories of the Year*. He has won the Bill Crider Prize for Short Fiction. He also won the Al Blanchard Award in 2019 and 2021.

**Andrew Welsh-Huggins** (www.andrewwelshhuggins.com) is the Shamus, Derringer, and ITW-award-nominated author of the Andy Hayes Private Eye series and editor of *Columbus Noir*. Kirkus called his latest crime novel, *The End of The Road,* "A crackerjack crime yarn chockablock with miscreants and a supersonic pace." His short fiction has appeared in multiple magazines and anthologies. His nonfiction book, *No Winners Here Tonight,* is the definitive history of the death penalty in Ohio.

# About the Editors

**Michael Bracken** (www.CrimeFictionWriter.com), the author of more than 1,300 short stories, is an Edgar- and Shamus-award nominee and four-time Derringer award-winner. His crime fiction has appeared in *The Best American Mystery Stories, The Best Mystery Stories of the Year,* and many other publications. Additionally, Bracken is the editor or co-editor of three dozen anthologies, including a Derringer Award winner and three Anthony Award finalists. He is the 2016 recipient of the Edward D. Hoch Memorial Golden Derringer for lifetime achievement in short mystery fiction, and, in 2024, he was inducted into the Texas Institute of Letters for his contributions to Texas literature.

**Stacy Woodson** (www.stacywoodson.com) made her crime fiction debut in *Ellery Queen's Mystery Magazine*'s Department of First Stories and won the 2018 Readers Award. It is the second time in the award's history that a debut took first place. Since her debut, she has placed more than forty stories in publications—three winning the Derringer award for excellence in short mystery fiction. She is a five-time nominee. Her short fiction has also been nominated for a Macavity Award, Anthony Award, and a Thriller Award, selected for *The Best Mystery Stories of the Year*, and adapted for animation. She is also a co-editor of three crime fiction anthologies and a recent graduate of the Writers Guild Foundation's Veterans Writing Project program. Her pilot script, "Poppins," was named a second-rounder at the Austin Film Festival's screenwriting competition, a quarterfinalist at CineStory, and a quarterfinalist in the Stage 32 + DramaBox Screenwriting Competition/ Vertical Drama Incubator.

# Also by Michael Bracken and Stacy Woodson, Editors

## BOOKS BY MICHAEL BRACKEN

*All White Girls*
*Bad Girls*
*Deadly Campaign*
*Psi Cops*
*Tequila Sunrise*
*Yesterday in Blood and Bone*

### As Editor
The *Chop Shop* series
The *Fedora* series
*Boots, BBQ, and Bloodshed*
*Groovy Gumshoes*
*More Groovy Gumshoes*
*Hardbroiled*
*Janie's Got a Gun*
The *Mickey Finn* series
*Notorious in North Texas*
*Private Dicks and Disco Balls*
*Sleuths Just Wanna Have Fun*
*Small Crimes*
*The Eyes of Texas*
*Trouble in Texas*

Edited with John Betancourt and Carla Coupe
*Malice Domestic 18: Mystery Most Devious*
*Malice Domestic 19: Mystery Most Humorous*
*Malice Domestic 20: Mystery Most Senior*

Edited with Barb Goffman
*Murder, Neat*

Edited with Gary Phillips
*Jukes & Tonks*

Edited with Trey R. Barker
The *Guns + Tacos* series

Edited with Stacy Woodson
*Scattered, Smothered, Covered & Chunked*

## NOVELLAS BY STACY WOODSON

*Two Tamales, One Tokarev, and a Lifetime of Broken Promises*
*The Cadillac Job*

Edited with Michael Bracken
*Scattered, Smothered, Covered & Chunked*